THE
QUALLSFORD
I·N·H·E·R·I·T·A·N·C·E

THE
QUALLSFORD
I·N·HER·I·TA·N·CE

A Memoir of Sherlock Holmes
From the Papers of Edward Porter Jones,
His Late Assistant

by

Lloyd Biggle, Jr.

A Joan Kahn BOOK

St. Martin's Press
New York

Design by Amy Bernstein

Copyeditor: Ann Adelman

Library of Congress Cataloging in Publication Data

Biggle, Lloyd, 1923–
    The Quallsford inheritance.

    "A Joan Kahn Book"

    I. Title.
PS3552.I43Q34   1986   813'.54   86-3877
ISBN 0-312-65813-3

First Edition

10 9 8 7 6 5 4 3 2 1

THE
QUALLSFORD
I·N·H·E·R·I·T·A·N·C·E

CHAPTER 1

I was christened Edward Porter Jones—"Edward" after the Prince of Wales, later His Majesty, King Edward VII, and "Porter" after my father, who was one, just in case the "Edward" proved too grand for me to handle. I have always been called "Porter." I first met Mr. Sherlock Holmes by way of a group made immortal in the writings of his long-time friend, Dr. John Watson: The Baker Street Irregulars. I was an Irregular. Sherlock Holmes even honoured me by calling me his most irregular Irregular, and he kindly singled me out for special assignments.

Those extra shillings were colossally important to me. I was the sole support of an invalid mother and two younger sisters, a heavy burden indeed for a young lad, and I was immensely grateful for Sherlock Holmes's kindness and the opportunities he gave to me.

His presumed death in 1891 was a shattering blow, and his astonishing resurrection three years later was the most joyous event of my life. I continued to perform special errands for him until I was sixteen. He was a man to be admired, emulated—at that age, worshipped. It was on my sixteenth birthday that I finally summoned my courage and asked if he would take an apprentice.

The suggestion first irritated and then amused him. He had never thought about teaching and training others in those special talents that were so intrinsically a part of his own genius. He doubted that it would be possible; but when he reflected on our relationship, he realized that he had in actual fact been training me according to my own capabilities for several years. He frequently encountered situations where an assistant could be invaluable to him, and he often had to make do with such help as he could acquire on the spur of the moment. In his younger days, Dr. Watson had accompanied him on many of his cases, but Dr. Watson was more of a companion and an observer than an assistant.

The result was that I became his apprentice. Eventually, when Dr. Watson acquired rooms of his own, I moved into Sherlock Holmes's rooms at 221B Baker Street. I shared his life as his assistant until he retired, and then I set up my own inquiry agency and made it my life's work.

Dr. Watson was an immensely kind-hearted man—courteous, considerate, a gentlemen in all of his acts and thoughts—but I fear that he was more than a trifle jealous of my association with Sherlock Holmes. Nowhere in his writings, even in his accounts of those adventures in which I had a part, did he mention my name. He did acknowledge that the great detective sometimes called upon others for assistance, but it was in reference to my old friend Shinwell Johnson, who acted occasionally as Sherlock Holmes's agent and contact with the underworld and later served me in the same capacity; or Charlie Mercer, who operated his own inquiry agency in London and performed local investigations for us when we needed additional assistance.

Dr. Watson even assigned earlier dates to some of the cases I worked on, suggesting that they occurred before I joined Sherlock Holmes, but this could have been due to carelessness. He often made factual errors in his reports, and a number of them are misdated. I regarded his attitude towards me as the amusing quirk of a splendid gentleman. Jealous or not, he never failed to treat me with utmost courtesy, and he never uttered an unkind word to me.

The adventure I am about to describe took place at the end of summer in 1900, when I was approaching twenty years of age. I had completed my apprenticeship with honours. Sherlock Holmes not only trained me; he also gave me an education, and no university could have bettered it in the subjects he chose to emphasize. My employer and I worked well together, and our combined efforts enabled him to handle a far larger number of cases than he had in the past. Although he never sought financial rewards, this did in fact increase his income considerably. He honoured me with the status of a trusted associate and paid me a salary that was generous for those times. I was able to keep my mother and sisters in comfort, and that was all that I asked.

I refer to my employer as "Sherlock Holmes" in this account, but I always addressed him as "Mr. Holmes," or as "sir." I was properly brought up, and never, as long as he lived, did I presume to call him "Holmes," as Dr. Watson did, or "Sherlock."

We had just finished the Darbler Case, in which Sherlock Holmes brilliantly succeeded in locating a missing will by studying the organization of the deceased testator's coin collection. At breakfast on that Monday in late August, he ordered me with mock sternness to enjoy a holiday. I took my two sisters on an outing by boat to Richmond.

It was late when I returned to Baker Street, and I found Dr. Watson there. The two old friends were arguing politics—Dr. Watson would have insisted that it was merely a discussion—and their pipes had filled the room with a veritable fog-bank of smoke.

Dr. Watson greeted me with his usual bluff warmth, though he had the air of wounded petulance that my employer's relentless logic always produced in him. Sherlock Holmes had been pacing the floor with that impatient, morose restlessness that quickly manifested itself when he had no challenging problem to exercise his wonderful mind on. His tall, enormously thin form always conveyed the impression of a tightly wound spring in danger of destroying itself if it could find no useful work to do. He turned his mind to everyday commonplaces like politics only when he had nothing better to occupy it with, and he analyzed a political question as incisively as he would a question of criminal evidence. This always disconcerted Dr. Watson.

He interrupted his pacing and pushed aside the crumpled accumulation of newspapers to make room for me on the sofa, hopefully expectant that my outing had churned up some small puzzle that would relieve the day's tedium for him. Alas, it had not, but I told him what my younger sister Bertha had said about two boatmen on the Thames who blamed each other for a near collision in language decidedly unfit for her tender years. "How very fortunate for them that it isn't Sunday!" she exclaimed.

He laughed heartily; Doctor Watson merely looked puzzled. I went to my room, which formerly had been Dr. Watson's, intending to read for a time before retiring, but I was soon interrupted.

Sherlock Holmes tapped at my door. "Radbert is here!" he called gleefully. "Will you join us?"

Radbert, whom everyone but Sherlock Holmes called Rabby, was a street Arab, one of the new generation of Baker Street Irregulars whom Mr. Holmes employed when he had need of such a group; but he found more frequent uses for Rabby as he once had for me in my time as an Irregular.

Rabby was a ragged little chap who supported himself on the odd shillings he was able to earn. Perhaps "supported" is an exaggerated way to describe Rabby's financial affairs. It cost him nothing to live, so he saved all of his earnings. An ostler permitted him to sleep in the stables and gave him occasional employment in looking after horses. His long days were otherwise occupied with his own business affairs, which consisted of carrying messages or running errands all over London. Whatever the task and wherever it took him, he managed to enjoy himself immensely along the way.

He was a likable lad with a charming smile, and there had been many efforts by well-meaning people to rehabilitate him and improve his station in life, but he resisted these with an adroitness that sometimes seemed inspired. He was perfectly content to be where he was and what he was, and he was especially pleased with the assignment that Sherlock Holmes had given to him.

The streets of London were Rabby's personal domain; he roved them day and night in all seasons and turns of weather, and no one observed what went on there more sharply than he. Sherlock Holmes's commission was a simple one: Any time that Rabby encountered anything that was truly odd or unusual, he was to come to Baker Street as soon as he was free and describe what he had seen. He usually came late at night when his round of chores was finished. He knew that Sherlock Holmes was as likely to be accessible at midnight as at noon, and he never left the streets until all opportunities for employment by late diners and the theatrical crowds had been exhausted. Both of us suspected that Rabby was an incipient capitalist. He was so bright and capable that his services were always in demand, and his clients paid him well, but he was never known to spend money.

When I reached the sitting room, Mrs. Hudson, our landlady, was urging Rabby up the stairs. "Come along," she said. "It's only Dr. Watson, and he won't mind." On one of Rabby's unannounced and informal visits, Sherlock Holmes had introduced him to a duke. As a result of that momentous evening, Rabby turned shy whenever he found us with company. I also think that Mrs. Hudson frightened him when he called late at night; her preparations for bed converted her into a formidable mummy-like apparition enveloped in a vast, shapeless white wrapper that terminated implausibly in a clutter of variously coloured strips of cloth that she used to do up her hair, and she suspended her normal warm friendliness promptly at midnight. She felt an obligation to wait up whenever Sherlock Holmes had a late guest, even if that guest were a street Arab, and to have tea ready in case it should be required, and she resented late visitors because they kept her from going to bed.

When Rabby called on us, Mr. Holmes always asked Mrs. Hudson to send up whatever food she could provide on short notice along with the tea. He feared that Rabby's efforts to live exclusively on charity and save his money would undermine his health.

"Come along, Radbert," Sherlock Holmes called. I never learned how he had discovered Rabby's real name, but once he had done so, he not only insisted on using it, but periodically he would ponder for Rabby the linguistic vagaries by which "Radbert" had been corrupted to "Rabby."

"Dr. Watson is waiting to talk politics with you," he said as the grinning Rabby slipped into the room. He gave Mrs. Hudson instructions about the tea, and then we began a game that over the course of many visits had evolved into a ceremony. Sherlock Holmes often remarked that the greatest scope for observation and analysis came in unimportant but bizarre matters where the crime was minor or non-existent. Rabby periodically brought to him a gleaning of such strange events upon which he could practise his wonderful powers of detection.

Rabby himself was an important part of the game. We scrutinized him intently; Rabby, who enjoyed the ceremony as much as Sherlock Holmes did, boldly scrutinized us in return. He must have found us a droll study in contrasts. Dr. Watson occupied "his" chair —it had been his when he lived with Sherlock Holmes, and his chair it remained. I never presumed to sit in it, and Sherlock Holmes, who thought that excessive comfort interfered with the mental processes, did not like it. He kept it only for visitors and for Dr. Watson's occasional use. It was a massive affair of bulging cushions, designed for relaxed lounging, but Dr. Watson sat stiffly erect in it, and his posture and formal attire—he had taken an evening round of calls on patients for a medical friend who was ill—made him look like an uncomfortable spectator at a Royal Ball. He would not have removed either coat or waistcoat in public for a Queen's ransom.

Sherlock Holmes's shirt sleeves and slippers were not in evidence. As usual, he had enveloped his tall figure in one of a long succession of lavender dressing-gowns. With the passage of time, a gown became faded and acquired stains and even a few holes from his chemical experiments, but he resisted discarding it as one would hesitate to cast off an old friend. While talking with Dr. Watson, he had been pacing a favourite circuit of his that led from the bearskin hearthrug to his desk; from his desk to the scarred old mahogany table in the centre of the room where we took our meals; around the table to a window; and finally back to the hearthrug. Now he had found something to focus his restless intellect on, and he halted his pacing to study Rabby with an intense concentration of attention.

My own costume may have been the strangest of the three. I was still attired in the striped shirt and trousers I had worn on the river —at that age and time I was inordinately proud of them—but I had donned the elaborately beaded American Indian moccasins that a client of Sherlock Holmes's had given to me. Rabby's sharp eyes must have found us an extraordinary threesome.

"Yours is just the fresh face I like to see on a dull night, Radbert," Sherlock Holmes said. "Tell me—what is your opinion of the South African situation?"

"I haven't any, sir," Rabby said promptly.

Sherlock Holmes laughed merrily. "An eminently sensible attitude. Dr. Watson and I have far too many opinions about far too many things." He turned to Dr. Watson. "You remember Radbert, don't you? He is the fifth best observer in all of London, and if he continues to improve as he has this past year, he will soon be third."

"Of course I remember him," Dr. Watson said. He sniffed and wrinkled his nose. "Stable hand, isn't he?"

Sherlock Holmes chuckled. "Come, Watson. Surely you can look—or smell—beyond the blatantly obvious. What sort of stable? But we should not squander your deductive genius on matters that Porter and I are already familiar with. What can you tell us about Radbert's more recent activities?"

Dr. Watson pursed his lips. "He has been about the streets, I suppose. No routine employment would keep a young lad out so late."

Sherlock Holmes laughed and clapped his hands. "Excellent, Watson! Your observations are far sharper than your political arguments. Radbert certainly has been about the streets, and he has a highly unusual occupation. He is an entrepreneur. He operates his own messenger and errand service. Porter and I consider him a capitalist."

Dr. Watson studied Rabby doubtfully, head cocked to one side, a frown on his face. "Indeed," he murmured. "Does he actually secure that much custom?"

"So much that I have to wait my turn when I need him. He also has a roving commission from me. Because he works for so many different employers, on so many different kinds of errands, he spends his days rambling all over London. When he encounters anything likely to appeal to my jaded taste for the bizarre, he stops by to tell me about it. He also provides us with a challenge. As our honoured guest, Watson, you shall have first turn. Where has Radbert been today and what has he been doing?"

Sherlock Holmes had undergone a transformation. The air of restless boredom had vanished. His face was alert and eager, and he pointed his sharp nose at Rabby like a bloodhound straining for a scent to follow.

Rabby was grinning with anticipation. He entered into these games with all of his native shrewdness and wit. He had quickly understood that an inability to make deductions about his day's activities disappointed Sherlock Holmes severely, so he always managed to have a clue or two about him. He would deliberately ornament his trousers with distinctive varieties of mud. "'E's a great one for smears and smudges," he once confided to me admiringly when Sherlock Holmes detected a short cut taken through Lincoln's Inn Fields on the basis of a soiled trouser cuff. Or he would wear a sprig in his cap or leave a tram ticket protruding from a pocket.

His face would pucker as with a private joke when Sherlock Holmes or I pounced on these too-obvious clues, and he would burst into laughter if we missed something that he expected us to notice.

His greatest pleasure came when Sherlock Holmes adroitly discerned a clue Rabby was not aware that he had about him. Then his eyes would sparkle with admiration. Occasionally he would turn the tables on us with a clue that led us astray. I am certain that he managed such deceits with waggish deliberation.

On this evening, Rabby had tucked a flower into the button hole of his ragged coat. It was a lovely yellow bloom, with several blossoms drooping from a single stem, and it gave Rabby a jaunty air that perfectly matched his character. He seemed to go through life laughing at everyone and everything.

I could not remember seeing such a flower before—the streets of London, where I grew up, are not the best place to study botany —and I scrutinized it perplexedly. Rabby obviously intended it to be a clue—but of what?

Dr. Watson pounced on it immediately. "He passed through Covent Garden on his way here," he said confidently. "Where else would he get a flower like that at this time of year?"

"Really, Watson," Sherlock Holmes said. "Each time you call on me you reach new heights of observation."

"I am right, I suppose," Dr. Watson said to Rabby.

"No, sir," Rabby said.

"What?" Dr. Watson exclaimed. "You did not get it at Covent Garden?"

"No, sir."

Dr. Watson humphed disgustedly.

Sherlock Holmes had been enjoying a silent laugh. "You should have noted the kind of flower more carefully, Watson. No London vendor handles a simple wild bloom like that. If it has medicinal qualities, the Physick Gardens might have it, but I doubt that the Apothecaries would permit Radbert to select a 'Button Hole.' Have you been to Chelsea, Radbert?"

"No, sir," Rabby said.

Sherlock Holmes seated himself on the sofa and regarded Rabby gravely. "These are deep waters indeed, Watson! An ordinary wild cowslip finds its way to the heart of London—at the end of summer, in full bloom—and appears in Radbert's button hole. Where did it come from? What is your deduction, Porter?"

"Rabby *has* been to Spitalfields Market," I said.

The mud on his right trouser leg perfectly matched an excavation I had seen there. Sherlock Holmes nodded approvingly; he already had formed that conclusion.

"But I don't know of any Spitalfields proprietor who would offer that kind of flower," I added.

"Very good, Porter," Sherlock Holmes said. "Did the flower come from Spitalfields, Radbert?"

"No, sir," Rabby said.

"I refuse to believe that the flower girls at Oxford Circus are offering out-of-season cowslips."

"No, sir."

"Then where did it come from?"

"Mrs. Mullens grew it in a pot," Rabby said.

Sherlock Holmes stared at him. Then he burst into laughter. Dr. Watson and I joined in.

"He has got us there, Watson," Sherlock Holmes said. "Let that be a lesson to us. No chain of logic is safe when it can be disrupted by women who grow things in pots. The ostler you stay with is named Mullens, is he not? Then Mrs. Mullens is his wife?"

"His mother, sir."

"She grows handsome flowers."

"Thank you, sir. I'll tell her you said so."

"And you *have* been to Covent Garden today—or as near there as Maiden Lane—even if your 'Button Hole' has not."

Rabby looked startled. I had noticed the small, yellowish smudge on his left trouser leg, but until Sherlock Holmes spoke, I could not remember where I had seen that type of excavated soil.

"You strolled along the pavement there," Sherlock Holmes went on, "and instead of taking to the street, you carelessly stepped around and over the untidy geological exhibit that has been blocking Maiden Lane pedestrian traffic for five days. Did you dine at Rules this evening, Radbert?"

"I took a message to a gentleman that was dining there," Rabby said.

"Just so," Sherlock Holmes said with a nod. "You also have been in Leicester Place. Have you and your friends been baiting that French porter at the Hotel de l'Europe again?"

"Only a little, sir," Rabby said confusedly.

"*He* thought it excessive. It was he who threw the tomato at you, was it not?"

"How do you know that?" Rabby exclaimed in alarm. "He missed me!"

"But he missed you closely enough to spatter seeds on your trouser leg. If you are not careful, one of these days he may throw something harder that will not miss. But enough of that. What do you have for me this evening?"

"Pitahaygas, sir," Rabby said.

"*Pitahaygas?*" Sherlock Holmes echoed, a note of genuine interest in his voice.

"Pitahaygas?" Dr. Watson exclaimed. "What is, or are, or were, pitahaygas?"

"I don't know, sir," Rabby said.

Sherlock Holmes reached for one of the thick volumes that sometimes lay scattered about as though the ceiling had been raining books.

"Pitahaya," he said finally when he found the place he sought. He spelled the word. "This must be it. Radbert has a fine gift for observation, but I have noticed that his ear is erratic in matters of pronunciation. You have had a far-ranging day, Radbert. This word refers to the fruit from *cereus variabilis* of the cactus family *cactaceae,* found in Mexico and the south-western United States. According to the description, beautiful to look at and delicious to eat. Sometimes attains a size as large as a vegetable marrow, varying in colour according to variety and habitat. Well known in the markets of Mexico. We are left to deduce that it is an unobtainable rarity in those of England. Was the word 'pitahayas' rather than 'pitahaygas,' Radbert?"

"I expect so," Rabby admitted.

"How does it happen that you have encountered an exotic fruit like this among the flora of London, Radbert? Does your Mrs. Mullens also grow pitahayas in a pot?"

"No, sir."

"Or has the porter of the Hotel de l'Europe taken to throwing less prosaic things than tomatoes?"

"No, sir. This afternoon, as I was passing through Spitalfields Market, I heard a woman asking for pitahayas."

Dr. Watson had lost interest. He began hunching himself about in his comfortable chair, the inevitable prelude to an announcement of his departure. Sherlock Holmes was leaning forward excitedly, his keen, grey eyes gleaming, his thin face tensed. He looked like a beast of prey about to spring.

"What sort of woman?" he asked.

"An old woman. Her clothes were dirty and patched. Her shoes were worn out. She carried an empty old basket that had holes in it."

"Hum," Sherlock Holmes mused. "And what did you think of this badly attired crone, Radbert?"

"I thought there was something odd about her, sir. She had dirty old clothes on, but she looked clean about her person, what I could see, and she was particular about what she touched. She pulled away from people and cringed when someone brushed past her. She moved around horse droppings. Old women with dirty clothes usually don't. Also, her face was white. She had not been out in the weather at all. And her talk hadn't any rough edges. Neither did her manners."

"Excellent!" Sherlock Holmes exclaimed. "What about the possibility that this elderly crone was a young woman in disguise?"

Rabby shook his head firmly. "Not any, sir. Her wrinkles were real."

Sherlock Holmes rubbed his slender hands together with delight. "Admirable! So we have an elderly woman, clean and fastidious, who is disguised in patched and dirty clothing—certainly we can consider it a disguise—in order to ask for pitahayas in a wholesale market where both her speech and her manners are out of place. Does that describe the situation accurately?"

"Not quite, sir," Rabby said. "She was—"

"Just a moment, Radbert. I have done no meaningful work at all today. Let us consider the options. Someone was playing a prank on the poor woman. She was sent to Spitalfields to buy something that the prankster knew would be virtually impossible to find in any London market. Is that possibility worth considering?"

"No, sir."

"Why do you say that so positively?"

"Because she didn't expect to find any pitahaygas—I mean, pitahayas. Or she didn't really want any. She went from stall to stall, and she kept asking the question, 'Do you have pitahayas?' but she didn't wait for an answer. She asked, and then she hurried away."

"Hum. Did any of the proprietors know what pitahayas are?"

"No, sir. They were puzzled. Some tried to find out what the old woman wanted, but she rushed off without waiting to talk. I asked around afterwards, and no one had heard of such a thing."

Sherlock Holmes was rubbing his hands again. "I am grateful to you, Radbert. This is the prettiest little problem to come my way in more than a month. Watson, what do you make of these doings?"

Dr. Watson got to his feet. "It seems simple enough," he said. "The woman was having guests, or a party, or some harmless celebration, and she wanted to serve something unusual. Someone had told her about pitahayas, innocently or—if you will—as a joke.

Or she had read about pitahayas and did not realize that they are unavailable in London. She had the whim to serve them, and she went off to the market to buy some. By the time Rabby encountered her, she had begun to realize that she had been duped or made a foolish mistake. Hence her haste and her refusal to converse."

"But what about the patched and dirty clothing, Watson? Why get herself up so outlandishly for a simple shopping expedition?"

"Oh, well—that." Dr. Watson shrugged indifferently. "She needed the pitahayas urgently, and no servant was available, or she wanted them as a surprise, but she didn't want to be recognized while performing such a humble chore. I am certain that you would find the matter to be absurdly simple."

"Perhaps so, Watson," Sherlock Holmes murmured. "Perhaps so. Must you leave now?"

"My colleague's wife will be wondering what has happened to me," Dr. Watson said. "I promised her that I would look in on him when I finished his calls. It is good to see you again, Rabby. I don't have to be Sherlock Holmes to deduce that you have grown since the last time. I can tell from the amount of shin displayed below your trousers. Observation and deduction, eh, Holmes?"

"Profoundly correct, Watson," Sherlock Holmes chuckled. "Growth is a natural affliction at that age."

Dr. Watson bade me good evening, and Sherlock Holmes went to the stairs with him to exchange farewells. Then he returned, made Rabby comfortable at the table with a tin of biscuits, called down to Mrs. Hudson to hurry the tea, and seated himself on the sofa, hands held in front of him, fingertips together, eyes closed—a favourite posture of his for meditation.

"What is your opinion of the lady's behaviour, Porter?" he asked me finally. "Was she searching for titbits for a party?"

"No, sir," I said.

Sherlock Holmes gave me a sharp glance, and then he transferred his gaze to the ceiling. "What was she doing?"

"She was delivering a message," I answered.

"Indeed. Then you think 'pitahayas' was a signal or a code word directed at the market proprietors?"

"At one of them, sir, but obviously she did not know which one. That is why she questioned every proprietor in the market. There was to be no acknowledgement or return message, which accounts for her peculiar conduct once she had asked her question."

Sherlock Holmes nodded thoughtfully. "But we cannot be certain that her message was intended for a proprietor, Porter. Its destination could have been a bystander waiting for someone to mention the word 'pitahayas.'" He paused. "What do you make of the inept disguise?"

"It is what I would expect of a woman who wanted to disguise herself and did not know how to go about it."

"Hum. Either that, or the disguise was the best she could manage on short notice. I have no doubt that you are right, but why entrust such an errand to an inexperienced person who was so obviously unsuitable for it? Could she have been a substitute, pressed into service at the last moment without fully understanding what it was that she was doing? It is possible. Yes, certainly it is possible."

He returned his gaze to the ceiling and sank into one of his profound meditations, but he wrenched himself back to present reality when Mrs. Hudson arrived with tea and a plate of sandwiches.

"Help yourself, Radbert," he said. "How long has it been since you have eaten?"

"Not since morning, thank you," Rabby said.

Sherlock Holmes sat back with a chuckle to watch Rabby's ravenous assault on the food. I had eaten lightly myself, so I joined in. When we had finished and pushed our chairs back, Sherlock Holmes said, "Now we must have the complete story, Radbert. What were you doing in the market, and how long did you follow the woman?"

"I was on my way to Aldgate High Street with an order for trimmings for Mr. Pettigrew."

Sherlock Holmes nodded. "The tailor. I suppose he had run out of buttons or some such thing. He often does."

"Yes, sir. As I passed the market, I overheard the old woman asking her question. So I followed her as long as I dared. Mr. Pettigrew was in an enormous hurry."

"He would be," Sherlock Holmes agreed. "Was there any other mark of distinction about this elderly woman?"

"She had a hook nose," Rabby said. "A big one. It looked funny on a woman."

"Then it could have been a false nose," Sherlock Holmes suggested.

Rabby was uncertain about that. He had accepted it as genuine.

"Very well," Sherlock Holmes said. "You followed her as long as you dared. And then?"

"On my way back through the market, I looked for her again. She was gone. After I delivered Mr. Pettigrew's trimmings, I went back and asked some of the proprietors if they had ever heard of pitahayas."

"And none of them had."

"No, sir. They thought someone was trying to play a prank on them. That happens sometimes. None of them had seen the old lady before, either."

"It is unfortunate that you were not able to follow her, but I quite understand that you could not offend a good customer by dawdling during an urgent errand. It is an unusual mystery, Radbert. It almost achieves uniqueness. If you happen onto anything else, bring it along. Here is your pay." He clinked a shilling onto the table and then added a second as a bonus.

With Rabby fed, paid, and sent on his way, Sherlock Holmes turned to me. "What about it, Porter?" he asked.

"It should be worth a cast or two," I said. "Do you want me to try in the morning?"

"Almost certainly, Porter, this is one more humdrum specimen of that family of a thousand and one shoddy little crimes that infest the human habitat as fleas do that of dogs. As you well know, the more bizarre a thing seems, the more ordinary the result. 'Pitahayas' is a tip to housebreakers from a servant who thought to disguise herself. Or a message to thieves regarding a share-out. Or any of a long list of similar dodges. But the word 'pitahayas' is an original twist. No underworld riffraff thought that up. It perfectly illustrates those extraordinary combinations and effects that make reality so much stranger than fiction. This definitely is worth a cast or two, but don't be disappointed if that particular pond contains only minnows."

I agreed with him—which only demonstrates that a mystery's first vague stirrings could be as obscure to a genius like Sherlock Holmes as they were to a mere journeyman such as myself. Rabby's chance encounter with the word "pitahayas" was our introduction to one of the most astounding enigmas that either of us experienced in long careers of exploring the darker side of human behaviour.

CHAPTER
2

Sherlock Holmes said nothing more that evening about pitahayas or casts at Spitalfields Market. His normal practice, at the time I am writing of, was to leave the method of investigation entirely to me on cases where we had no client. If I erred, he would point this out to me afterwards.

According to my diary, we talked instead about the electrification of London's tramways, which was then in progress. For years he had closely followed the many experiments in mechanical traction, and on this evening we had a wide-ranging discussion of the impact on crime of improvements in public transportation. He had twice had the experience of having his prey escape on a horse tram—once when he was following with a trained tracking dog—and London's Underground was only too obviously an enormous convenience for the fleeing criminal. Sherlock Holmes was in no way opposed to progress, but he believed that the ingenuity of lawbreakers in exploiting these developments should not only be recognized but anticipated.

I arose at four the next morning and dressed in the work clothing that I kept for such excursions. It was not unusual for me to find Sherlock Holmes reading, or meditating some problem, or conducting a chemical experiment when I had an errand at an early hour, but on that morning there was no sign of him. All of Baker Street seemed as somnolent as the dwelling at 221. I walked through a sleeping London with gas lights working their usual grotesque transformations on my shadow.

Joshua Wirt was a greengrocer who had been a friend of my father's. I had known him all of my life. Occasionally I did his marketing as a favour when his rheumatics were bothering him, and he was more than willing for me to assume the role of greengrocer whenever I needed that disguise. He lived above his shop near Great Portland Street, and he was still in bed when I arrived.

He greeted me jovially. He had been in pain and wondering how he could drag himself out that morning; now he had the delightful prospect of dragging himself back to bed. While I was harnessing his horse, he made a purchase list for me with notes about prices. I drove the cart out of the narrow, empty lane that served as his mews and into the wide thoroughfares of a London that never slept.

It was a long, tedious drive to Spitalfields. Normally my friend patronized Covent Garden, which was much closer. His good horse and I had to plod our way across much of an increasingly wakeful city. Traffic thickened steadily, and when we finally reached Commercial Street and the neighbourhood of the market, the horse and cart were flecks in a seething chaos. I loaded up with potatoes and onions, checked the available green vegetables according to my friend's instructions, and finally found some cabbages at a price and quality that would please him. All of this brought me into close contact with a number of proprietors in the most favoured role possible, that of a customer; and, when I had transacted my friend's business, I inquired of each one, "Ever have any pitahayas?"

Sherlock Holmes had taught me that London was a city of experts. Even the humble wagoner memorized every defective cobblestone along the routes that he travelled, and he knew wagons, and horses, and other wagoners. No scientist, no university professor, no police detective could approach his richly detailed knowledge in those subjects that necessity made him the daily master of.

The Spitalfields proprietors possessed a different kind of expert knowledge. They knew fruits and vegetables. They could discourse at length on the virtues and defects of the current Lincolnshire potato crop as opposed to those of Yorkshire, Cambridgeshire, or Scotland. Of onions from anywhere. Of apples and plums. Of rhubarb, beans, green peas, celery.

But even experts have their blind spots. I had to consider the possibility that one of the market proprietors might be handling small quantities of special fruits and vegetables—or of one special fruit—for a limited clientele, in which case even his near neighbours might know little or nothing about it. That was the person I had to find—if he existed.

The first man I asked about pitahayas stared at me, spat disgustedly, and remarked, "I been hearing too much about pit-a-hay-as or whatever they are."

I spat in turn. "Had a customer asking. Promised to see if I could find some. Ever have any?"

"Never heard of pit-a-hay-as before someone came asking about them yesterday," the proprietor said. "Still don't know what they are."

"Some kind of fruit, my customer said."

"It's no fruit that's ever been sold in London."

I nodded gloomily. "Never heard of it myself. This customer offered a fancy price."

"Don't start counting your profit," the proprietor said. "You might have to pay a fancier price."

I displayed an understandable curiosity as to who had been asking about pitahayas. Naturally I wondered whether my customer had called at the market after she talked with me. If she had already found what she wanted, she might renege on the bargain we made.

The proprietor guffawed. "She didn't find pitahayas in this market."

"What did she look like?" I asked.

"Like a nasty old hag." The brief description he added was of a kind not normally applied to a female who might be someone's mother.

I shook my head. "No. It was an attractive young woman—in fact, a lady."

The proprietor snorted. "This is a wholesale market. What would a lady be doing here?"

This brief scenario, with slight modifications, was repeated with each proprietor I questioned. I was able to confirm Rabby's description in several of its details, but I could not amplify it. Sherlock Holmes was right—Rabby certainly was one of the finest observers in London, and no one at the market had noticed the old woman's manners and conduct as carefully as he had.

I made the weary return trip across a London now wide awake and bustling with work and trade. When I had delivered my purchases and put my friend's horse away, I returned to Baker Street.

Sherlock Holmes was not at home. "Went off with a dressed-up gentleman in a carriage," Mrs. Hudson told me.

It was a common occurrence. With his growing fame, he was much in demand as a consultant, and often he would consent to render opinions on minor matters that held some interest for him but which seemed too insubstantial to merit a formal investigation. Heads of commercial establishments were learning that his relentless logic could save them money or increase their profits.

I altered my appearance and returned to the market to join the ranks of boys hanging about in hope of casual employment, though I was a bit old for the role. I spent the remainder of the day there, and I had to accept an occasional chore to verify my disguise. Younger boys were handed the light errands; I was favoured for such tasks as loading and unloading wagons, and I had never worked harder for so little information.

In slack periods, I talked with the other labourers. The few who remembered the old woman well had been impressed by her haste. She asked her question about pitahayas and then rushed off—but Rabby had already told us that.

The problem seemed as unpromising as any I had worked on. We had no expectation that the old woman would ever return to the market. She had delivered her message. There were only two forlorn possibilities of tracing her. One was that a proprietor or market hanger-on might have seen her previously and recognized her. The other was that one of them had seen her in conversation with someone. Both possibilities drew emphatic negatives.

By afternoon, I knew that all of my casts had failed utterly. The crowds had begun to thin out. I drifted about with the remaining customers, determined to make a last attempt if my imagination could invent something useable.

Suddenly I heard a shrill male voice pronounce a familiar word: pitahayas. I turned alertly and hurried towards it. An elderly farmer with a small handcart was talking with one of the proprietors.

"Fresh and delicious," his cracked voice shrilled. "Let you have a bushel or a wagonload."

The proprietor was regarding him curiously. "I never heard of pitahayas until yesterday," he said. "Since then, I've heard of nothing else. The others were wanting to buy, and here you are trying to sell, and I still have no notion of what they are."

The old farmer reached into a bag on his cart, took something, and offered it to him. Pressing closer, I saw that it looked like a small plum.

The proprietor stared at it. "That is an ordinary Damson plum," he said.

"We always call them pitahayas," the old farmer said. "Very mellow flavoured, they are. Go ahead—try it."

The proprietor rubbed the plum on his sleeve, bringing the dusky surface to a fine polish. Then he bit it, chewed, stuffed the remainder into his mouth, and finally spat out the stone.

"Not bad," he said. "What's your price?"

"Twelve bob."

The proprietor stared at him. "For a bushel?" He turned away disgustedly. "You can't triple the price of plums by calling them pitahayas."

"You can when they're special," the old farmer said calmly.

"That's an outrage!" the proprietor ranted. "That's thievery. The police should take notice of such things. Ordinary Damson plums—"

"They ain't ordinary," the old farmer said. "They're pitahayas. You don't have to buy them. Someone else will if you don't."

He turned his cart and pushed it away.

I followed on his heels. He tottered over to the next proprietor, paused to elaborately mop his brow, and then asked, in his shrill, cackling voice, "Like some pitahayas to sell?"

A similar dialogue followed. The proprietor knew nothing about pitahayas but was curious because customers had been asking about them. The notion of anyone trying to charge twelve shillings the bushel for Damson plums, no matter what fancy name he called them by, enraged him, and the insults he shouted at the farmer's retreating back were of a sort better left unuttered in public. The old farmer calmly made his unsteady way to the next proprietor, where the scene was repeated.

I followed him for half an hour as he went from stall to stall, leaving behind him a trail of enraged proprietors. Not until it seemed certain that he actually was trying to sell plums as pitahayas did I turn away. At least I had picked up another interesting item for Sherlock Holmes, and I looked forward to telling him about it.

At that moment, the old farmer spun his cart around and all but ran over me on his way to the next stall. As he passed me, he glanced slyly in my direction and winked.

It *was* Sherlock Holmes.

Dr. Watson often remarked that the stage lost a great actor when Sherlock Holmes decided to become a detective. His astonishing talent for disguise, for flawless impersonation, is reflected in the fact that even a person such as myself, who knew his talent well and who had learned to anticipate such transformations, was nevertheless taken by surprise almost every time it occurred. This was not Sherlock Holmes playing the role of a farmer; this *was* a farmer, totally different in stature, in facial expressions, in mannerisms, in speech.

When we met back at Baker Street, and Sherlock Holmes had removed his disguise, he opened one of a pile of books that he had acquired somewhere during the day and showed me a coloured drawing of a pitahaya.

"Have you ever seen one under any name?" he asked.

"No, sir," I said.

"Neither have I. I wonder—"

He often did not say what he wondered. I returned to my chair and waited. Some minutes went by before he remembered that I was there.

He came to himself with a start. "Tell Mrs. Hudson to bring our tea, please. I have eaten nothing since morning."

I rang the bell. When I regained my chair, Sherlock Holmes said, "I have not been able to decide whether this is one of the more notable puzzles to come our way or a meaningless triviality. Did your cast get any rise at all?"

I described my day to him.

"It is no more than could be expected," he said when I had finished. "Now that line of inquiry is closed to us. The proprietors may inflict physical violence on the next person who mentions pitahayas to them. We will have to think of a different approach."

That was kind of him—saying that *we* would have to think of a different approach. When our problems passed a certain level of perplexity—and this one already had done so—it was Sherlock Holmes who did the thinking for both of us.

But Sherlock Holmes was an exceptionally kind man. Dr. Watson also was a kind man, but he was kind in different ways. It was as though Dr. Watson thought that he was expected to be kind, and so he was. He did everything that a kind man could be expected to do. Sherlock Holmes was kind in unexpected ways. He could apply the same energy and deep thought to being kind that he did to solving mysteries, but he also could be kind in unexpected ways without thinking about it at all. Dr. Watson does him rank injustice by constantly alluding to his cold manner and the machine-like qualities of his intellect. Such a description applied to him only when he was actually on the chase; otherwise, either Dr. Watson is guilty of gross exaggeration or Sherlock Holmes behaved far differently towards him than he did towards me. I remember him with great affection as a warm and exceptionally kind human being.

The next day, following Sherlock Holmes's instructions, I returned to the market and had conversations with four of the proprietors in widely scattered locations. I selected them with care, and I gave each of them a tale about a wealthy man trying to locate an elderly maiden aunt who was harmless but a bit strange in the head and who had run away from home. It was she, I explained, who had been asking for pitahayas. If they caught a glimpse of her in the market again, they were to send a messenger at once to Mr. Sherlock Holmes, 221B Baker Street, and try to detain her until he arrived. They would be rewarded handsomely.

"I fear that it is much too late for this ploy," Sherlock Holmes told me. "But we are bound to try it."

My fear was that the proprietors would recognize me from my own inquiries of the previous day and react with the violence Sherlock Holmes had predicted, but his name was well known to all four of them, and—having nothing to lose—they agreed to keep their eyes open for the old woman who had asked for pitahayas.

But of course none of them saw her.

That week passed, and the next, and it seemed that the pitahayas mystery was doomed to be filed with what my employer called his inexplicables. I virtually forgot about it myself. Sherlock Holmes was consulted on a blackmailing case involving the son of one of England's most illustrious families, and both of us were in Oxford for several days in connection with that case. So it happened that when Rabby called on us again, pitahayas were the furthest thing from my mind.

They also were the furthest thing from Rabby's mind. It was a Sunday evening, and he arrived early enough to share our regular tea with us.

"More pitahayas, Radbert?" Sherlock Holmes asked him jokingly as Rabby got himself settled at the big dining table.

Rabby blinked his surprise. He had to confess that he had forgotten all about the pitahayas.

"What bizarre event do you have for us today?" Sherlock Holmes asked.

The occurrence that Rabby described to us certainly was an oddity. He had seen, late that afternoon, strolling in Piccadilly Circus and surrounded by a crowd of jeering street Arabs and not a few laughing adults, a gentleman in full evening dress with a goat on a leash. The goat, Rabby observed, was a rather large animal, and it did not seem to be enjoying its walk. The gentleman was rather hard put to make it go in the direction he had chosen. Rabby had followed this procession down the Haymarket and ultimately to Northumberland Avenue and the Hotel Metropole, where gentleman and goat caused consternation, first with the outside porter and then with several employees who came to his assistance when the gentleman insisted on taking the goat into the hotel with him.

"He was staying at the hotel," Rabby said, "and he claimed the right to entertain a guest of his choice."

"Did he succeed?" Sherlock Holmes asked.

"No, sir."

Sherlock Holmes shook his head sadly. "You disappoint me, Radbert. The man with the strange taste in walking companions represents no mystery. There was a boxing match last evening between Millingford and an American challenger, Bartlett, and Millingford won. Americans can be somewhat fanciful in their wagers. I saw two that were equally droll being paid off in Trafalgar

Square this morning. Haven't you heard anything at all about pitahayas?"

Rabby had not given pitahayas a thought since his original report.

"Radbert," Sherlock Holmes said sternly, with an air of extreme disappointment, "when Mrs. Hudson announced you, I felt confident that you were bringing us the identity of your mysterious crone. At the very least, you should be able to offer a suggestion for our investigation."

His eyes were twinkling, but Rabby reacted with genuine alarm. After a moment of hesitation, he blurted desperately, "A notice in the newspapers?" Rabby frequently served as messenger for such notices.

"What should the notice say?" Sherlock Holmes asked. His eyes were still twinkling. " 'If the woman who was looking for pitahayas in Spitalfields Market a fortnight ago will present herself at 221B Baker Street, we have an ample supply available?' "

Rabby nodded eagerly.

Sherlock Holmes shook his head. Now his gloom was genuine. "You are forgetting that she did not want pitahayas. Probably she had no interest at all in them. She was only a messenger delivering a word. She would know that such an advertisement could not possibly concern her."

"If she did not know the person the message was intended for, she may have had no way of knowing whether it actually was received," I ventured to point out. "She might respond to an advertisement for that reason. And what if it wasn't received? Then the person it was directed at might respond to an advertisement."

"If the message miscarried," Sherlock Holmes said, "it would have been sent again another day—with a different code word and also a different messenger, since the old crone almost certainly was a substitute."

"But what if the *sender* doesn't know that it miscarried?" I asked.

Sherlock Holmes meditated for a moment; neither Rabby nor I dared to speak.

"It seems like a forlorn hope," he said finally, "but if two parties were communicating by code through an ignorant messenger, I suppose it is remotely possible that a message could fail to reach its destination without either of them knowing it. The supposed recipient would not know that it had been sent, and the sender would be unaware that it had not been received."

He took pen and paper and scribbled briefly. "We'll try this. The agony column of the *Times* and one or two other papers. 'Those desiring information about pitahayas can obtain the same by applying to Mr. Sherlock Holmes at 221B Baker Street.'"

Rabby, after enjoying Mrs. Hudson's ample tea, pocketed his shilling and hurried away with the notice.

Our blackmailing case, concerning which I have already said too much, was rapidly approaching a climax. The best weapon against a blackmailer is—blackmail. Faced with certain destruction from the exposure of sordid events in his own life, no blackmailer will persist. I brought conclusive evidence with me when I returned from Oxford the following evening, and Sherlock Holmes immediately made arrangements to confront the blackmailer with it.

Not until that had been taken care of did I think to inquire about responses to the advertisement.

"There was only one," Sherlock Holmes said. "A proprietor from Spitalfields Market called in person. He remembered the inquiries about pitahayas at the market, and he thought he might be missing out on something profitable. I told him that the advertisement referred to a special type of foreign investment we were making available to a limited clientele."

I was disappointed.

"Never mind," Sherlock Holmes said. "It was an unpromising venture from the beginning. We need an occasional setback to remind us that human vagaries must by definition occasionally defy logic. Perhaps this will bring us a more interesting and satisfactory problem."

He passed a telegram to me. It read, "Urgently need to consult you concerning family tragedy. Please inform me at Charing Cross Hotel whether you will be available at nine tomorrow morning." It was signed "Emmeline Quallsford."

"What do you make of it?" Sherlock Holmes asked as I pondered the brief message with a frown.

I continued to frown at it. A telegram seldom conveys more than the facts stated by the sender. A letter, on the other hand, offers a rich assortment of information for deductive speculation: stationery, handwriting, and, usually, a far longer message that reveals much about the writer. I regretted that Emmeline Quallsford had been too rushed to pen a letter.

One of the most disconcerting things about working for Sherlock Holmes was the way in which he seemed to know my exact thoughts even before I had finished thinking them. "Never mind, Porter," he said with a smile. "The most terse telegram can divulge more than the sender intended. This one was handed in at Rye this afternoon. Pass me the Bradshaw, please. Here we are—the South Eastern and Chatham line. Hastings to London by way of Rye and Ashford. We may safely assume that she will travel from the vicinity of Rye, since the telegram was dispatched there. No morning train is listed that would reach London in time for a nine o'clock appointment. She must come up on an afternoon or evening train, stay overnight at the hotel, and see us in the morning. Hence the request to send confirmation of the appointment to the hotel, which I have done."

"Then the 'family tragedy' occurred today, perhaps even this afternoon, and she immediately decided to consult you," I said. "She dispatched the telegram, and she took the first available train."

"No, Porter. The family tragedy *may* have occurred today, but it could have happened last week or years ago. It was the *urgent need* that arose this afternoon, suddenly and unexpectedly. That is what makes the message seem promising."

I reminded myself that a notable family tragedy, even one that occurred on the south coast, should have been mentioned in the London newspapers. Of course if it actually had happened that afternoon, they would not have the story until the next morning.

I was reaching for the day's accumulation when Sherlock Holmes smiled again and said, "Most families keep their tragedies private if they can manage that. Does the message convey anything to you about the sender?"

"She is unfamiliar with telegrams. She uses half again as many words as are really necessary."

"True, but she obviously was at great pains to make her meaning clear to us. The family tragedy, whatever it may be, has not affected her mental processes. There is a brisk and business-like air to her message, but she does leave us several avenues for speculation. For example, if the urgency is genuine, why has she not rushed from the railway station to Baker Street? Why arrive today and stay overnight at the hotel for a morning appointment? If the urgency is no more urgent than that, she could have taken an early train tomorrow and reached London in ample time for an appointment at eleven—only two hours later than the time she specified. Does my reasoning impress you, Porter?"

"Yes, sir. According to the information we have, her conduct makes no sense at all."

"I am glad to hear you express it in that way, Porter. 'According to the information we have.' If we knew more about her, her conduct might seem eminently sensible. She may have more than one urgent errand to attend to in London, for example. It is an excellent illustration of the danger of theorizing before one has sufficient data. Never mind. I think we can expect Miss or Mrs. Quallsford promptly at nine, and she will tell us all about her family tragedy. I want you here in case any activity is required."

"Activity" meant that he might want me to follow her.

She did arrive promptly at nine, and to my youthful eyes she looked like one of those untouchable creatures rarely encountered outside of story books—a beautiful lady. She was dressed in black, from which I deduced that Sherlock Holmes had been wrong in his suggestion that the tragedy could have occurred years before—surely she would not have remained in mourning for so long—and also that I had erred in assuming that it had happened the previous day. I did not see how she could have attired herself so elaborately in mourning on such short notice.

Her luxurious gown was soft and clinging; it moulded her figure beautifully and looked very fashionable to me. She also wore a long, flowing black cloak and an unadorned black hat. The shoe that I glimpsed was just as stylish and indicated an exceptionally small foot. She raised her heavy veil as soon as she seated herself. She was fresh looking and pretty, like a princess just arrived from the country. She had very light brown hair and steady blue eyes.

Most of Sherlock Holmes's visitors have troubles, and many of them have very serious troubles. Emmeline Quallsford looked like a young lady carrying a crushing burden. With a distraught manner and eyes that were shadowed as though worn out from weeping, her tragic mien matched the blackness of her gown.

As soon as she entered, Sherlock Holmes graciously set about making her comfortable. He took her cloak and escorted her to Dr. Watson's chair, the one usually allotted to visitors.

"Pray make yourself comfortable," he told her. He introduced me as his assistant, but Miss Quallsford took no notice either of the introduction or of its subject.

Sherlock Holmes often professed to know nothing at all about women, whom he liked to refer to as the enigmatic sex. "That is a book I have not been able to decipher," he once remarked, and he would slyly refer puzzles about feminine behaviour to Dr. Watson or myself. Dr. Watson had been married, and I had two sisters, and either circumstance, Sherlock Holmes pretended to believe, should have produced a qualified expert.

I wondered whether this attitude might be due to the fact that many women possessed a natural immunity to his methods. Sherlock Holmes could indeed read his male clients like a book. Their hands told him their occupations; a splash of mud on boots or trousers revealed their recent wanderings. Items of jewelry worn by men—rings, pins, fobs, chains—almost always possessed a significance, to Sherlock Holmes's keen mind and observing eyes, that their owners considered supernatural.

Women *were* an enigma by comparison. Infallible clues to a man's background and associations merely indicated whim or current fashion in a woman. There were few occupations open to women of the classes most likely to consult Sherlock Holmes and almost no professions. They took cabs or carriages more frequently than men. Their long skirts concealed their shoes, and a splash of mud that a man would ignore was removed by a woman at the earliest opportunity. Sherlock Holmes always looked first at a woman's sleeves and hands for tell-tale evidence of such activities as typewriting or music, but my own eyes told me that there was absolutely nothing to be deduced from Emmeline Quallsford's stylish and probably quite new dress except that she was in mourning, and that there were no abnormalities about her hands except for a small ink stain on her left first finger. Even without the attendant emotional complexities, Sherlock Holmes would have found women a difficult book to read.

Now he faced another of this disconcerting species, who fixed her blue eyes on him and said, with a faint smile, "I suppose you know all about me, Mr. Holmes. I've heard of the uncanny way you detect things about people."

"Not quite all," Sherlock Holmes said brusquely. "It is obvious that you are left-handed, that you are unmarried, and that you associate with children frequently but not, I think, as an ordinary hired governess. You have an incisive character. You make decisions quickly and act on them. These are only probabilities, of course. I could offer a long list of them, but they would not tell me all about you. For example, I have no notion of why you have come to see me."

The left-handedness was deduced from the ink stain, which she certainly had acquired in writing. She wore no wedding ring. An ordinary governess could not afford such an expensive gown. I missed the clue to her association with children because I had not handled her cloak; she had brushed against a chalk board. Her character, of course, was evident from the telegram.

She was staring at him. Her lips were parted in astonishment. "You really are uncanny," she murmured.

She ended the sparring with a shrug, took a deep breath as though to collect herself, and announced, "I am here because a friend chanced to bring a copy of the *Times* back from London yesterday. I have heard that people who are caught up in tragedy do irrational things, and I believe it. I did something I had never done before in my life—I read the agony column. When I saw your reference to pitahayas, I knew that I had to talk with you."

"Strange," Sherlock Holmes murmured. "What connection do you have with pitahayas?"

"Absolutely none. But Edmund, my brother, used the word for years, Mr. Holmes. 'It is going to rain pitahayas,' he would say. Or, 'It is pitahaya time.' Or, 'Today we add up the pitahayas.' I thought it was a nonsensical word that he made up to make us laugh." She caught her breath. "So when I saw your newspaper notice—"

Sherlock Holmes was shaking his head gently. "My pitahayas have no connection with your brother's nonsensical word," he said. "You should have asked him about it and saved yourself a journey."

She winced as though he had struck her. "I could not ask him," she said in a choked voice. "The day before yesterday, my brother was horribly murdered."

Then she fainted.

CHAPTER
3

I leaped to the sideboard for a glass of water, and Sherlock Holmes, who had caught Miss Quallsford as she pitched forward, gently helped her back into her chair. He moistened a handkerchief with the water and dabbed at her face. At the same time, he told me to ask Mrs. Hudson for tea.

Miss Quallsford recovered quickly and murmured an embarrassed apology. "Edmund's death was such a shock," she said. "Such a total shock. So inexplicable! The moment I learned that you were investigating it, I decided to consult you."

"But I am not investigating it," Sherlock Holmes protested soberly. "I had never heard of your brother until you mentioned him, so of course I did not know that he was dead."

She stared at him. "But you published that notice the day after he died. There must be a connection. No one except him ever used that word. I don't even know what pitahayas are. I would ask him, jokingly, and he would joke back and refuse to tell me. 'Look it up,' he would say, but I never did. I was afraid that it would turn out to be something he had made up, and he would have more cause to poke fun at me." She squared herself in the chair and faced him with intense seriousness. "Mr. Holmes, what *are* pitahayas?"

Mrs. Hudson interrupted, bringing tea. Miss Quallsford admitted

· 34 ·

that she had not eaten breakfast, and Sherlock Holmes insisted that she drink her tea and eat some toast before talking further. She reluctantly sipped the tea and nibbled in a desultory manner at a piece of toast. Finally she pushed the tray aside.

"What are pitahayas?" she demanded.

"They are the fruit of an American cactus," Sherlock Holmes told her.

"But—what could that possibly have to do with my brother?" she asked wonderingly.

Sherlock Holmes shook his head. "I have no evidence to suggest that it has anything to do with your brother."

"It does not seem possible that there would be no connection at all. He used that word so frequently, and none of our acquaintances had any idea of what it meant. I had never seen it in print. Suddenly there it was, in the newspaper, the day after he died. What information are you offering, Mr. Holmes? I want it."

"That information concerns something that happened in London a fortnight ago," Sherlock Holmes said. "I know of no possible link with either you or your brother. A most unfortunate misunderstanding has compelled you to travel to London at a tragic time. I offer my apologies, Miss Quallsford."

"No!" she exclaimed. "The notice said that those wanting information about pitahayas should apply here. I insist upon knowing what it is. If you are selling it, I will pay. Well, Mr. Holmes?"

Sherlock Holmes shook his head again. "It is connected with an investigation I am conducting at Spitalfields Market."

"Are pitahayas sold at Spitalfields?" she asked incredulously. When he did not answer, she went on slowly, "I can understand your reluctance to discuss one of your cases with a stranger whom it does not seem to concern. All the same, anything involving pitahayas, occurring at the time of my brother's murder, is an exceedingly strange coincidence."

"Tell us about your brother," Sherlock Holmes suggested. "It is an even stranger coincidence that there could be such a sensational crime as murder in the south of England two days ago without word of it reaching the London papers."

"The police are convinced that it was suicide," she said scornfully. "The doctor, my brother's wife, her solicitor, even the vicar are trying to make out that it was an accident so as to lessen the embarrassment to the family, and the coroner is more concerned with obliging them than with discovering the truth. I know that it was murder. But the pitahayas that you mentioned—"

Sherlock Holmes said gravely, "I can assure you, Miss Quallsford, that the possible murder of your brother is a far more important matter than our trivial little inquiry at Spitalfields Market. Please tell us about it."

She leaned back and closed her eyes. I poured her another cup of tea, and she sipped absently.

"My family have been graziers on the Isle of Graesney for more than a hundred years," she said finally. "Our home is called Sea Cliffs. Graesney is one of the land islands of Kent, and it is located a short distance north of Rye. Its one village is named Havenchurch.

"My brother—" tears filled her eyes—"my brother and I were very close. When we were young, we were much alone. We were our own friends and playmates; we had no others. When we grew up, we remained close to each other. He was my last surviving relative—and my only close friend."

Sherlock Holmes loved to marshal facts in array like an army being prepared for battle. This was an exasperating beginning for him, but he sat back patiently. "There must have been some tragedy or overwhelming unhappiness in his life to make the police accept the idea of suicide so readily," he observed.

"There was," Miss Quallsford agreed. "He was married, he had two lovely children and a beautiful, loving wife, but something was twisting his life. He began to avoid his loved ones. There is a strange, half-ruined tower on our estate, Mr. Holmes. Some people think it looks like a relic from ancient times, but it is not. My grandfather, who was slightly mad, began the tower, and my father, who inher-

THE FOOTPRINTS OF A
GIGANTIC HOUND LTD.

a mystery bookstore

16 Broadway Village
123 South Eastbourne
Tucson, Arizona 85716

(602) 326-8533

Date 2/7

NAME

ADDRESS

CITY

SOLD BY		CASH	CHARGE	ON ACCT.	CREDIT	
QUAN.	**DESCRIPTION**				**AMOUNT**	
1	Quillford 1595-480				11	15
						78
					11	93

000901   **PURCHASED BY**

All claims and returned goods must be accompanied by this bill.

ited his affliction, finished it—for no reason that anyone now remembers. My brother carried a few conveniences to the tower— a chair, a cot, an old table—and he spent more and more of his time there. At night he would sit there for hours, brooding in the dark. We knew that something was troubling him, but he would confide in no one. His wife tried; I tried. Neither of us could reach him, and finally the very sinews of his existence were corroded. He rejected his family. He would explode into terrible oaths at anyone who tried to approach him—he who was the gentlest of men! And now he has been murdered. Because you mentioned pitahayas in your newspaper notice, I hoped and expected that you were already on the criminal's track. Since you are not—" She hesitated. "Mr. Holmes," she said slowly, "will you investigate my brother's murder?"

"It would have to be an investigation of your brother's *death*," Sherlock Holmes said. "You say that he was murdered, but the police would not readily accept a suicide verdict in the face of contrary evidence, and there may have been reasons other than family embarrassment for calling it an accident. The first objective must be to determine how he died. Once that is done—unless the cause *was* murder—there may be nothing further to investigate. Unfortunately, it would be impossible for me to leave London at this time. No, I could not consider it. A matter of enormous importance is approaching a crisis. But I can send my assistant. He will handle the preliminaries just as capably as I could."

Miss Quallsford turned and looked at me for the first time. Her calm, blue eyes examined me critically. "He is young," she announced.

"Mr. Jones has been assisting me since he was a child," Sherlock Holmes said. "Except for myself, there is no other private inquiry agent in London with his experience and competence. He can return with you today, and I will join him as soon as circumstances permit."

Miss Quallsford was, only too obviously, a strong-willed young woman who was accustomed to having exactly what she wanted. Sherlock Holmes's suggestion did not please her, but she soon saw that neither argument nor wiles would change his mind. The result was an agreement that I should meet her at Charing Cross Station and travel to Havenchurch with her on the evening train.

She took her leave of us.

"Evening train," Sherlock Holmes mused. "I was wondering why she came to London yesterday in order to see us today. Now I am wondering what urgent matters require her presence in London for an entire day when her brother is—according to her—lying in Havenchurch horribly murdered." He was consulting the Bradshaw. "She could take a late morning train and be home by midafternoon. Find out what she is doing."

Miss Quallsford had a hansom cab waiting for her. As soon as she was safely under way, I whistled up a four-wheeler and followed. She went first to a draper's shop in Regent Street, and she was occupied there for so long that I risked peeking in to see what was happening.

She was buying black cloth for mourning clothes—probably for the entire household, for she bought quantities of it. She made her selections carefully, and, when she had finished, she instructed the attentive clerk to send her purchases to her hotel. From Regent Street, she went—by way of Pall Mall and the Strand—to the Temple, where she dismissed her cab. She was greeted with affectionate concern by a plump, elderly barrister named Ginter. I heard his welcome from the stairs below and caught a glimpse of him as he escorted her into his chambers.

"My dear Emmeline! I was astonished and grieved by your message. What on earth happened?"

The door cut off their voices. I waited; an hour passed, and then a servant left in a great hurry and returned balancing a heavy tray that obviously contained an ample luncheon for two. I went back to Baker Street and enlightened Sherlock Holmes as to what a young lady with a recently murdered brother had to do in London.

"Mr. Ginter is obviously a family friend who has known her from childhood," I said. "She may spend the afternoon with him. Do you want me to keep on following her?"

If he had been expecting dramatic revelations, he showed no sign of disappointment. He shook his head. "Ask Mrs. Hudson what she can provide for our luncheon," he said. "Then we must consider what can be accomplished at Havenchurch."

After we had eaten, Sherlock Holmes packed a pipe with his favourite shag tobacco and, while he meditated, he smoked with that peculiar intensity that quickly filled the room with pungent fumes. Finally he said, "You may find it an obvious suicide. Miss Quallsford is adamant that her brother would never take his own life, but people frequently think that of a loved one who has in fact done so. According to her own story, madness may run in the family. The police would not call it suicide if the indications were not strongly in that direction. As an additional complication, if the young man's wife is determined to make his death an accident, she may refuse to permit any investigation at all, which will severely limit the scope of your inquiries. But speculation is futile when we have so few facts to work with. You know how to proceed."

"Apart from Edmund's death, we have only one fact," I said. "His odd use of the word 'pitahayas.' "

"That one fact is my only justification for accepting this case. A link between Edmund's pitahayas and the Spitalfields pitahayas may be too tenuous to trace even if one exists, but we can oblige a charming young lady and attempt to satisfy our own curiosity at the same time. Did you find Miss Quallsford attractive, Porter?"

"Very," I said. "And also frightening. I can understand why she wears no wedding ring."

Sherlock Holmes looked at me alertly. "What an interesting observation! Are you rejecting the obvious deduction that she is unmarried?"

"I would conclude that she is probably unmarried; at the same time, it would not surprise me if a young woman with her strength of character spurned such a symbol of servility even if she were married."

"Indeed. Porter, sometimes you display more wisdom than your years can safely accommodate. I expected you to say that her devotion to her brother is much better evidence that she is unmarried. No matter—anyone at all in the village of Havenchurch will be able to tell you all about her. I have a slight recollection of the Quallsford family, and I refreshed it last evening after you went to bed. I believe that it was her father, Oswald Quallsford, who was involved in a mild scandal some years back—something about a foreign actress, if I remember correctly. The connection was said to be his ruin, but there are degrees of ruination, and Miss Quallsford certainly displays none of the obvious symptoms of poverty. You will find the Quallsfords to be an old and—except for the foreign actress—respected family."

"How shall I report?" I asked.

"In the usual way. A modern contrivance such as the telephone will not be available in Havenchurch, and you may have to telegraph from Rye, as Miss Quallsford did, but the distance is not great. Wire only in an emergency or if you uncover something significant."

"What would constitute an emergency, sir?" I asked. "The brother is dead. Police or family will have tidied up most of the evidence. There won't be anything for me to do except collect gossip."

Sherlock Holmes smiled. "But you do that superbly well. Either this is a mere family tragedy, insignificant to outsiders except for its pathos, or you are about to try a cast over exceptionally deep waters. Use the telegraph in an emergency. Do you know anything about the Marshes?"

"Marshes?" I echoed blankly.

He reached for a book that lay open on the floor beside his chair. "The Marshes of south-east England—Romney, Walland, Guldeford, and so on. Eleven hundred years ago, a work called the

Catalogue of British Wonders described the Marsh country like this: 'In it are three hundred and forty islands with men living on them. It is girt by three hundred and forty rocks and in every rock is an eagle's nest. Three hundred and forty rivers flow into it and there goes into the sea but one river which is called the Limen. . . .' Eleven hundred years have brought about a few changes. The three hundred and forty rivers probably were tidal creeks that long since dried up. Both the eagles and the marshes have been gone for centuries, but there is a strangeness about that country that is difficult to describe. Whether the strangeness has anything at all to do with the strangeness of Edmund Quallsford's death is something we will have to determine."

He spread out a map and showed me how the triangle of East Sussex lay between western Kent and the sea, and how the boundary between them followed the winding path of the River Rother and then made its own looping way to the coast east of Rye. Graesney —and Havenchurch—were located in Kent, a few miles north of Rye and just north of the Sussex boundary.

"This wretched business at Oxford may drag on for days if the blackmailer persists in trying to play when all of his cards have been trumped," Sherlock Holmes said. "I will come to Havenchurch as soon as it is finished."

Miss Quallsford's manner, when I met her at Charing Cross Station, was that of an employer towards a new servant. She was uncertain as to my competence and my reliability, but she was willing to give me every opportunity to prove myself.

Since she obviously considered me to be little more than a child, there was no possibility of her treating me as a confidant, as she might have Sherlock Holmes. The journey lasted almost two and a half hours, and during that time we did not exchange half a dozen words. She took a book from the bag she carried and concentrated her thoughts upon it. I performed my first feat of detection on this case and concluded that the Quallsfords possessed a noteworthy library. The volume she was reading was expensively and ornately bound in leather, and a large, florid "Q" had been tooled onto the spine in gold. Unfortunately I could not read the title from where I was sitting, so I had to suspend judgement both as to her taste in literature and as to the library's contents.

Several times she turned her large blue eyes in my direction, but it was no more than a passing glance, a fulfilment of her responsibility to make certain that I was comfortable and wanted nothing.

At Ashford we changed to the Ashford and Hastings Branch of the South Eastern and Chatham Railway, which runs southward through the Marshes to Rye and Hastings. I peered curiously from the train window when we entered the strange country Sherlock Holmes had referred to, but it was shrouded in the darkness of an overcast, moonless night, and the few impressions I received revealed nothing out of the ordinary.

We halted briefly at Appledore Station, a cluster of poorly lighted buildings. When we moved on, Miss Quallsford got to her feet and began collecting her belongings. I assisted her by taking the bundle of cloth she had purchased. The train came to a stop at Havenchurch Halt, and I opened the door and stepped down. I turned to assist Miss Quallsford, but an elderly groom in livery had hurried forward to take her overnight bag and offer her a hand.

"Evening, Miss Emmeline," he said.

"Good evening, Ralph," she replied. "How is Mrs. Quallsford?"

"A little better, Miss Emmeline."

"Has the doctor called?"

"He stopped this afternoon."

The train was already in motion again. Its lights vanished into the distance, leaving us in darkness. The groom took charge of bags and bundles with surprising dispatch and led us to a waiting trap. He handed Miss Quallsford into it. I stood back, waiting for him to light the lamps, but the trap had none.

I knew that there would be room on the box only for the driver and one passenger; I was about to find a place for myself with the luggage, but Miss Quallsford, with an invitation that sounded like an order, summoned me to the seat beside her and took the reins herself. I had a momentary apprehension about her driving home in total darkness. Then I reminded myself that she certainly had made the trip dozens or perhaps even hundreds of times. More important, so had the horse. I climbed up, ignoring the helping hand that Ralph offered to me, and he perched on the luggage. A moment later we were following a rough rural road into the night, and I sensed, rather than saw, the strangeness of the land that closed in on us.

It was a land without landmarks. The darkness blended with level ground that had once been sea bottom—as I learned the following day—and each became a part of the other.

The world I had occupied until now conveyed a reassuring impression of permanence. When God made hills or valleys, He left them undisturbed until they acquired an antiquity far beyond the imaginings of a mere mortal. This land was different. Here God performed experiments, trying out new blendings of sea and land and changing His mind catastrophically within the span of recorded history, so that former seaports were stranded miles inland, islands came to rest surrounded by farms instead of by water, and valleys lost their rivers. Humankind had entered its own puny experiments in direct competition with the Almighty.

And the land seemed enshrouded in a suspenseful stillness, spiritually unmarked by the inconsequential frenzies of those peoples who inhabited the Marshes for the brief hours or centuries allotted to them and then moved on, leaving behind them a mystery that only the awakening touch of God could fathom.

We plodded on into a night that was one with the land that it enfolded, following an invisible road with endless windings and zigzags that not even daylight could have satisfactorily accounted for. Suddenly the hoof beats rang hollow as the horse trotted onto a bridge. The road became smoother, with a gravelled surface. It began to point upward. Ahead and above us were the scattered lights of a village.

Havenchurch consisted of two long, unlit streets of old buildings in various stages of decay. I would have seen very little of it had the clouds not parted opportunely. The moon, though still low in the sky, had waned but little from the full, and its touch of ghostly silver softened the village's shabbiness.

A windmill with a disused look about it stood at the end of the row of houses like a sentinel long deceased. We moved onto the smoother surface of the village's High Street, and I looked about curiously. Beyond an open door, a smith was shoeing a horse while a stout farmer watched critically in the light of the forge. A prosperous smith, I told myself, would not interrupt his leisure to do a job better left for morning. There was an inn, a grocer, a draper, a baker, a wheelwright, another grocer—the usual establishments offering goods and services in a rural village. From the general air of shabbiness, I deduced that these local merchants sold barely enough to survive and that the young doctor who looked curiously at our trap from his surgery window received part of his income in local produce and the remainder in unpaid accounts. Even the public houses had a dim, unpatronized air about them.

Church bells chimed the quarter hour, sounding as though they were tolling just above our heads, but I could see no church. It was a spectral reverberation that hung in the air around us.

The flash of a lantern directed my attention to a shop that looked different from the others. It had recently been painted, and the name, prominent in large, gilt letters, read: "Quallsford Importing Company."

"Is that a family firm?" I asked Miss Quallsford.

She had lost herself in her own thoughts; she started when I spoke, and then she was disconcerted to find that she had no comprehension of what I had asked. I repeated the question.

"It is my brother's firm," she answered. "He had great expectations for it."

An importing company remote from any seaport could have been viewed as one more indication of the land's strangeness; or perhaps it merely gave credence to her brother's suicide. If he had entertained great expectations for such a firm, he had been doomed to a great disappointment. I wondered whether he had already experienced it.

There was a lovely old inn called the Royal Swan. As we passed it, I said awkwardly, "I had planned on staying in the village."

"There is plenty of room at Sea Cliffs," she answered impatiently, "but first we must see what my brother's wife says. Sea Cliffs belongs to her, now."

We left the High Street for the rough, unsurfaced road beyond, which continued to point upward. Suddenly an enormous shadow loomed on our left: the church. After we passed it, the road closed in on us and became a winding, rutted country lane. The moon had disappeared again, and the trap lurched and bounced along in darkness with branches occasionally scraping it on either side. I could not see the road, and neither could Miss Quallsford, but the horse plodded forward confidently.

Neither could I see much of Sea Cliffs when we arrived. We made an abrupt turn, climbed steeply, turned again, and suddenly, at the end of a park, a large building stood before us with several lighted windows. The trap halted in front of it; the groom sprang down and assisted Miss Quallsford to dismount. She spoke softly to him, but there was a note of urgency in her voice. I leaped down on the other side and turned to assist the groom with our bags and packages. Miss Quallsford placed her hand on my arm and said, "Come."

We walked towards the house. As we crossed the portico, the massive door swung open and light poured from within. A strange apparition stood poised there, but whether it intended to greet us or drive us off was not immediately evident. It was a woman, perhaps of the same age as Miss Quallsford and also dressed in black, but her opposite in appearance and manner: Tall, dark, and slender, with an exotic, foreign air about her where Miss Quallsford seemed the very embodiment of English femininity.

She stood in sullen silence while Miss Quallsford introduced us.

"Larissa Quallsford, my brother's widow. Larissa, this is Mr. Jones. He is Sherlock Holmes's assistant. He has come to investigate Edmund's murder."

"Murder!"

She shrieked the word at us. "There has been no murder. You—" she pointed a quivering finger at her sister-in-law—"you drove him to it. You. You did it. You made Edmund kill himself! Go away. Both of you—go away!"

She whirled abruptly and ran down the corridor to vanish into the house.

This would have been disconcerting enough without Emmeline Quallsford's reaction. She stood for a long moment with head bowed. When she looked at me again, there were tears in her eyes.

"I am so sorry," she said. "You have wasted a journey. I should have known that it would be impossible. Obviously you cannot investigate Edmund's death if she will not admit you to the house."

"Many people feel that a tragedy has been compounded if a death is called murder," I said. "Perhaps in a day or two—"

"Perhaps," Miss Quallsford agreed. "Will you return to London? I could write to you or telegraph when she seems more—more in control of herself."

"I shall have to ask Mr. Holmes for instructions," I said. "There are certain to be inquiries that I can make without disturbing you here. If there is accommodation, I will stay at the inn we passed."

"The Swan," she agreed. "It is the better of the two available. Very well. Ralph will take you. If I have a message for you, I will send it to the Swan."

We walked back to the waiting trap. Ralph had removed Miss Quallsford's bags and bundles, but he had left my bag. The instruction that she murmured to him when we arrived must have been to wait with it until she saw how the mistress of the house would receive us.

I protested that I could easily walk, but she firmly dismissed that thought as nonsense.

"It would take you for ever in the dark. It is a poor road, and it can be dangerous at night. Ralph will drive you."

No doubt she was right, but I would have welcomed a long walk after the interminable, cramped train ride and the rough, uncomfortable road. I needed to think about the report that I would wire to Sherlock Holmes.

For I had seen, in the corridor behind Larissa Quallsford, peering out of a doorway, an ugly, elderly woman with a prominent hook nose, and I knew, in a sudden flash of intuition, that I had discovered the identity of the old crone who asked for pitahayas in Spitalfields Market.

CHAPTER
4

I now describe my Havenchurch investigation in detail as an illustration of the way I worked for and with Sherlock Holmes. My task was to cover as much ground as possible as quickly as I could, and to apply his methods as effectively as my own training and imagination permitted, so that all of the data that a finished case required would be assembled for him when he arrived on the scene. This ideal was rarely achieved, but it always remained foremost in my mind as I worked.

At the time of the Quallsford Case, Sherlock Holmes was in his late forties. He seemed to be enjoying an astonishingly energetic, vigorous middle-age, but the rigours he had imposed upon himself for so many years with his arduous methods of investigation had exacted a punishing toll, and he was increasingly appreciative of the value of youthful energy and youthful legs to relieve him of a portion of this strenuous effort.

As for the effectiveness of my work, Dr. Watson frequently complained that his own efforts at independent investigation were always scorned by Sherlock Holmes because everything of importance had been missed. I occasionally missed something of importance, but Sherlock Holmes never criticized me for that. The most difficult task the detective faces is to recognize, in a vast accumulation of data, those few facts that are of genuine significance. Sherlock Holmes had no equal at this. When I failed, he was amused and possibly even gratified. Even though I had taken enormous strides towards professional competence, it pleased him to know that he was still the master.

I presented myself at the Royal Swan, where Mr. Werner, the landlord, a small, rotund man whose waistline was vibrant testimony to the excellence of his wife's cooking, greeted me with surprised enthusiasm. It was past the season for summer visitors, and guests were infrequent. He agreed that I could have a late supper, or even two or three of them, if I so desired.

"The wife's got no one to cook for but me and the help," he confided. "Have your meals whenever you like."

I settled comfortably into a cheerful, large, first-floor room that overlooked the High Street. Before going down to eat, I composed a cryptic telegram for Sherlock Holmes and dated it the following morning. It read: "Staying Royal Swan Havenchurch. Will study Quallsford Importing Company inventory and records. Old friend from Spitalfields asks to be remembered."

Then I sat back and pondered how I should dispatch it. Emmeline Quallsford had sent her telegram from Rye. I felt certain that she would have done so even if the village had its own telegraph office. She would not want all of Havenchurch to know that she was in contact with Sherlock Holmes, and, until he chose to make his interest in the Quallsford tragedy public knowledge, neither did I. I also had a presentiment that Sherlock Holmes's growing fame might extend to the Rye telegraph office. My instinct was to keep even an ambiguous message as private as possible.

I addressed the telegraph form to Loxton & Lagg, Importers, 221B Baker Street, London, and sealed it into an envelope. Then I took another envelope, stuffed several blank pages into it, sealed it, and addressed it to Her Majesty's Customs House, Rye.

I called down to the landlord and asked him if he had anyone who could carry important papers to Rye in the morning.

"Joe can ride over on the pony any time you like," he said.

"Excellent," I said. "Send him to me as soon as he has had breakfast."

At such moments I deeply missed Rabby's resourcefulness and reliability. There was a matter that I urgently needed to investigate in Rye, but I had to give my first attention to Havenchurch. I considered telegraphing for him, and then I decided to wait until I had seen Joe perform.

Mr. Werner asked permission to join me at the lavish cold supper that his wife had laid out. We discussed the weather, which had been unseasonably cool, and the South African situation, concerning which he displayed a surprising sympathy for the Boers. We had finished the meal and adjourned to the parlour with a pint each of his home-made bitter before curiosity burst through his friendly restraint.

"Came down with Miss Quallsford, didn't you?" he asked.

"That I did," I agreed noncommittally.

"Solicitors' clerk?"

"Clerk," I admitted. "Not solicitors'. Importers'. Loxton & Lagg. London importing firm."

He evidenced astonishment. "That so? I would have thought solicitors'. Emmeline is going to need her own solicitor before this is finished. She and Larissa will be fighting like tomcats over the estate. They'll never get along under one roof without Edmund to keep the peace."

"Miss Quallsford is a friend of the niece of one of our directors," I said. "She is concerned about her brother's importing business, and I was sent down here to inspect the inventory and the books and appraise its potential."

"That so? I suppose most people would say it has no potential. Myself, I am not so sure about that. Edmund Quallsford was a dreamer, but that importing firm was a dream he and several others believed in." He sighed. "It is a great pity things ended the way they did. It is sad. That business might have been a grand thing for Havenchurch."

"You believed in it?"

"Aye. That I did. I suppose there is no chance, now, that a grand firm from Lunnon would try to carry on a business here. Piddling thing it must seem to anyone accustomed to dealing in shiploads from real ships, but it promised a lot to a little village like ours."

"I know nothing at all about it except that it exists," I said. "I never heard of Edmund Quallsford before today. Suppose you tell me about him and this promising business."

"Aye. Glad to." He went to refill his glass. I had scarcely touched mine, and he asked anxiously, "Too bitter for you?"

"Too *much* for me," I said, "after that splendid supper. I will have to digest a bit before I can drink."

"Aye." He settled himself again and took a long draught. "Edmund and Emmeline Quallsford. Those two were a pair. I always said that Emmeline should have been the boy. Edmund was a gentle, slight, retiring type, often sickly, and Emmeline was the tomboy daring him to jump this or climb that. They were left to themselves too much—no doubt at all about that. Being two or three or maybe ten cuts above all the other children hereabouts, they weren't permitted to associate. Mostly they went nowhere. They had their governess, a rarely well-educated woman, and she kept them to their books and taught them well—maybe too well. Edmund went directly to Oxford without ever having been to school, though one always wonders whether his father's influence helped him out. Oswald Quallsford was a bit of a wastrel, but he had friends in high places. No doubt Edmund's book learning proved valuable to him, but Emmeline got her head packed with things she had no use for. Gave her the wrong ideas, I would say. Nice-looking young woman like her, from a good family, she could have married well, but she wouldn't, and neither her father nor her brother could make her do what she wouldn't do."

He paused for breath and raised his glass.

I had an inspiration. "Governess still with them?" I asked.

"That she is. Doris Fowler. Came from a local family. Had a rich aunt who educated her beyond her prospects, as we used to say. She was a plain girl and a homely lady, and now she is an ugly old woman, but there never was any doubt that she had brains—all brains and no common sense. That must have been bad for the Quallsford children, too."

"Is the Quallsford family wealthy?" I asked.

"That's a good question. It *was* wealthy a long time back, and it was still well off when Oswald Quallsford set about squandering what money was left. By the time the children were grown, he had pretty much succeeded. There was enough to send Edmund to Oxford, though Oswald may have borrowed for that like he was borrowing for everything else. He died owing everyone in this part of the country who was foolish enough to lend to him or give him credit—not to mention a lot of firms in Lunnon, where he spent most of his time. But things have been looking up since the children started managing their own affairs. Edmund's wife brought him a nice bit of money, and he seems to have done well with his business interests. I know for a fact that he paid off all of Oswald's debts within a year or two of his marriage—that was his way."

"If the importing business was that profitable, why are people saying that it has no potential?" I asked.

"The importing business was just a sideline—something he did for Havenchurch. He never made any profit from that. His business interests were in Lunnon. No doubt it was his wife's money that saved the family, but he certainly made good use of it."

"His wife has a foreign look about her," I observed.

"Aye—that she does. Comes packed with silly foreign airs from France for all that she has spent most of her life in England. Her brother, name of Monier, was at Oxford with Edmund. They exchanged visits during holidays, and the young men were introduced to each other's sisters. Edmund and Larissa Monier fell in love, and Charles Monier would have been happy to make it a double wedding. Emmeline wouldn't have any part of that, even though it would have pleased Edmund. Emmeline always had a mind of her own."

"Would it be possible to send a note to Miss Quallsford?" I asked.

"To Emmeline? Certainly. I'll send it up right now."

I hesitated. "It's late. Perhaps it should wait until morning."

The landlord shrugged. "Edmund has been dead for two days, but I don't think there's much sleep going on at that house."

I went to my room to write the note. I told Emmeline Quallsford that I would like to look over the records of her brother's importing company in the morning, and I asked her to make the necessary arrangements. Joe and the pony were called into service, and they clumped away into the darkness. I went to bed thinking about the elderly crone, educated beyond her prospects, who had asked for pitahayas in Spitalfields Market. Until I fell asleep, some trick of the night air kept the quarter-hour chimes of the church bells reverberating weirdly just above my head.

In the morning I was up early for a walk and my first glimpse of Havenchurch by daylight. It was much larger than it had seemed at night, but it was also much more shabby and impoverished. It possessed an illustrious history that I was not yet aware of—no stranger could have suspected it—and it had once been a substantial, prosperous community. The church dated from the twelfth century, and the village was already an old settlement at that time. The sea had reached far inland, making Havenchurch a minor port, but access to shipping invited disaster as well as prosperity. Vikings had sacked the village in the early Middle Ages, and later the French fleet had done the same. King Alfred had defeated the Danish invaders a few miles from here. I looked across the peaceful, verdant countryside and tried to imagine a time when ocean vessels sailed proudly past. The notion seemed preposterous, but Tenterden, some miles further inland, had been one of the Cinque Ports. Havenchurch had shared in the great wool prosperity that the area enjoyed in the

Middle Ages, and its church, far too large even for a prosperous village, was testimony to this.

But now Havenchurch was a shabby, stagnated place. I strolled along the High Street looking at old buildings that had been built on the foundations of older buildings. There was an odd conglomeration of architectural styles, all venerable. Here was a black-and-white Tudor house next door to a cottage of indeterminate ancestry; the building nearby had an old upper storey imposed upon an older lower storey to which a rickety greengrocer's shop had been appended to displace the front garden. There were timbered buildings, and stone buildings, and brick buildings. This odd assortment of structures might have been picturesque had they not been so badly in need of repair. The few that had thatched roofs should have looked quaintly historical; instead, they left me wondering how such ragged thatching could survive the winter gales. The village's desperate economic straits were manifest in the fact that its residents had looked upon Edmund Quallsford's pathetic little importing business as their salvation.

I had seen a draper's sign on a building the night before; this belonged to the village's one prosperous-looking establishment, a large general store with premises formed by combining several adjoining shops. The long sign across the front informed customers that Geo. Adams was draper, grocer, and clothier; smaller signs extended his activities to include hats, boots, and shoes; and displays in the windows suggested that he offered for sale—or took orders for—almost anything. He also delivered to the surrounding countryside by horse and cart and to nearby customers by handcart, and at that early hour there already was a bustle about the store.

I walked to the end of the High Street and back. The only other evidences of activity were the squeals and bleating from animals in the slaughter houses behind the two butcher shops, and the cloud of smoke emitted by the bakery's chimney. The smoke hung low and formed a long, dark line across the level Marshland to the east.

I returned to the Royal Swan. Before I sat down to the lavish breakfast Mrs. Werner had prepared for me, I invited Joe up to my room for a conference. He was a sturdy, freckled lad of about twelve, and he followed after me twisting his cap nervously.

I closed the door and looked at him sternly. "Can you keep a secret, Joe?" I asked in a conspiratorial whisper.

He nodded excitedly.

"You are going to take something to Rye for me," I said, continuing to whisper. "Before you leave, you will show Mr. Werner this envelope." I handed him the package of blank paper addressed to Her Majesty's Customs House, Rye.

He nodded again, eyes sparkling. Excitement had rendered him mute.

"You will tell Mr. Werner that you are going to the Customs House in Rye. But when you are safely away from Havenchurch, you will find a secluded place and burn this envelope and its contents. It contains only blank paper."

Now his mouth was wide open.

"You are really going to Rye to do two things," I said. "The first is to hand in this telegram." I clinked coins into his hand to pay for it. Then I leaned closer to him. "The second is to find out at the railway station whether Doris Fowler made a trip to London two weeks ago." She would have taken the train from Rye, I thought, because her departure there would be less conspicuous than at Havenchurch Halt. "Do you know who Doris Fowler is?" I asked him.

He did. A boy of that age, working at a village inn, knew all about everyone.

"Mr. Werner thinks I am an importer's clerk, but I am not," I whispered. "I am a detective—and you are the only person in Havenchurch who knows that. Now you are a detective, too. You are working for me. Try to find out about Doris Fowler without letting on that you are interested. Do you understand?"

He understood. He confessed later that he had read more than a few stories about detectives. He even had read some about Sherlock Holmes.

"Say nothing to anyone," I told him. "The case will be ruined if the culprits even suspect that we are detectives. Now make haste!"

He was off like a shot.

Mr. Werner joined me for breakfast, and I encouraged him to talk about Havenchurch. "What do ordinary people do for a living?" I asked.

He shook his head sadly. "Sometimes I wonder myself. Labourers and farm hands don't earn much even when they can get work, and they are laid off for weeks during the winter. Poor relief keeps them going after a fashion. For years George Adams has held this village together. He lets needy people put things on the slate and pay later with their hops money."

"Hops money?" I echoed.

"The poor people pick hops every fall. A family can earn several pounds during the season."

"I suppose the Quallsford family is important to the village," I said.

"Not so much as it might be. Oswald was too la-di-da to buy in Havenchurch except on credit, which cost him nothing, and the Quallsford women always have had their clothes directly from Lunnon."

I thought of Emmeline Quallsford and her long shopping session with the Regent Street draper.

"Edmund was trying to change that," Mr. Werner said. "He bought a bit from the smaller merchants—a shilling now and then, here and there, it made a difference. And his importing business let poor people earn something. Now we've lost all of that."

Mrs. Werner interrupted us. Someone was asking to see me. "It's Nat Whyte," she said in an aside to Mr. Werner.

She was short and plump like her husband, and her manner was as friendly as his, but she escorted a gaunt, elderly man into the room as though she were holding him at arm's length. His white hair and deeply wrinkled face were suggestive of the Biblical three score years and ten, but there was nothing decrepit about his movements and manner. He had a nautical swing to his walk, his brown face evidenced days in an open boat, and he was as lithe and energetic as men a third his age.

He told me that Miss Quallsford had sent him a note asking him to show me anything I wanted to see about her brother's importing business.

I invited him to share my breakfast. That brought scowls from both the landlord and his wife—Nat Whyte's clothing looked and smelled as though he had just returned from a week at sea, and his person was no ornament to the inn's dining room—but there were no other guests, and his score would be billed to that wealthy firm of London importers, Loxton & Lagg, so the landlord subsided and signalled to his wife to bring more food.

The old sailor quickly consumed a breakfast that would have done credit to two hungry men. He was much too busy eating to talk, but later, as we strolled down the High Street towards the Quallsford Importing Company, he answered my questions willingly.

"Was Edmund Quallsford much of a sailor?" I asked him.

"Wasn't much for sailing," Nat Whyte said. "Never saw a man so awkward about handling a boat. He had no strength in his arms. But he liked being sailed."

"Did you have him often as a passenger?"

"Whenever I would," Nat Whyte said simply.

Listening to him talk, I tried to envision Edmund Quallsford as a boy, scion of a once wealthy family of graziers, and imagine whether some seemingly innocent event of his youth had fatally blighted his life. He had grown up a landlubber, as any grazier must be, and he was physically frail; and yet he lived tantalizingly close enough to the sea to be fatally imbued with its romance while failing to comprehend its grim reality. He went to Rye whenever he could, but he shunned the old town on its high hill and instead took the long walk to the harbour, there being no passenger transport at that time. He made friends with Nat Whyte and several other fishermen, who occasionally took him out in their boats.

He grew up, he went to Oxford, his father died, he married. When he finally returned home with his new wife, his friends had grown old. The arduous life of a fisherman was becoming difficult for them, and drift net fishing from small boats was losing out to the larger trawling smacks that were more efficient and forced prices down.

"But he knew we had a spot of work left in us," Nat Whyte said warmly. "He set up this company just to give us and a few others a bit of income. Old sailors, old carriers, and the like. There wasn't much in it for him, but it was nice for the rest of us."

I said incredulously, "Do you mean that his importing company used small fishing boats for transport?"

"Why not?" Nat Whyte asked. "It don't take the *Great Eastern* to cross the Channel in fair weather."

I questioned him until I had all of the story, and it still seemed unbelievable. Edmund Quallsford had been distressed that these friends of his youth were facing want in their old age, so he conceived the remarkable idea of an importing company that would use the old sailors and their small boats to bring goods from the Continent. Local carriers would deliver the goods to merchants in neighbouring communities. His ultimate goal was nothing less than the revitalization of Havenchurch. Profits from England's foreign trade normally went for the enrichment of London and other large ports. A generous share of the money from this little business would remain in the village, and be spent there, and the entire area would benefit.

And what did he import?

The building contained one large workroom and a storage room, with storage bins in the cellars. Sherlock Holmes possessed astonishingly minute information about almost anything; I, alas, did not. I had no idea what constituted a normal stock of goods for a small importing company. I set about forming a mental inventory so I could report to him in detail.

There was a bolt of silk with a singularly unattractive print pattern partially unrolled on a long table; someone had been cutting off lengths. I saw one more bolt of silk, untouched; scraps of lace; a number of small kegs of French brandy; bottles of French wine of various vintages; a large sack of coarsely shredded tobacco from which someone had been weighing out and packaging small bags. There were cartons of coloured silk thread; variously shaped glass bottles; a box of corks; a case of small animals carved from wood. The commercial manipulations involved in culling such odds and ends from the Continent, transporting them to Rye by small boat, bringing them inland to Havenchurch by whatever means, and then peddling them about the countryside by wagon, were awesome to contemplate. Could Edmund Quallsford actually offer these items to local merchants for a few pence less than goods could be supplied by train from London?

I indicated the carved animals to Nat Whyte. "Where did he sell them?" I asked.

"Here and there," Nat Whyte said with a shrug. "When something was offered cheap, he would pick up a bit to see if he could make a go of it."

"Those don't seem to have gone," I observed.

He shrugged again. "Some things take time."

In a corner of the room, a ledger lay open on the rickety table that Edmund Quallsford had used as a desk. I thumbed through a few pages and then pushed it aside. My education was not equal to account books. I could learn what I needed to know much more quickly by talking with Nat Whyte.

He told me that Edmund Quallsford had contacts with merchants in France who found for him remnants of merchandise that could be purchased cheaply for cash. The old sailors provided cheap transport and were pleased to earn a bit for easy runs in nice weather.

Carriers who conveyed merchandise about the Marsh area with horse and wagon could toss Edmund Quallsford's small shipments on top of their regular loads and take the few pence they earned as a bonus. Their employers, if they had any, probably knew nothing about this or winked at it.

A number of local people earned an occasional shilling cutting up bolts of silk or packaging small items. Village merchants who never would have been able to dispose of an entire bolt of a single pattern of cloth could buy short lengths of several patterns, each long enough to make a garment or trim one. People in Havenchurch and the surrounding communities were able to save a few pence on the goods they bought. The merchants made a small profit they otherwise would have missed. Village tradesmen about the Marsh considered Edmund Quallsford a resourceful young man from whom great things might come. The impoverished people at the lower end of the village, who were his firm's incidental beneficiaries, venerated him.

"He'll be missed," Nat Whyte said sadly. "I'll tell you this—there will be a crowd at his funeral, and the tears will be genuine."

I opened the ledger again and found an accounts summary showing a loss of six pounds for the month of August. "He wasn't making much for himself," I observed.

"He said that didn't matter. First he had to get the business going and develop a list of regular customers. Then there would be something for him. It was doing well, it was. He seemed pleased. What will come of it now? No toff up in London could make the arrangements Mr. Quallsford did and tell us when to sail."

"How did he get word that the merchandise was ready in France?" I asked.

"Don't know," Nat Whyte said. "Letter, I suppose. Then he would come and ask me how the weather looked, and I would say, 'Two trips tomorrow,' and he would give me the nod. He knew I would know. Never told me what to do. Never asked me to do anything. Just asked what I could do, and I would tell him, and he would give me the nod."

There was no file of correspondence, but Edmund Quallsford might have handled that at home. I sat back and thought. Throughout my years of training, Sherlock Holmes had emphasized over and over again that facts were useless when the investigator was blind to their implications, and there was an obvious tilt to this business that I did not care for. A small concern like the Quallsford Importing Company, in a quiet, out-of-the-way location so conveniently near the coast, with an unlikely owner and a volume of trade that amounted to no more than a dribbling pretence, looked too obviously like a front for smuggling.

There was no point in asking the old sailor whether everything brought from the Continent got entered into this ledger. Instead, I asked him whether Edmund Quallsford had looked after the bookkeeping himself.

"No, sir," he said. "Mr. Herks did that."

"Who is Mr. Herks?" I asked.

"Chemist. Greengrocer. Postmaster. He did all of Mr. Quallsford's record keeping."

Sherlock Holmes's method was founded on the observation of trifles and the ability to see what others overlooked. I could not pretend to his genius for intuitively knowing which trifles were important, but I could strive not to overlook anything. While Nat Whyte waited with increasing impatience, I went through the building again, noting all the goods on hand and even sifting the dust of empty bins for clues as to their former contents. I also made a thorough search for tell-tale signs of secret rooms or compartments, but I found none.

"I'd like to talk with Mr. Herks," I said finally. "When would be a good time to see him?"

"Any time you like. Miss Quallsford sent him a note. By me. She told him to tell you anything you wanted to know. He's waiting for you now."

Nat Whyte locked up the building, and we walked back along the High Street towards the shabby shop where Mr. Herks eked out a living from his combined enterprises. Probably he, too, would miss the small income he received from the Quallsford Importing Company.

"Why would Edmund Quallsford want to kill himself?" I asked. "He seemed to have everything to live for."

Nat Whyte's face was a study in blankness. "That wife of his—" he began. Then he caught himself and said brusquely, "I don't know."

"Did you ever hear him use the word 'pitahayas'?"

"Lots of times," Nat Whyte said. "Talking to other people, he used it to make jokes, or what he thought was jokes. I didn't understand them, and he never made jokes to me."

"Never?" I asked.

"No, sir. He didn't like it when people poked fun at his importing business. It was a very serious thing to him. When he talked with me, he never made jokes."

CHAPTER
5

M r. Herks was a robust, red-faced man who looked out of place dispensing pills, or vegetables, or postage stamps. The display of sheep dip in one corner of the cluttered shop seemed to offer something more in his line. He greeted me matter-of-factly when Nat Whyte introduced me.

"If I'm needed again, come and tell me," the old sailor said as he took his leave of me. "I live in the cottage with green shutters near the school."

Mr. Herks led me to his living quarters at the rear of the shop. "A great tragedy," he said. "I spoke with Edmund that morning at church. He seemed cheerful, though he was looking a bit pale."

"Was there anything about his behaviour to suggest that he might take his life?" I asked.

"Nothing. His mind was full of business. He had the opportunity to buy up some print cloth at a good price, and he had several prospective customers for it."

"How much tobacco and brandy did the firm handle?" I asked.

Mr. Herks pointed a finger. "I know what you are thinking, and you could not be more mistaken. Every item that Edmund Qualls-ford imported was properly declared, and I have the customs receipts to prove it. That was the reason he hired me. He said, 'Herks,

I don't want any suspicions at all about this company of mine. I don't know anything about keeping records, but I want books that no one can find fault with, least of all the excisemen. I'm leaving it to you. See that everything is done lawfully.' And I did."

Not only had he recorded every item that Edmund imported, but he had records to show where it had been disposed of. Edmund Quallsford, Mr. Herks said fervently, was one of the world's few honest men, and anyone trying to besmirch his memory would have him, Harry Herks, to contend with.

Finally I took my leave of him and returned to the Royal Swan. Mr. Werner greeted me eagerly. He wanted to know whether the great Lunnon firm of Loxton & Lagg was ready to take over the Quallsford Importing Company. I paused long enough to explain that the decision was not mine to make. I was only gathering information for my superiors.

I went to my room to write a full report for Sherlock Holmes. A few minutes later there was a soft tap on the door. Joe's freckled face looked in, grinning broadly. He slipped into the room and closed the door silently.

"Two weeks ago. Either Monday or Tuesday," he whispered. "She took the early train to Lunnon. The porter can't remember which train she came back on. He doesn't think it was the late train. Ralph, the Quallsfords' groom, took her to the station and met her."

"Joe," I said solemnly, "you are not only a detective, you are a *good* detective." I tossed a florin to him, and he caught it elatedly. "Has Havenchurch had any rumours or gossip about smugglers lately?" I asked him.

He shook his head perplexedly.

"Start listening, Joe. But remember—don't let anyone know you are interested."

He nodded and went out quietly.

I wrote my report, addressed the envelope to Loxton & Lagg at 221B Baker Street, London, and took it to the post office corner of Mr. Herks's shop. Then I returned to the Royal Swan for lunch.

When I finished eating, there was another visitor waiting to see me. This one was of a type that could no more be mistaken in a small English village than a Turkish sultan—a rural sergeant of police.

Mr. Werner, who hovered curiously in the background while our meeting took place, was too obviously having sober second thoughts about the harmless importer's clerk he had been sheltering. In his experience, respectable clerks did not have the police seeking them out the day after they arrived.

The sergeant, a large, middle-aged man of serious mien, stepped forward and offered me his hand. "Mr. Jones? Sergeant Donley."

I shook the hand warmly. "Glad to see you again, Sergeant. I was hoping you would have time for a visit."

The landlord relaxed visibly. He had the sergeant's broad back turned towards him, and he was unable to see his puzzled reaction. I invited the sergeant to my room, calling an order to the landlord for two pints of his excellent bitter as we turned towards the stairs.

The sergeant did not speak again until I had closed the door behind us. Then he said, with a ponderousness that matched his appearance, "I had a telegram from Mr. Holmes. He did me a considerable service once, years ago. Solved a case for me and let me take the whole credit for it. He asked me to look you up and assist you if I could, either officially or privately, and of course I will be glad to do anything I can. But I don't remember that you and I have ever met."

I explained the role that I had assumed and my concern for avoiding local gossip, and his puzzlement vanished as he eased his bulk into the larger of the room's two chairs.

"That is quite all right," he said. "Mr. Holmes is a great one for disguises—no one has better reason to know that than I—and I see the need for them on occasion, though of course they are not practical for the local police. Everyone knows us too well. But I must confess that I cannot think of anything in this quiet neighbourhood that Mr. Holmes would find interesting."

There was a knock at the door, and the landlord entered with the two pints of his home-made bitter.

"Just what we needed," I exclaimed. "Mr. Werner, there is no better accompaniment to a reunion of old friends than a finely brewed beer."

"True enough," the sergeant said, following my lead with a good-natured jollity. "But a pint may not be sufficient to drink to the last meeting, and the present one, and also the next."

The beaming landlord promised that he would not let us run out.

When the door had closed behind him, the sergeant resumed his attitude of puzzlement. "Mr. Holmes is welcome to anything he asks for if I have it. What is it that you are investigating?"

"The murder of Edmund Quallsford," I said.

The sergeant stared at me in astonishment. "The *murder*—does Mr. Holmes say it was *murder?*"

"No," I said. "Miss Emmeline Quallsford says it was murder. She asked Mr. Holmes to investigate."

"Oh, well. Miss Emmeline." The sergeant shrugged. "I didn't know that she was saying that, but the family was understandably upset, and both she and Mrs. Quallsford have said a lot of things that made no sense, some of them about each other. I find it hard to believe that Mr. Holmes would accept that kind of statement without evidence just because it came from a pretty face. Edmund Quallsford committed suicide. He wrote a farewell letter to his wife. Then he laid down on his bed, pressed the muzzle of a revolver to the side of his head, and pulled the trigger. Not even a wizard like Mr. Holmes can make murder of that."

"Was there any sign of a struggle?" I asked.

"None."

"How do you know that he wrote the letter?"

"It was his writing. There is no doubt at all about that."

"Who was in the house at the time?"

"Two servants and the old governess. It was Sunday afternoon, you know. Miss Quallsford had gone for a long walk along the cliffs. Mrs. Quallsford had taken the children to visit a friend near Stone. Edmund Quallsford went to see someone—about something connected with his importing company, it was thought. The servants had the impression that he would be gone all afternoon, but he returned unexpectedly about an hour later, and he told them he wasn't feeling well—he had a bad headache and was going to bed. That old house is solidly built, and the servants were in the kitchen, which is in the west wing. They didn't hear the shot. Larissa found his body when she returned."

"Where was the governess?" I asked.

"Sleeping. In the east wing. She and Miss Quallsford have that wing of the house to themselves except for the children's schoolroom. She is elderly and sometimes a bit confused. She knew nothing at all about it until one of the servants thought to wake her up long afterwards and tell her.

"Havenchurch is a goodly distance from London, Mr. Jones, but that doesn't mean that we are simpletons here. I have heard one or two things about motives for murder and murders disguised as suicide, and I have even seen a few oddities myself. I personally made certain that all of those people were where they said they were. Miss Quallsford walked all the way to the Iden Road and stopped to call on an elderly woman who once was a servant at Sea Cliffs. She was seen by several people along the way, going and coming. I have a note of the exact time that Mrs. Quallsford and the children arrived at the friend's house in Stone and the time that they left—with the names of several witnesses. The servants alibi each other. So do the labourers who were on the estate, and I have their testimony that no one went near the house. A good investigator takes nothing for granted, Mr. Jones—not even an obvious suicide like this one. Mr. Holmes taught me that."

"He would be proud to hear you say it," I said. "Whose revolver was it?"

For the first time the sergeant hesitated. "We make it out to be old Oswald's. Supposedly it disappeared years ago, but indications are that Edmund had it all the time."

I shook my head. "Mr. Holmes will want something better than 'indications.' He will also want to see the farewell letter and samples of Edmund's handwriting."

"He is welcome. I can tell you positively that there is no mistaking the writing. It is distinctive. I compared it with several letters that Edmund had written."

"Distinctive handwriting is the easiest to forge," I said. "It is also a simple matter to murder a sleeping man and make it look like suicide. Place the revolver against his head and pull the trigger before he is aware of it. Make his dead hand grip the pistol in a natural position. Walk out. With the servants in another part of the house, anyone could have done it. The labourers may say that no one went near the house, but they certainly were not watching it alertly and continuously. The forged letter would have been prepared in advance, of course."

The sergeant was staring at me. "You actually believe that Edmund Quallsford was murdered? But why?"

"I don't believe anything at all. I am investigating, and my first question is whether the circumstances of the supposed suicide eliminate the possibility of murder. Since they do not, more questions have to be asked. For example, what reason did he have for committing suicide? Did he have money problems? Could he afford to sink money into a business that showed no profit? Was his marriage a happy one? Whom did he see just before he died? Did something happen at that interview that made him ill? Was the relationship between his wife and his sister as stormy before his death as it is now? Did anyone have a reason to want him dead? When we have enough answers to enough questions, then we will know. That is the trusted method of investigation for ordinary mortals such as us. Mr. Holmes has his own methods, of course. Have you ever heard the word 'pitahaya'?"

"Edmund Quallsford used it when he was joking. Some kind of nonsense word. I never figured out what he meant by it."

"How well did you know him?"

"Mr. Jones, a country policeman knows *everyone*. I have known Edmund Quallsford ever since he was born."

I shook my head. "How *well* did you know him? Can you answer all of the questions that I suggested?"

He was scowling at me.

"Who were his close friends?" I asked.

The scowl became troubled. "Everyone was his friend. Everyone liked him, but I don't suppose he had any really close friends. His only intimates were his own family."

"Did he have any enemies?"

"None," the sergeant said emphatically.

There was little more that he could tell me. I said ruefully, "My job is to collect facts for Mr. Holmes. Thus far, the crop is a meagre one: Edmund Quallsford had no enemies and no reason to want to die; he used the word 'pitahaya' as a joke; and he is dead."

"That last is true enough," the sergeant said with grim satisfaction. "Dead by his own hand."

"But that isn't a fact—yet," I pointed out.

We ordered another round of Mr. Werner's bitter for the sake of appearances, and he described the case that Sherlock Holmes had solved for him—but that is a tale for another time.

After he left, I composed a second cryptic telegram and sent it off to Rye with an elated Joe. Probably the pony was less enthusiastic, but Sherlock Holmes would want to know immediately that the police description of Edmund Quallsford's death did not exclude the possibility of murder.

I spent a long, unprofitable afternoon and evening wandering about Havenchurch and talking with anyone who had time for conversation. Dr. Watson customarily omitted such activity from his accounts. Often he was not even aware of it, and he conveyed the impression that Sherlock Holmes always went intuitively to the one person who could tell him what he wanted to know or to the one vital clue. He did not. He worked long and tirelessly for the results that Dr. Watson summarized so dramatically, and Sherlock Holmes's own complaint, frequently expressed, that Dr. Watson emphasized only the sensational aspects of his cases, was certainly justified.

Now much of that investigative tedium fell to me, and I worked the remainder of the day at it. I first went to the one prosperous-looking establishment in Havenchurch, the enterprising general store that sold everything. Its owner, George Adams, was a small, peppery, energetic man, too restless to talk for long about anything that did not relate to his business—a thin man who would never sit still long enough to become fat. He was very neatly dressed. He had removed his coat while rearranging some merchandise, and he carefully donned it again before he came to talk with me.

I explained my fictitious errand in Havenchurch.

"What do you want to know?" he asked.

"Anything you would care to tell me," I said. "Until yesterday, I had never heard of either Edmund Quallsford or his company."

"There never was a more honest, and upright, and kind man," George Adams said firmly. "He gave me the biggest surprise of my life when he walked into this store, asked for the balance due on Oswald Quallsford's account, and paid it in cash. It was more than six hundred pounds, and it came close to ruining my father. No one expected Edmund to make good on those old debts. The mortgages, yes, he would have to pay them off if he could or lose the land, but Oswald's small creditors, in Havenchurch and elsewhere, had long since written the accounts off to experience. It was a matter of honour to Edmund, and he did it at a time when he could have used the money himself. I happen to know that the Quallsfords were living very frugally just then, but it was important to Edmund to clear the family name. I don't know of anyone in this village who could possibly have an unkind thing to say about Edmund Qualls-ford."

"Did you ever hear him use the word 'pitahaya'?" I asked.

"Many times. There was some joke involved, but I never rightly understood what it was. Edmund expected people to laugh when he said that, so we laughed. Matter of being polite, you know."

"Why did he kill himself?" I asked.

Adams shook his head soberly. "I will always believe that it was an accident. Edmund was a sane, level-headed, practical man, and as far as I know, he had absolutely no reason for killing himself. If he pulled that trigger intentionally, he must have been demented."

"Did you ever notice any sign of his being demented?"

"Never," Adams said.

As for the importing company, Adams stocked several items Edmund Quallsford had offered. One or two of them had done very well. He thought it an excellent idea, and it certainly was very good for Havenchurch.

I talked with Sam Bates, the muscular blacksmith, who had never got over his astonishment at the way in which Edmund repaid his father's debts. "Quiet fellow," Bates said. "Frail. No push at all about him. I never saw much of him. He wasn't the type to bring in his own horses or come himself with a thing that needed fixing —he would send someone. But he was always polite and friendly and interested and willing to stop when you met and listen to anything you had to tell him about your family or your business. Why did he kill himself? He had no reason I know of. He certainly had no money problems, and he had a beautiful wife and two lovely children, and he had Sea Cliffs, a fine farm. The only thing I could think of was that he was off his head. The vicar says it was an accident, and that makes a lot more sense."

Wilbert Harman, an elderly man and one of Havenchurch's two butchers, was almost as tall and slender as Sherlock Holmes but with a perpetually mournful face. He described Edmund's repayment of his father's debts as though it were something read out of the Bible.

"I hated to cut them off, the Quallsfords," he said apologetically. "They had been buying from me for years. They bought from my father and probably from his father. Suddenly Oswald couldn't pay. When the account went past three hundred pounds, I had to choose between losing their business or going out of business. But I hated to do it. Edmund paid the account in full and started buying again, so there was no hard feeling on either side."

"And why would Edmund commit suicide?" I asked him.

Harman's mournful face underwent a convulsion of emotion. "Sergeant Donley said suicide, but I don't believe him. There just wasn't no reason for it. The coroner said an accident, and it must have been that way. Edmund was having a wonderfully successful life, and he was a man that could be successful without making anyone jealous. People loved him. We will never see another like him."

William Price, manure agent and corn dealer; Charles Walker, water bailiff; Thomas Strickney, saddler; Richard Lyster, shoemaker; David Wyatt, wheelwright and builder—all had kind things to say about Edmund Quallsford and the diligence with which he had paid off his father's debts. All had heard him use the word "pitahaya" and thought it a joke. None could suggest a reason for his wanting to kill himself, and all were reluctant to believe that his death was suicide.

One of the most interesting remarks came from Ben Paine, the mole catcher. Despite his odd occupation, Paine seemed much better educated than the usual rural labourer and far more articulate. "Edmund Quallsford wasn't just a gentleman," he said. "He was *gentlemanly*—to everyone. Most gentlemen are only gentlemanly to ladies or to other gentlemen."

I talked with all of the merchants and craftsmen on the High Street and with everyone else who was available. I looked Havenchurch over carefully from one end to the other, and I found only three mysteries that seemed worth pondering.

One concerned the identity of the person who left the circular imprint of a wooden stump throughout the village. By the time I finally staggered back to my room that night with an aching head,

I had seen and talked with much of the population of Havenchurch. I thought it mysterious that I had encountered the stump's imprint everywhere without ever glimpsing the one-legged man who owned it. I knew that it was a man. Employing Sherlock Holmes's methods, I measured his stride and the depth of the impressions he left with his natural foot. I estimated his height at more than six feet and his weight at almost fifteen stone, and the woman who matched that description would have been a spectacle. Probably anyone in Havenchurch could have told me who it was, but I did not want to appear curious until I had learned more about him.

An unknown one-legged man who had no established connection with the Quallsfords did not justify another report to Sherlock Holmes, so I wrote none.

The second mystery was more complicated. Graesney points an angular corner towards the intersection of the River Rother and the Royal Military Canal. When I strolled to the edge of the village to look out across the Marsh country and see if I could detect by daylight the strangeness that Sherlock Holmes had mentioned, I was surprised to see a long barge with a single sail moving up the river. Appended to that rural landscape, it looked as out of place as a Thames barge would have looked sailing along Oxford Street. As it tied up at a small landing stage, a wagon passed me, moving briskly towards the Rye Road. One of the two men seated on the box was Nat Whyte. The wagon turned south, took another turn towards the river, and I watched while it loaded goods from the barge.

That mystery evaporated while I thought about it. Whatever the fate of the Quallsford Importing Company, goods already ordered had to be dealt with.

The third mystery concerned the dead man. It did not seem possible to me that any human being could be so universally loved and respected and admired as Edmund Quallsford was by his fellow citizens of Havenchurch. I was sufficiently sceptical to extend my investigation far into the night in an attempt to find one person who disliked him. The village had two inns and a public house; after I had eaten another of Mrs. Werner's lavish meals, I sampled the beer —and the customers—in all three, and I actually found the person I was looking for. In fact, I found three witnesses whose attitudes towards Edmund Quallsford were in striking contrast to those of the other citizens of Havenchurch.

I investigated them carefully. Edmund Quallsford had discharged one of them for stealing and had refused employment to the second because of a bad reputation.

The third was more interesting. He was a morose, middle-aged man named Derwin Smith—a prosperous-looking man—who described Edmund Quallsford with such restrained enthusiasm that I wondered whether he might be the enemy that everyone had called non-existent.

"Why did Edmund commit suicide?" I asked.

"Ask the police," Smith said. "They say he did. I don't. I don't think he would have had the nerve to do it. Everyone says he was gentle, which is true, but he was also cowardly. As far as I know, he never owned a gun. He was afraid of guns. That revolver couldn't have been his father's. Oswald would have pawned that one years ago. Edmund simply did not have the character to kill himself, either accidentally or on purpose. He must have been murdered."

In all of those conversations about the death of Edmund Quallsford, Smith was the only person who used the word "murder." I resolved to learn more about him.

As for the others, the common people of Havenchurch were as distressed, and as perplexed, about Edmund Quallsford's death as the shopkeepers and tradesmen had been. Jack Browne, a stout, muscular man who operated his own carrier business and had transported goods about the Marsh for the Quallsford Importing Company, told me gloomily, "A lot of people will have less to eat with him gone."

Taff Harris, the man he was drinking with, grinned and patted Browne's protruding stomach with mock concern. "Wasting away already, you are. Don't tell me Edmund Quallsford's death means much out of your pocket."

"He gave me a fair piece of business," Browne said.

"A bit of lace and now and then a keg of brandy. If you don't carry it for him, you'll carry it for someone else."

Browne growled something in response and signalled the publican, who brought him another half-pint of mild. We were drinking in Havenchurch's Victoria Inn, a very shabby establishment, though the owners seemed to be working hard to make it respectable.

Harris turned to me. "Look," he said. "I didn't know Edmund Quallsford. I don't know if I ever laid eyes on him. I live over by New Romney. Work for Derwin Smith, he pays me more than I could earn around home. I heard all about the wonderful things Mr. Quallsford was doing, but none of them made my walk to work or my walk home any shorter. It is a good ten miles either way."

"Takes him two hours and a half in the morning," Browne said, "but it takes him four hours and a half going home because he has to stop and pay his respects at every inn he passes."

"Indeed I do," Harris said with a grin. "It is a long and lonely walk."

"Costs him more than the extra money he earns to lubricate his way home at night," Browne said.

"That it does not. But about Edmund Quallsford. People were excited when he started that business, but it never made me richer by half a tuppence. But everyone speaks well of him, and he did help a lot of people, and now those people have no one at all to help them, and they are the ones I feel sorry for. If Mr. Smith gives us the time off, I'll go to Edmund Quallsford's funeral with the rest of the hands and pray for him just as hard as the people who knew him well, because he deserves it, but I will also pray for the people who no longer have him to help them, because they are going to need prayers more than he will."

That was the way it went.

At breakfast the next morning, I asked Mr. Werner about Derwin Smith.

"Grazier," he said. "Owns about half of Graesney. The Quallsfords own the other half."

"Edmund's rival?" I suggested.

"Aye. In a manner of speaking. He is a very capable grazier. So was his father. The Quallsfords used to be very capable, too. The first one was a dealer who came wandering through here and liked the place and settled. He had gypsy blood, or so people say. He made a lot of money, and bought some land, and made a lot more money. He was a genuine expert with sheep, but by the time the line got to Oswald, there wasn't any expertness left. Maybe the gypsy blood had thinned out.

"Both Derwin Smith and his father tried to give advice to Oswald, who would have been wise to take it, but Oswald wasn't wise about anything. Derwin also tried to give advice to Edmund, but Edmund didn't need it. He was smart enough to hire an expert of his own to run Sea Cliffs for him—name of Walter Bates, he's the blacksmith's cousin and an outstanding good man. Edmund hired him away from the Warnleys over by Lydd. Walter has never said what his wage is, but it would have to be very good to make him leave a job he had held for more than twenty years. Edmund hired him and told him to put Sea Cliffs in order—and he has done that. Sea Cliffs must be showing a nice profit these days. So when Edmund needed advice, he naturally turned to Walter Bates for it, not to Derwin Smith. Smith felt snubbed about that. The Smiths have been nettled for years by the fact that the Quallsfords, who were inept graziers and eventually squandered all of their money, were looked up to by everyone and associated naturally with important people not only here but even in Lunnon, and no one paid much attention to the Smiths, who have always been sober, hard-working, prosperous citizens."

It sounded like a very poor motive for murder, but it had to be considered. The case might turn on the question of whether Derwin

Smith had been expressing an opinion or stating a fact when he said that Edmund Quallsford had been murdered.

I had decided to go to Rye to find out what the excisemen thought of the Quallsford Importing Company. I was discussing with Mr. Werner whether I should walk or hire a horse when a message arrived that changed all of my plans.

Larissa Quallsford wanted to see me.

Her note asked when I wanted the trap sent for me. I told the stable boy who brought it that I preferred to walk. I started out at once along the steep road that led upward past the church, which by daylight seemed to hover protectingly over the town. Its tower had battlements and no spire, and from a distance, thrust above the trees that grew closely about it, the grim stone structure looked startlingly like a castle.

As I strolled along, I noted that my villager with the wooden stump had a pious vein; the hard surface of the road preserved no marks, but in a few low places along the edge, where water had stood, I found evidence that he had walked between the church and the village numerous times, coming and going, since the last rain.

The level ground on the south side of the church, away from the road, was crammed with mossy monuments and tombstones; these spilled down a slope to another level where the vicarage stood, an old, well-kept stone house in a hedge-enclosed garden. I strolled on, past a lonely stone cottage where a score of all-white sheep grazed contentedly about the doorstep, dissociating themselves from the single cow in evidence. They were accustomed to passers-by; they looked up at me indifferently. The road, which had a wild, uncared-for look about it, became as narrow and winding and overgrown as it had seemed in darkness.

Then I saw the mansion rising above the trees that lined the road. Sea Cliffs was a large, gloomy, square-looking brick building, festooned with chimneys, and its graceless appearance seemed more suitable to a factory than to a country estate. The impression it conveyed was one that Sherlock Holmes had once laughingly pointed out to me: Threadbare luxury. The highly ornate barge-board that framed the roof lines of its gables had the look of having been added as an afterthought in an effort to create the atmosphere of elegance that the building denied.

There were massive stone posts on either side of the drive that led up a slope towards the house, but there was no gate, and the fence that at one time had lined the road had all but disintegrated. At the top of the slope, I found myself in a well-kept park. The drive wound through it to the small, square portico that ornamented the front entrance. A branch angled off towards the stable. By daylight, Sea Cliffs was much larger than it had seemed when shrouded in darkness. I gave Sergeant Donley full credit on one point: A single revolver shot in a closed room on an upper floor probably would not have been audible in the large, low wings that had been added like untidy afterthoughts at either side and in the rear.

I tried to conjure up an image of that curving drive lined with grand carriages that had brought the well-dressed gentry of the surrounding villages and estates to a Quallsford fête. My imagination failed me. Despite its pleasant park, the stark old manor did not look like one to be visited for pleasure. Then I turned in the other direction and caught my breath. The view, although partially screened by trees, was breathtaking. I could see far across the level land of the Marshes to the dim, dark line of hills on the other side. From the upper storeys of the house, that view must have been spectacular.

Off to the south-east, perhaps a quarter of a mile or more from the manor, and standing on the edge of the cliffs, was the crumbling stone tower that Miss Quallsford had mentioned, the place where Edmund Quallsford had retreated to brood in lonely solitude. I looked at it curiously, reflecting that the view it offered would be even more awesome than the one seen from the house. Edmund Quallsford was a peculiar man indeed to take his troubled soul there in darkness when he could have brooded by day with a spectacular sweep of the strange Marsh country at his feet.

The tower seemed to have been built in sections. A slender finger with crumbled tip thrust upward from a ponderous base. I was tempted to go and examine it and also to stand at the edge of the cliffs and look down on the Marsh. I had been perplexed by the name, Sea Cliffs, on an estate so remote from the coast, and I was intrigued to learn that the sea had indeed lapped the Graesney cliffs as recently as Roman times and only artificial barriers prevented it from still doing so at high tide.

But my errand at the manor house was the more urgent one. I walked on, crossed the portico, raised the ornate knocker.

It was wrenched from my hand by the opening door. A very young maid in a black dress bobbed a curtsey at me.

"I am Mr. Jones," I said. "Mrs. Quallsford asked me to call."

She stepped back and allowed me to enter. "If you will wait there, please," she said, indicating an open door and speaking in a singsong the lines that someone had taught to her, "I will tell Mrs. Quallsford that you have arrived."

I paused for a moment to look about me. Farther along the corridor was the door where I had seen Doris Fowler. Probably it led to the east wing that she shared with Emmeline Quallsford. The room where Edmund Quallsford's body was found would be on the floor above. Regretfully I followed the maid's pointing finger.

I found myself in a study or library. One wall was lined with books, each with the same ornate "Q" on its spine that I had admired on the book that Emmeline Quallsford was reading on the train. There was a fireplace with a carved mantelpiece and a large mirror above it. There was a faded carpet, a worn settee, and a desk that even I could appraise as a valuable relic from the Quallsfords' prosperous past. "Threadbare luxury" seemed like an apt description of the mansion's interior as well. I seated myself on the settee, then jumped to my feet immediately as Larissa Quallsford swept into the room.

Although she faced me calmly, she looked paler and more frenzied than she had the first time I saw her. She was taller than I, and lovely even in the depths of her tragedy. Her black gown moulded her figure almost too stylishly for mourning. Mr. Werner would have viewed that as one more manifestation of the foreign airs he had described to me so resentfully; but she came by those airs naturally and probably was not aware of them. Her black eyes had an unwonted dullness.

I thought, "Her husband committed suicide or was murdered, and she is the ghost."

She said accusingly, "You walked." Her voice sounded hoarse.

I nodded. "It is a lovely day, and this is lovely country."

"I am sorry that you wasted your time," she said. "I only wanted to say this to you. Sea Cliffs has belonged to my husband's family for more than a hundred years. Edmund was born here and grew up here. His children were born here and I am determined that they shall grow up here. I will fight to the death anyone who tries to take this heritage away from them. Tell your employer that. Think about it while you disturb the privacy of a grieving family and count the bones of the dead."

She was gone before I could open my mouth to answer.

The maid returned. "Mrs. Quallsford said I am to order the trap for you if you want it."

I shook my head. "No, thank you. I still prefer to walk." I had turned away and actually started out of the door when another thought occurred to me. "Is Miss Quallsford at home?" I asked.

"Miss Emmeline? No. She left early this morning."

The maid volunteered no more information, and I did not ask for any. I thanked her and walked off down the drive. The old tower tempted me a second time, but I feared that someone from the house might see me walking in that direction and report it to the mistress.

I kept to the drive and took the turn towards Havenchurch.

When I reached the High Street, I saw a brewer's dray approaching the Royal Swan. There were two men seated on the box. One, the driver, gave me a friendly nod as I approached. The other, a lank, surly-looking character in a badly worn jacket and a filthy cap, did not look in my direction.

I abandoned my intention to go to my room and write another report. Instead, I walked to the end of the High Street and down the slope towards the Rye Road a half-mile beyond. I crossed the road and followed a well-worn fisherman's path to the bank of the Royal Military Canal. I seated myself by the quiet water and waited.

Glancing over my shoulder, I had seen the dray's lank passenger dismount, pause for a few parting words with the driver, and then amble after me.

Sherlock Holmes had come to Havenchurch.

CHAPTER
6

The familiar lank form eased itself down beside me. Sherlock Holmes folded his long legs in front of him, embraced them with his arms, and thoughtfully pointed his fingers together. For a time neither of us spoke; the horse bus from Rye passed on the road and took the turn to Havenchurch. A soft breeze rippled the water, which seemed currentless. The canal possessed its own zigzagging strangeness, but that was for military reasons.

"The blackmailer?" I asked finally.

Sherlock Holmes shrugged and smiled. That case was finished, and he preferred to say nothing more about it. Now Miss Quallsford's problem could have his full attention.

"I thought it best not to make an official appearance until we decide what it is that we are investigating," he said. "Tell me what has happened."

He had received my two telegrams, but he left London before my written report reached him. He leaned back and produced a pipe from the depths of his soiled clothing. "Details," he said. "Whom have you talked with?"

He wanted to know everything. He always wanted to know everything. No fact was too trivial for his marvellous talents to scrutinize, and some of his most spectacular exploits were made possible, as he himself explained, by the meticulous observation of trifles.

I described the railway journey with Emmeline Quallsford, my two receptions at Sea Cliffs, my inventory of the Quallsford Importing Company, Joe's detective work in Rye, Sergeant Donley's report. I paused only when the horse bus reappeared and turned northward, towards Appledore. I concluded with impressions gleaned in my afternoon ramble about the village and my evening conversations over more beer than I normally chose to drink.

"Except for those two men who have personal grudges—and Derwin Smith, who was a rival—the people of Havenchurch revered Edmund Quallsford," I said. "Everyone in the village knew him and liked him and admired him. On the other hand, none of the women claims a close acquaintance with either his sister or his wife."

"Probably there are few village social events that young women of their standing can take part in," Sherlock Holmes said. "Are they actually unpopular?"

"Emmeline has been one of a pair with her brother for so long that she shares in the affection the villagers had for him. Edmund's French wife is another matter. She is much admired for her beauty and social graces and thoroughly disliked for her foreign airs."

Sherlock Holmes questioned me closely on my own impressions of Larissa Quallsford. "The rural police have a stultifying occupation," he remarked finally. "Their lives revolve around missing pigs and hayrick fires, and their imaginations become atrophied. The good Sergeant Donley believes that Edmund Quallsford could not have been murdered because there were only a couple of servants and the elderly governess in the house. It is in no way unique for a servant to kill a master, and it would have been a simple matter for a clever murderer to find his way into that house at an opportune time. As for the motive—Edmund was one of the world's few honest men in Havenchurch, but you have talked with two persons who bore him grudges, and we don't know how he was regarded elsewhere."

"I realize that he could have had many enemies," I said. "Even a man whom he treated honestly and justly might think himself wronged. But how could an outsider guess that the servants were in remote parts of the house and that Edmund was sleeping? Derwin Smith lives nearby, but he would not know the routine of the house that intimately."

"Certainly there are objections, and it is always sound practice first to eliminate possible suspects in the victim's own household and among his close associates before we address ourselves to the world at large. As for the conflict between wife and sister, that would be of vital interest only if one of them had been murdered. It may have no connection with Edmund's death. I have read that the Chinese ideogram for disharmony is a graphic representation of two women under one roof. In such an atmosphere, servants take sides as passionately as their mistresses, and the home quickly becomes a battleground, but the master of the house may not have been a party to the conflict or even aware of it."

"Evidence seems to indicate that both women were devoted to Edmund," I said.

"I hope that this case will not turn upon our ability to unravel a woman's motives. Her slightest actions may be fraught with significance, and her most significant actions may mean nothing at all. Well, Porter, all of this could be dismissed as a sordid domestic entanglement, not worth soiling our hands upon, except for two things."

"What are they, sir?" I asked.

"For one, the pitahayas. Don't lose sight of the pitahayas, Porter. Always look for the unusual, the out of the ordinary. The pitahayas, and the conduct of the elderly governess in asking for them at Spitalfields Market, are one of the two remarkable features of this case. The second is the ruined tower and Edmund Quallsford's use of it as a retreat. Have you seen it?"

"Only from a distance, sir."

"For shame, Porter!" He spoke sternly, but there was a twinkle in his eyes. "You haven't even the excuse of the missing pigs or the burning hayricks! The tower is an anomaly. The pitahayas are an anomaly. Always begin with the singularities. Make that your first principle of criminal investigation."

I explained how the interview with Larissa Quallsford had diverted me from the tower.

He shook his head disapprovingly. "Diligence is not a virtue unless it is addressed to the proper object. You should have done more with the pitahayas; you should not have neglected the tower. Fortunately we are not at a total loss for information. My friend Mr. Sims, the dray driver, acquainted me with a fair parcel of tower lore on the ride from Rye. He also informed me that there is a centuries-old right-of-way that passes near to it. The footpath begins just west of the schoolhouse. I intend to visit the place now and see what kind of a tale it has to unfold. There are critical questions that must be answered before we can proceed further. If a well-loved and successful Edmund Quallsford had no reason to brood his lonely nights away in a crumbling tower, what was he doing there —or did he visit the tower at all? The facts you have assembled are not without interest, but they lead nowhere. We must see whether the tower points a direction for us."

We found the public footpath easily. "An old right-of-way like this," Sherlock Holmes said, scrutinizing it carefully before he would permit me to set foot on it, "could furnish us with a remarkable history if any scholar could read what is written here. Who knows what armies have marched this way, what goods from Rome and Byzantium have been laboriously carried over it, what momentous events occurred because the path climbed the cliffs instead of going around? Even in comparatively recent times, it must have been a useful road link. Now it leads from Havenchurch to nowhere in particular, but that rich unknown history guarantees its continued existence."

We followed it. Sherlock Holmes strode ahead with his usual long, deliberate steps, studying every inch of the ground he was covering. The path was partially overgrown; the soil was hard, and only in an occasional place where rainwater had produced mud was there any possibility of clues. Sherlock Holmes often remarked that the reading of footprints, a skill that he had been at great pains to develop, was one of the more neglected essentials in criminal research, but on this path there was little scope for his talent.

When he did discover marks of any kind, he whipped out the large magnifying glass that he always carried and scrutinized them with his usual meticulousness. While he was thus occupied, I ranged widely, looking for related clues. Sometimes even a cigarette stub or cigar stump revealed a great deal more than its discarder intended, but the working-class people who used this path were not smokers. I found nothing.

From a distance, the old sea cliffs looked like a difficult climb, but the path followed an easy gradient in a looping ascent from terrace to terrace. At the top, Sherlock Holmes paused to admire the full sweep of the Marshes. The day had become overcast, but the view was still spectacular. I had already seen it, and I was impatient to push on.

"Do you notice anything different about the Marsh country, Porter?" he asked.

"It is unusually flat and uninteresting," I said.

"It is uninteresting only in its lack of topographical variety. It once was sea bottom, you know. Havenchurch was a seaport. Look again. Where are the villages? And where are the hedges? How are the fields divided?"

I stared. Those very points had disturbed me, but my mind had not fixed firmly enough on them to form questions. "Is it common land?" I asked.

Sherlock Holmes shook his head. "The divisions are there, but they are not visible from this distance. The fields are marked off by drainage ditches. If you tried to walk across that country on a dark night, my friend, or even by daylight, you would find the going far more difficult than any system of hedges could make it. What a splendid vantage point! On a clear day, one could easily see the cities of the south coast!"

"I would be satisfied just to see my way through this mystery," I said.

Sherlock Holmes chuckled, and we moved on. There were hedges on the Isle of Graesney, with gates for the public footpath, and we carefully secured them behind us. The path crossed one sparkling pasture after another with grass cropped so closely that it looked like green cloth underfoot. Sheep, glistening white against the dark background of hedge and pasture, regarded us warily from a distance. On one of Sherlock Holmes's earlier cases in the Midlands, we had encountered black-faced sheep, and I remarked on the whiteness of these.

"They are Romney Sheep," Sherlock Holmes said. "It is a famous breed. What puzzles you most about the mystery?"

"Many things puzzle me. Right now I am wondering whether honest men commit suicide."

"Your greatest handicap, Porter, is that you keep asking yourself the wrong questions. You should be wondering under what circumstances an honest man would take his own life. According to the information you have assembled, the suicide is inexplicable—but so is the murder, and not even Sergeant Donley would credit the possibility that Edmund Quallsford left a suicide note and then shot himself accidentally while sleeping. Everything is inexplicable; but he is, in actual fact, dead, and therefore we need more data. Are you quite convinced that he was not a smuggler?"

"I am convinced that his importing company did not handle smuggled goods."

Sherlock Holmes smiled. "Very well put, Porter. The customs

official I talked with in Rye last evening agrees with you. Edmund Quallsford's tiny importing business is regarded with affectionate amusement at the Customs House. It has had the interesting effect of placing French brandy on sale in a scattering of public houses from Hastings to Folkestone. Small quantities of French silks and other luxuries, not to mention exotic tobaccos, may be unexpectedly encountered in village shops throughout the same region. Edmund Quallsford did indeed secure bargains on the Continent, transport them cheaply, and sell them at cost—perhaps even a trifle below cost, since he was trying to build a business. In a very minor way, his importing company has provided a stimulus to trade in this corner of England."

"How much money did he lose?" I asked.

"Not a great deal for a person who actually had money, but it should have been a significant amount to Edmund Quallsford. His business could not have lasted, you know. That is the official view, held with deep regret. It should not have lasted as long as it did. A business cannot survive indefinitely on no profit. And yet, it did survive."

"He had money," I protested. "He wasn't dependent on the importing business."

"Wasn't he? Then from what mysterious source did his money come?"

"He married an heiress," I said. "Doesn't that account for it?"

"He did not, and it does not. He married the daughter of a wealthy man—who strongly objected to the match. I was unable to learn whether Larissa Monier was actually disinherited, but she certainly did not bring a dowry to her marriage. That is a fact."

I turned to him in surprise. "After the marriage, Edmund began to pay off the family's debts and involve himself in business ventures."

"That is another fact," Sherlock Holmes said. "The missing fact is where the money came from. I have been asking questions of friends of Oswald Quallsford and also of connections of the

Moniers. Edmund Quallsford was the impoverished son of a ruined family. The Quallsfords have been prominent graziers since the eighteenth century, and the family estate is a valuable holding, but the income it produced did not suffice to pay the interest on Oswald's indebtedness. Creditors were refusing further credit and pressing for payment. Edmund was about to lose everything. He married; his father-in-law opposed the match, but the young people were very much in love. The father-in-law said to them, 'Do what you like, but expect no help from me until you prove yourselves worthy of it.' And he has given them none.

"Eventually he extended a rather grudging, perplexed acceptance to his son-in-law. He was relieved at the young couple's improving finances but at the same time suspicious. As a practical businessman, he could not understand how Edmund had managed it, and a practical businessman does not believe what he does not understand. The verdict of suicide was no surprise to him, though of course he is grieved for his daughter. Edmund's reputation as one of the world's few honest men was not endorsed by his father-in-law; but then, Lambert Monier knew Oswald Quallsford well and could be called prejudiced: 'Like father, like son.' Guilt is much more easily presumed than innocence."

"What did he think of the possibility that his son-in-law was murdered?"

"He did not think of it. It did not even occur to him. Officialdom has spoken; the suicide verdict has an imprimatur and so does the verdict of accidental death. There is as yet no evidence of any kind to suggest that Edmund Quallsford was murdered. All that we have, Porter, are our two anomalies and an awareness that the known facts do not exclude the possibility of murder."

"Our two anomalies are evidence," I protested.

"That is true. But we don't know what they are evidence of."

Again Sherlock Holmes stopped abruptly and knelt to examine the ground with his lens. I immediately ranged about looking for clues. When I returned and knelt down beside him, I found him studying an impression that had become only too familiar to me.

"Your friend the one-legged man," Sherlock Holmes said. "As you remarked, he has left his sign all over Havenchurch. I saw it in the High Street and also in the school yard. There was no trace of him on the path up the cliffs, so he has reached this place by cutting across private land from the road. Was he alone? The path is too overgrown and the grass too closely grazed to tell us. The mark is recent, though. See—he broke through the mud crust, and the edges and bottom of the indentation are still soft. He passed this way no longer ago than yesterday."

We docketed the fact about the one-legged man—for later use in case he entered our investigation again—and moved on.

Sherlock Holmes resumed our interrupted conversation. "Regardless of what Miss Quallsford believes, we must give equal attention to the possibilities of suicide and murder. If one of the world's few honest men faced ruin in some way, and if he knew that his wealthy father-in-law would restore the fortunes of his wife and children after his death, might he be tempted to take his own life?"

"He might if he were about to be overwhelmed by a disgrace that would reflect on his family," I said, "but certainly there is no evidence of that."

"There is too little evidence of anything," Sherlock Holmes said. "I have never seen a more unpromising beginning, Porter. What we have is a thin assortment of facts that direct our attention to every point on the compass. Perhaps the old tower—here it is up ahead of us."

The footpath had wound its way through a small grove of trees, and when we emerged on the other side, we saw the tower looming on a rise of ground almost directly in front of us. Both of us halted and studied it. It stood on a point of land near the edge of the old sea cliffs, and it looked like no architectural style I remembered in any tower I had seen before. It began as a vast, ungraceful, circular structure with sides that tapered inward slightly. After forty feet or so, a slender tower arose from the centre of the massive base. The stones of the upper tower were darkly weathered; the base had been given a smooth coat of plaster that had crumbled away in places to reveal similar but less weathered stonework underneath.

"It might be a lighthouse on the shore of the ancient sea, warning ships away from these cliffs," Sherlock Holmes said. "A lighthouse of peculiar design, to be sure, but that would be appropriate to one built by denizens of a long-forgotten race."

I mentioned that the upper structure looked like an afterthought, and he told me that I was correct. "Oswald's father built the base," he said. "He had a friend who owned coastal property near Folkestone, and the friend had a Martello Tower as a neighbour."

"What is a Martello Tower?" I asked.

"Porter!" Sherlock Holmes exclaimed. "Napoleon would feel offended! It was the threat of an invasion by Napoleon that led to the digging of the Royal Military Canal, beside which we just had our chat, and the building of Martello Towers at strategic places along the eastern and south-eastern coasts. The friend of Oswald's father was excessively proud of that Martello Tower. He actually had a proprietary affection for it, and Oswald's father finally retaliated by having one built for himself. Of course it does not have the massively thick walls of the Martello fortresses, which are virtually impervious to cannon fire, but it looks very like one, and it is as out of place in this peaceful countryside as the originals on the coast now seem to be. When Oswald inherited the property, he thought the thing hideous, and he beautified it by adding the upper tower, thus converting an oddity into an absurdity. Our concern is for the role that it played in his son's life. Did Edmund actually come here to brood? It looks like a brooding kind of place, does it not?"

The path we were following curved to the right as though to avoid the scowling sentinel on the hill. We left it and started up the slope towards the tower. There was no sign of a path there, but we soon encountered unmistakable evidence that a number of people had trod that thick turf, both coming and going.

Both of us dropped to our knees to study the marks.

"How many?" Sherlock Holmes asked me.

"Six, at least," I said.

"At least," he agreed. "I would say eight. How recently?"

"Within the last day or two."

He nodded. "In any case, *after* Edmund's death. That may be important. Our problem now is to determine whether this visitation was in any way connected with him and whether Miss Quallsford's absence in London had anything to do with its timing."

He swept his hands over the crushed turf as though seeking to draw out its secrets. Then he stiffened and leaned forward intently, a look of triumph on his keen face. "What is this? Porter, your eyes are failing you. Also, your sense of priorities. You should have been up here yesterday instead of jollying the local entrepreneurs and unsettling Sergeant Donley."

It was a circular indentation in the ground, the unmistakable mark of our one-legged man.

Sherlock Holmes got to his feet and brushed off his trousers. "It is interesting that you failed to see him yesterday," he said thoughtfully. "Are there many seafaring types in the village?"

"I only met one—Nat Whyte."

"You say that One-Leg left his mark on the road to the church. Of course that is no guarantee of piousness. He may live somewhere nearby. Was he one of the eight, or did he visit the tower alone?"

"He was one of the eight," I said.

"I agree. Now let us see what our visitors were about."

As we approached the tower, the grass thinned out. The ground became stony, but the wind had spread dust thinly in the hollows. Sherlock Holmes held up his hand, and the two of us, with lenses and tape measures, busied ourselves with that fragile record. He was a whirlwind of activity at such moments: He knelt, he measured, he peered through his lens, he rose to his full height and took sightings, he knelt again, talking all of the time to himself, or to me, or to the footprints. An observer might have thought me the teacher and him the pupil, because—not being as quick in my perceptions as he—I moved more deliberately and had to study and meditate longer to reach a conclusion.

"Here is a woman's print!" Sherlock Holmes exclaimed suddenly. "She came before the others—they have almost obliterated it. See, only the toe is visible. What do you make the total now?"

"I make it eight men, including One-Leg, and one woman."

"What else can you deduce?"

"Except for One-Leg, the men are all labourers wearing heavy boots. They came directly here; they left the way they came. There isn't enough of the woman's print to say much about her."

"Except that she wore expensive footwear—no Havenchurch shoemaker made that shoe—and she had an exceptionally small foot."

"Emmeline Quallsford!" I exclaimed.

"Undoubtedly, unless there is another woman in Havenchurch with an equally small foot and a similar taste in stylish shoes. At a guess, these came from Regent Street. Hold a moment—one of the maids could have been wearing Emmeline's cast-off shoes if they chanced to fit."

"They wouldn't have fit the maid I saw this morning," I said. "She was a young girl with large feet."

"But where is Edmund? He is the one who supposedly visited the tower regularly."

I searched again, but I found no footprints that I could attribute to Edmund Quallsford—unless he wore labourer's shoes and came with the group.

"Edmund Quallsford did no brooding for some days before he died," Sherlock Holmes said finally. "That bodes ill for the suicide theory. He certainly did not kill himself because he was feeling more cheerful. As for the others—they came directly here, they approached the tower, they left the way they came. Did they go inside?"

We circled so as to approach the tower's gaping, doorless entrance obliquely and thus avoid muddling the marks with our own footprints. Inside, the stone floor was heavily covered with dust and blown debris except where the visitors had walked. It was certain to be a page with the history of weeks or even months written upon it. Sherlock Holmes, his arms extended to prevent my tramping over this new evidence—an action that reflected his years of bitter experience with blundering police officers and amateurs such as Dr. Watson—examined the marks with a scowling face.

He uttered an exclamation. "Here is Edmund," he said. "Patent-leather boots, good quality. Coming and going numerous times but almost wiped out by the others. He always went directly to the stairway. Miss Quallsford also went directly to the stairway."

There was a single enormous circular room with a central hub that served as the foundation to the upper tower and also enclosed the stairs. In the years of its existence, the vast, cavernous place had been used for many kinds of storage. Straw was scattered about, as were strands of wool. Light came from the door and from the high slits that were the only windows. Even in that dim illumination, footmarks were vividly evident. The seven men and One-Leg had marched completely around the room like a procession, stopping several times with unmistakable signs of milling about. Thick dust preserved the marks perfectly; even where the feet of those following had smudged the tracks ahead of them, there was an occasional well-defined print that showed the direction the toes were pointing. Finally the group had proceeded to the stairway. In leaving the tower, it had emerged from the stairway and gone directly to the door.

I exclaimed suddenly, "One-Leg was the leader!"

Wherever the group had halted, the marks of the wooden stump moved apart, pranced about, rejoined the group.

We followed the trail of the procession up the winding stone staircase to the first floor, where identical movements had been performed. Neither Edmund's nor Emmeline's prints were in evidence; they had not left the stairway.

I said glumly, "This makes no sense at all. There is no sign of any attempt to search these rooms or to look for hiding places." Sherlock Holmes made no comment.

We returned to the narrow, curving stairs and made our way up to the third level. The stairs were lit by window slits that emitted only the light from the dim rooms that surrounded them, and our long climb was like stumbling upward along an ascending tunnel.

We gave the enormous room on the third level a cursory inspection, and then we began the climb into the upper tower, where we found one small, well-lighted room on each floor with windows that faced north, south, and east. The curving stairway blocked off the west side. Again Edmund's and Emmeline's footprints did not leave the stairway. The visitors had remained in a milling crowd while One-Leg cavorted about the room.

The room on the sixth level differed from those below. It contained a cot with a tattered blanket and a rough table and chair— exactly as Emmeline Quallsford had described them. This was her brother's domain. His footprints were everywhere. Hers entered the room, paused by the table to shift this way and that, and then retreated. The group of visitors had halted by the stairway while One-Leg moved from bed to chair, paced the floor, and then rejoined the others.

The group had not climbed beyond that level. Following the stairway, we quickly found out why. The roof had collapsed into the floor above. At the point where the stairs curved out of sight, they became impassable.

We returned to the room that Edmund Quallsford had used for his retreat. Sherlock Holmes seated himself on the stairs, got out his pipe, and looked up at me quizzically. "What were the visitors doing, Porter?"

"They behaved like sightseers touring a museum," I said. "They looked into each room, and they courteously observed the ropes placed there to protect the treasures on display. Except that there were no ropes and no treasures, but they courteously observed them anyway. One-Leg was the guide, and he lectured to them each time that they stopped."

Sherlock Holmes nodded delightedly. "An excellent reconstruction, Porter. It was exactly like that. How do you account for it?"

"I don't."

He chuckled. "No? You have overlooked the most important clue of all. What about Miss Quallsford?"

"She came and looked. She took nothing away with her unless it was something on the table."

He began his examination of the room, scrutinizing every mark on the floor, studying with great interest a plug knocked from a pipe, and finally turning his attention to table, chair, and cot. Then he moved to one of the windows, and I began my own study of the room.

A crumpled object under the cot caught my eye; it was a hastily folded horse blanket. On the floor at one end of the cot I found a circle marked in the dust. I had already seen similar marks on the table. I sniffed them carefully. Then I turned my own lens on the tobacco plug. The circles were repeated on the east window ledge. Again I sniffed carefully. When I looked up, Sherlock Holmes was watching me with interest.

"What was it, Porter?" he asked.

"A lantern," I said. "At least Edmund Quallsford did not conduct his meditations in total darkness—unless he only used it to light his way here and back."

"No, Porter. The lantern was used here. The marks on the floor are especially interesting. What do you make of them?"

I looked at them again. "He lit the lantern under the horse blanket!" I exclaimed suddenly. "He also read here, lying on the cot with lantern and book on the floor under the blanket. I see the mark of a book in the dust."

"Which proves that some of the time, at least, he did not want to show a light. Look again, Porter. Do you see it? No? There were *two* lanterns here, Porter. One had a smaller base. Probably the larger of the two was an ordinary dark lantern. The other has its own unique features. See where it tipped?"

The smudges in the dust suggested nothing to me.

"Never mind," Sherlock Holmes said. "It *is* rather indistinct. I only saw it because I was looking for it. Here are more pipe dottles. What do you make of them?"

"I don't recognize the tobacco," I said.

"Nor do I. As you know, I have enlarged the list of tobaccos that I am familiar with to a hundred and fifty-six, but I have never seen this one. What about the tobacco you saw at the Quallsford Importing Company?"

"It was different from this."

"But this also might be from a foreign source. A negative always cuts two ways, Porter. A broken link can be a confirmation. What do you make of these marks on the window ledge?"

I made nothing of the marks on the window ledge.

Sherlock Holmes deftly flipped the blanket from the cot, shook it, and spread it out again. "Can you suggest a species of melancholy that would have impelled an intelligent young man, an honest young man of good character and no known vices, to abandon his lovely wife and children and his comfortable ancestral home to brood in these barren, comfortless surroundings?"

"In a sense, this also is his ancestral home," I said.

"That won't do, Porter. He did not come here to lament the lost glories of the Quallsfords."

"An old building like this might have many secret hiding places —even a secret room. And what about the dungeon?"

"If there are hiding places in any of the rooms, no one has had access to them lately, or their footprints would have given them away. As for the dungeon, there is none. Corby's *Kent Monuments* includes an ironical description of this tower—the author heaps his scorn on such a pseudo-monument. He obtained his information directly from Oswald Quallsford, and Oswald would have boasted about a dungeon if the tower had one."

I had joined him at the window. The view was as magnificent as I had anticipated. The Rother was a silver thread far below; the line of the Royal Military Canal was marked by shrubs and trees. The whole of the Marsh country lay at my feet.

"It does seem odd that the tower is visited so infrequently," I said. "Except for the museum tour and the Quallsfords themselves, no one has been here. I would have thought that the village children would come frequently to play and climb the stairs on a dare."

"When we locate the wooden leg and its owner, Porter, both the museum tour and the missing children will be made clear to you." Sherlock Holmes dropped into Edmund Quallsford's rickety chair, sat there for a moment with an intense expression on his face as though he were striving to emulate the dead owner's brooding, and then got to his feet. "There is nothing more to be done here. At least our researches have placed this tower, and Edmund Quallsford's behaviour, in their proper perspective and made the dimensions of our case clear enough. Now we know what we have to deal with. We have framed the picture, even though many of its details still fall into those realms of conjecture where logic cannot guide us."

I was astonished. I saw nothing except a welter of facts that could not yet be forced into any pattern.

He wagged a finger at me. "Remember, Porter, the more bizarre and inexplicable a thing seems, the simpler the explanation is likely to be. We no longer need the one-legged man, but we will visit him next just to tidy up our case."

"Do you mean that you know why Edmund Quallsford came here to brood?" I asked.

"I know what he came here to do. He may or may not have brooded while he did it. I expect that he did. I expect that he devoted long periods to brooding, but that was not his primary purpose in coming here."

"Was he murdered?"

"That corner of the picture is still obscure, but his death is part of it. I am certain about that. He was an honest man, Porter. All of your witnesses say so. I don't know whether that was reason enough for him to commit suicide. If it was, it was also sufficient cause for any of a number of people to want to murder him."

CHAPTER
7

In his dealings with the police, Sherlock Holmes always insisted on his right to reveal his conclusions when he chose, and he rarely chose to do so until his case was complete. He followed the same practice with me, except that he was much freer in pointing out clues and discussing them than he would have been with an outsider. I gave him my findings and conclusions whenever he asked for them; and, when a case was finished, he always reviewed my work in detail, pointing out what I had missed and where I had been negligent. In this way, I gained experience and knowledge with each case that we handled, and my work became increasingly valuable to him. He was now able to send me out alone on any case that he accepted, confident that I would have much of the investigation completed when he joined me.

On this case, however, I seemed to have gone badly astray. I could not understand how its dimensions could be clear to him when we had so little data.

We descended the stairs and retraced our steps towards Havenchurch.

"Mr. Werner, the landlord at the Royal Swan, will certainly know who One-Leg is," I suggested.

"I would prefer not to make myself known to Mr. Werner just

yet," Sherlock Holmes said. "No doubt you are correct in assuming that everyone in the village knows this person and can recount the intimate details of his genealogy, but for the moment I choose to be careful whom I ask. The postmaster would be a better choice. Or the vicar, since you have evidence that One-Leg numbers an unlikely piousness among his character traits."

"That piousness may be accounted for by his planning to rob the church," I suggested darkly.

Sherlock Holmes laughed merrily. "So it may. In that case, it is the vicar whom we must consult—first to find out whether his church has been robbed; then to identify our missing witness. I trust that we can reach the vicarage without parading in the village's High Street."

That was not a problem. Rural areas may have a dearth of thoroughfares, but they are always well supplied with paths. We had no difficulty in finding one that led directly to the vicarage, that rambling old stone dwelling I had already seen below the church.

As we approached it, Sherlock Holmes abandoned his posture as an itinerant working man. He reversed his coat, an ingenious garment that an excellent tailor had crafted with the dual personality of gentleman's leisure coat and labourer's squalid attire. He gave his shoes a polish. He found a red cravat in his pocket and utilized it to conceal his disreputable shirt. He brushed off his trousers. He pocketed his filthy cap.

He would be calling on the vicar in the role of himself, Sherlock Holmes, and a certain standard of dress was essential for that. "I can work comfortably in disordered surroundings," he once remarked to me. "I find that such an environment stimulates the mental processes without disrupting them. But it would not do to have Sherlock Holmes considered slovenly." Except when he was disguised, he was remarkably fastidious about his dress. It was only in his housekeeping that he was habitually untidy.

The vicar, wearing his cassock, was seated on his veranda—about to leave for some official function or having just returned from one.

Seeing two strangers approaching with himself as their obvious objective, he got to his feet and came to meet us.

He was enormously tall, almost a hand taller than Sherlock Holmes, with a barrel-like body and dark, shaggy hair that framed a large, good-natured face.

And he had a wooden leg.

I was dumbfounded—not because our missing witness had turned out to be the vicar, but because Sherlock Holmes had deduced that from the scanty evidence at the tower and slyly arranged to make the vicarage our next objective.

He obviously was delighted in the dramatic revelation he had produced for me. He introduced the two of us. In response, the vicar introduced himself as Gerald Russell, Vicar of Havenchurch. He absently shook hands with each of us in turn while muttering, "*Sherlock* Holmes? Sherlock *Holmes?*" His face brightened. "Was it you who recovered the chalice that was stolen from the church at Mengerton?"

"It was," Sherlock Holmes admitted. "But that was a rather trivial problem."

"The Vicar of Mengerton did not think so. He is a mentor of mine, and I heard all about your exploit when it happened. Please join me over here. This is a very comfortable place to sit in this mild weather. Excuse me—we will need another chair. I beg that you do not judge Havenchurch hospitality by my absent-mindedness. Mrs. Andrews? Mrs. Andrews?"

He bellowed into the vicarage, and a moment later an elderly woman appeared. She brought the needed chair, and the three of us seated ourselves.

When the housekeeper had departed after pausing to look us over curiously from the doorway, Sherlock Holmes said to the vicar, "I am telling you this in confidence. We have come here at Emmeline Quallsford's invitation. Naturally her brother's death has disturbed her deeply, and she wants to be assured that there was no foul play."

The vicar arched his heavy eyebrows in surprise. He was a

pleasant-looking man despite his bulk—middle-aged, the picture of exuberant good health, cheerful in manner—and he had comfortably accepted both his disability and his isolation in this out-of-the-way parish. The unexpected visit by a famous detective from London was startling enough for him, and the added suggestion that a tragic death in his parish might be murder was more than he could accept.

He began to protest. Sherlock Holmes interrupted him. "Do you know of any reason why Edmund Quallsford would want to kill himself?"

"None," the vicar said firmly. "That is why I consider his death an accident. He had a happy marriage, he had material success, he was proud of his immediate family and immensely proud and satisfied that he was restoring the family fortunes. In those circumstances, a man does not commit suicide."

"Did you ever hear him use the word 'pitahaya'?"

"That was his private joke."

"Was it never anything more than that?"

"What more could it be?" the vicar demanded bewilderedly.

"That is one of the things I am investigating," Sherlock Holmes said. "At the present time I really need only three items of information from you. At whose request did you perform the ceremony at the tower, who accompanied you there, and what were you exorcising?"

The vicar stared at him. Then he leaned back in his chair and uttered a great, booming laugh.

"The ceremony was my idea," he said finally. "There actually was talk about blowing up the tower, you know. Whoever or whatever is supposed to haunt the place has long been considered the author of every evil or tragic event the village has experienced. But it is a monument of sorts, even though a dubious one, and it should be preserved. Edmund Quallsford was fond of the ugly old thing, and he planned to restore it as soon as he could spare the money. He would have done so, too.

"For the villagers, his death was the proverbial last straw. He was a wonderfully talented man with a unique gift for friendliness, and many of the parishioners were proud to call him their benefactor. Everyone in Havenchurch was impressed by what he was trying to do with his importing company. He represented the future, full of hopes and expectations, and suddenly all of that was extinguished. Of course the evil spirit of the tower was blamed. It was as though the nether forces that concentrate their influence there resented the village having even that little ripple of prosperity and destroyed its source. I think there really would have been an attempt to blow it up. Something had to be done."

"What was the family's reaction?" Sherlock Holmes asked.

"I did not consult the family. Why bother Larissa and Emmeline at such a tragic time? It would have been one more worry for them and one more burden. No—I simply announced to a few men whom I considered the ringleaders that I was going to lay the tower's evil spirit to rest permanently. I invited them to be present as witnesses, and yesterday morning we went and did it. I made it as good a show as I could, and all of them enjoyed the ceremony enormously. There has been no more talk about blowing up the tower."

"What did you personally think of Edmund's plan for restoring the village's prosperity?" Sherlock Holmes asked.

The vicar laughed his booming laugh and then cut it off abruptly. "Please forgive me," he said. "In view of the tragic event that brought you to Havenchurch, such levity is most inappropriate, but Edmund would have understood that laugh. He would have joined in. He and I often laughed together over the fact that most of the village seemed to believe and accept that he intended to convert this decaying parish into a major trading center. He intended no such thing. Edmund Quallsford was a man of rare common sense. He established that shipping company as a means of letting some of the elderly friends of his youth earn a bit of money. They were far too proud to accept charity, but they delighted in sailing across the

Channel to pick up small loads of goods, and he paid them far too much for it. The same applied to the people he hired to cut up cloth and package things, and also to the carriers in the area, who were having hard times and appreciated an occasional extra delivery. The importing company was an act of charity from first to last. Also, it gave Edmund something to do when he was down from the city."

"Did he spend much time in the city?" Sherlock Holmes asked.

"A great deal of time there and in travelling to and fro. It was the cause of friction between himself and his wife, although she quite understood that the family fortunes had been in a sorry state of repair and would require years of hard work to restore."

"His real business was in London, then?" Sherlock Holmes asked thoughtfully.

"I would say so. London and perhaps other commercial centres —I really know none of the details. I only know that he was doing magnificently well. Business is a foreign country for me, but surely anyone who is active in London's Stock Exchange could tell you all about Edmund's success."

"Thank you," Sherlock Holmes said. "Obviously that is where we should inquire. When is Edmund's funeral?"

"Tomorrow morning. Eleven o'clock. Larissa's brother was in Scotland, and we had some difficulty in notifying him. The funeral had to be delayed. He will not arrive until this evening."

"And Edmund will be buried—where? In your churchyard?"

"There is a Quallsford family vault in the church's north chapel," the vicar said. "Of course he will be buried there."

Sherlock Holmes got to his feet. "Thank you. With your leave, we would like to visit the churchyard and the church. Churchyards are a special hobby of mine."

"Please do," the vicar said warmly, as though he considered this an appropriate interest for a detective. "We are proud of our church. The present building dates from the twelfth century, but there was probably a church on this site, and a haven for those who lived in the area, as early as the eighth century. One moment, please."

He stumped his way into the vicarage and returned with a thin pamphlet, which he thrust into Sherlock Holmes's hand. "A short history of the church. My own work. Not too scholarly, I am afraid, but I have assembled the known information to ease the labours of any qualified scholar who becomes interested."

We took our leave of the vicar and went to wander among the churchyard's weathered and crumbling tombstones. When Sherlock Holmes found a legible message, he paused to read it, sometimes rubbing his hands enthusiastically.

"These are admirable sentiments, Porter. Listen to this: 'We cannot tell who next may fall beneath thy chastening rod. One must be first, so let us all prepare to meet our God.' Here is another: 'The angels guard my sleeping dust, 'Till Christ return to raise the just. Then may I wake with sweet surprise, And in my saviour's image rise.' Think, Porter, how many thousands of people have been buried in this humble churchyard over the centuries. Most of the graves are lost and forgotten. These stones seem to date only from the past two centuries. They were erected with loving grief as permanent memorials, and now many of the names and the carefully chosen messages have weathered away. I wonder what message will be placed on Edmund Quallsford's grave."

I was wondering what his object was. He never did anything without a purpose. He seemed to be studying the tombstones in the manner of a man whose special hobby was indeed churchyards and churches, but from the quick glances he shot this way and that, I knew that he was hot on the scent of something. We circled the churchyard and moved down the slope to inspect the newer graves near the vicarage. The vicar, on his way to the church, turned aside to join us.

"The messages on tombstones epitomize human existence," Sherlock Holmes announced to him enthusiastically. "How many trage-dies are encapsulated in these brief summaries. Look at this one: 'In Loving Memory of Charles Jeffery, who, when boating with his friends, met an untimely death by drowning. June 3rd, 1842, aged nineteen years.' And pay close attention to the message, Porter. 'When blooming youth is snatched away by Death's resistless hand, Our hearts the mournful tribute pay which pity must demand. Let this vain world prevail no more. Behold the gaping tomb. It bids us seize the present hour. Tomorrow Death may come.' The hopeful expectations of an entire family may have died in that tragic accident. Look at this neighbouring tombstone. 'In Affectionate Remembrance of John Jeffery, who departed this life March 14th, 1843, aged forty-seven years. Also Henrietta, wife of the above, who died September 7th, 1844, aged forty-four years.' The grieving father followed his son in death by less than a year, and the mother died the following year. These are sad events, sir."

"True," the vicar murmured. "Profoundly true. But this churchyard does not record a sadder event than the burial that will take place tomorrow."

He hurried towards the church, and we followed after him in leisurely fashion with Sherlock Holmes continuing to inspect and comment on the tombstones.

I had been impressed by the size of the Church of St. John Havenchurch each time that I had passed it. From close by, it looked enormous. The door stood ajar; inside, men were at work preparing the Quallsford family vault for Edmund's burial, and they had spilled a small mound of dirt near the entrance. One of the workmen had stepped in it. Sherlock Holmes nudged me and pointed at the footprint.

"Do you recognize that badly nailed toe? Its owner helped to exorcise the tower yesterday morning. Today he is probing in the opposite direction. What a splendid topic for a sermon!"

The church had seemed impressively large from the outside; it looked gigantic from within. The dim interior had an austere loveliness, but the high box pews that crowded it gave it a ramshackle appearance. Sherlock Holmes moved through it in the same alert fashion as he had explored the churchyard. We made a complete circuit of the nave, but I had no time to do more than glimpse the simple Norman beauty of the place.

We were about to leave when the vicar caught up with us. "You must see the medieval font and the wall paintings," he said.

"We don't want to interfere with the sad preparations," Sherlock Holmes told him. "We will return another day when we can admire your treasures at leisure."

We were subjected to a lecture on the church bells and the clock before we finally made our escape and took the road to Havenchurch.

I have mentioned Sherlock Holmes's disturbing habit of answering the unasked questions of his companions. I wanted to know how he deduced that the one-legged man was the vicar performing an exorcism, but I hesitated to break in on his thoughts. When he finally spoke again, he said, "I told you that you were missing the most important clue, Porter. At every point where the vicar performed, he left marks in the dust where he sprinkled holy water. Even before that, you should have suspected—not known, but suspected—that One-Leg was the vicar. Who else visits all parts of a village and comes and goes repeatedly from the church?"

All I could say was "Yes, sir."

"At least you understand, now, why the children of the village don't play in the tower. You also know why the path loops around it. From some of the tales the dray driver related to me, I very much doubt that the men of the village would have had the courage to approach it with evil intent. No one goes there without a good reason, and few people are able to think of a reason."

He fell silent for a moment. Then he said, "The vicar's testimony does not help us, Porter. We already knew that Edmund Quallsford had a local reputation as a bright young businessman. Unfortunately, that does not answer the question of where his money came from."

"Would you like me to return to London and make inquiries at the Stock Exchange?" I asked. "Fortunes are made there—and lost, and restored—every day, or so I have heard. With a little capital to get started, he could have been doing well for himself. He sounds like the sort of young man who would take naturally to a such a business."

"I inquired yesterday," Sherlock Holmes said. "My friends on the Exchange have never heard of him."

I grappled with this riddle as we walked along. "Maybe there was a secret inheritance that the family doesn't know about," I said finally. "Mines in Wales, or tea plantations in India, or shares in the Suez Canal. That would explain where Edmund got his money and also provide a motive for his murder."

"This is not a romance, Porter," Sherlock Holmes said sternly. "At the time of Oswald Quallsford's death, he was in desperate financial straits and struggling to raise money any way he could. If there had been any kind of an inheritance, secret or otherwise, he would have found it and spent it."

He lost himself in thought until we approached the village and met Joe and the pony at the end of the High Street. They were on their way to the vicarage with a message. I introduced Sherlock Holmes to Joe, who sat with shining eyes while the great detective congratulated him on his own feat of detection.

"Did you find out anything about smugglers?" I asked Joe.

"My uncle says they were hanged and buried," Joe said.

"Your uncle is right," Sherlock Holmes told him. "Did he mention where they were buried?"

Joe's face puckered with the sudden strain placed on his memory.

"Was it Ruckinge?" Sherlock Holmes asked. His encyclopaedic knowledge of the history of crime enabled him to recite details about almost any locality in the world where an interesting event occurred.

Joe brightened. "Yes. That was it—Ruckinge."

"There is also supposed to be a hanged smuggler buried at Aldington," Sherlock Holmes said. "But all of that happened long ago. Have you heard anything about recent smuggling?"

Joe shook his head.

"Last month—or last week?" Sherlock Holmes persisted.

"Cor!" Joe exclaimed. "Last *week?* I never heard of smugglers doing anything *now.*"

"All right, Joe," Sherlock Holmes said. He tossed a shilling to him. "Keep your ears open, and remember—it's a secret. But here is something you *can* tell your uncle. Those smugglers who were hanged and buried were not hanged for smuggling. Two of them were highwaymen; the third was a murderer. Even a smuggler is not hanged these days unless he has committed murder."

Joe resumed his errand, and we turned our thoughts to food. The church clock had chimed twelve, which seemed a long time after my breakfast, and Sherlock Holmes had not eaten at all.

He suggested that we separate and meet again after lunch. He wanted to smoke a pipe or two on our morning's work, and then he would decide what our next move would be.

I returned to the Royal Swan, and he made his separate way to the Green Dragon, a pub whose name was far more colourful than the decrepit building that housed it.

Mr. Werner greeted me with his usual question about my progress in evaluating the assets of the Quallsford Importing Company.

"It gets more complicated by the hour," I complained fretfully. "I had no idea of the extent of the business Edmund handled. He was selling spirits and cloth and tobacco and other things all over southern Kent and Sussex."

"Is that so?" Mr. Werner asked. "I had no idea of that myself."

There was justification for his gloomy complaint that his wife had no one to cook for but himself and the help. Mrs. Werner offered, in her wholesome, inexpensive lunches and dinners, food of an unusual quality for a village inn, but it attracted few local patrons. Its fame extended beyond Havenchurch, however, and regular travellers on the Rye Road sometimes stopped at the Royal Swan for their meals. It was Mr. Werner's own friendly chatter that attracted crowds of locals for their afternoon or evening pints and half-pints.

Mrs. Werner brought me an enormous helping of shepherd's pie, and Mr. Werner joined me with his own full plate.

"How did your inn happened to be called 'The *Royal* Swan'?" I asked him.

"Queen Elizabeth stayed here in August of 1573," he said.

"Really!" I exclaimed. I was startled. I had admired the fine old building, but I found it difficult to imagine it housing a queen.

"No, not really," Mr. Werner said matter-of-factly. "She visited Rye in 1573, but no one knows where she stayed. Probably in Rye. The old vicar—not Mr. Russell, the one before him—wanted to make out that she came and went on the Rye Road and visited Havenchurch along the way, but that road belongs to the canal and wasn't even there in 1573. Of course she could have travelled by ship on the sea creek that led up to Appledore, but if she did, she sailed right past Havenchurch, as James the First's Queen Anne is said to have done later. No, I don't think Elizabeth ever saw this place, but she would have travelled in a large party, maybe hundreds of people, and Rye couldn't have held all of them, so *someone* royal may have stayed here in 1573. All I know is that this has been called the Royal Swan as long as there have been records. A cautious landlord took the sign down in Cromwell's time. It was the Royal Swan when he put it up again. It may have been the royal something else before then."

Mrs. Werner came scurrying in. She leaned over me and whispered breathlessly, "It's Miss Quallsford. She wants to see you."

I excused myself and followed her into the Werners' private parlour. Emmeline Quallsford was standing in the centre of the room. She looked agitated and deathly pale, and the simple black dress she wore offered a startling contrast to her stylish appearance in London.

"I am sorry to disturb you," she said. "I thought I should tell you that I am leaving Havenchurch." Her voice had sounded calm, but she gave a strange, sobbing little laugh and then burst into tears.

Mrs. Werner immediately provided a towel and appropriate motherly support, clasping Emmeline in her arms and making consoling noises. Emmeline shook her off. She wiped the tears away angrily.

"I'm sorry," she said. "Larissa insisted that I leave, and it is her right. Sea Cliffs was legally and properly my brother's, and his children should grow up there, and in due time it should pass to his son. I don't dispute any of that, though it is a shock be ordered out of the home that was my parents' and grandparents' and great-grandparents.' What hurts most is my sister-in-law's slanderous accusation that I caused my brother's death. Only time can cure that. I have great faith in time, Mr. Jones, and in your investigation."

I found my voice and asked, "Where are you going?"

"One of my friends in Rye will take me in temporarily, I am certain. I am trying to plan for the future. If I can find supporters, I would like to start a private school. I enjoy teaching children. I was governess for my niece and nephew, you know."

I was wishing that Sherlock Holmes had come to lunch with me. "No, I didn't realize that you were their governess," I said. "I thought perhaps Doris Fowler—"

"Gracious, no!" she exclaimed. "Dear Doris! She was the bright, shining light of our young lives, my brother's and mine. She represented knowledge, and fascinating books, and the wide world beyond Sea Cliffs, which we knew about only through her. We both loved her dearly. But she is awfully old, now, and muddle-headed, and sometimes definitely queer. She wanders about and does and says strange things. I will take her with me as soon as I can. Larissa dislikes her immensely, and I was sorry to leave her there, but I can't make a home for her until I am settled. If I have to take a position as governess for a time, looking after her will be difficult, but something must be managed."

"Will you let me know where you will be staying in Rye?"
I asked.

"Of course. As soon as I know. Please tell Mr. Holmes that I
expect him to continue the investigation. His fee will be paid. I
promise that. I am only sorry that I will be powerless to assist you,
but I could not return to Sea Cliffs for any reason."

She turned away muffling a sob and dashed from the room.

Mrs. Werner was still hovering nearby. "Poor Emmeline," she
murmured. Then she added, as though attempting to be strictly fair,
"Poor Larissa. This has torn both of their lives apart."

CHAPTER
8

I returned to my shepherd's pie, and Mr. Werner politely asked no questions. He knew that his wife would tell him all about it at the first opportunity. I had quite lost interest in the royal history of the Royal Swan, and we finished our meal in silence.

I declined Mr. Werner's invitation to join him for a pint and took my leave of him.

I found Sherlock Holmes in the Green Dragon making a meal of bread and cheese with beer from the Finn Brewery in Lydd—a popular variety that the locals called "Real Stingo." He had reverted to his disguise, and he looked fully as disreputable as the two men with whom he was talking. I took my pint to the next table and listened.

He was relating a sad history. He was a wagoner from Lewes, he told his companions. He had worked for the same farmer since he was a boy. The farmer—splendid chap—had known his business and treated his labourers well. In return, the labourers treated the farmer well.

"Always did our bestest for him," Sherlock Holmes murmured. The two men nodded approvingly.

But the old farmer had died, and his son was a drunken wastrel, cruel to his animals and worse to his labourers. A body could stand only so much of that, so here he was, on the road after almost forty years with one master. He found wages poor and work scarce at Lewes, so he had drifted east.

The other two expressed sympathy. "These be bad times," one of them said.

"Farm near Hastings was offering thirteen bob a week," Sherlock Holmes said. He shook his head. "Cruel for a man with a family. I heard wagoners do better around the Marsh."

"Farmers that have it will pay it," one of the men said. "Court Lodge Farm, at Appledore, pays wagoners fifteen bob, but they don't need any."

"They don't often need any," the other man said. " 'Sides, you have to be good."

"I be better than good," Sherlock Holmes said.

He was. He had a miraculous knack with horses. I had seen him demonstrate it.

The two men responded with shrugs but no challenge. They finished their beer and left. Sherlock Holmes and I exchanged polite comments on the weather, and I invited him to join me.

Quietly I described Emmeline Quallsford's dramatic message. He listened with a scowl.

"I must see Sea Cliffs," he said when I had finished. "Perhaps there is no longer anything to be learned there, but I must see it. Tomorrow at eleven is the time. Everyone should be at the funeral. This evening we will call on Sergeant Donley at his home, which will avoid the necessity of an official visit. We must see Edmund's suicide letter before we proceed further."

"What do you want me to do now?" I asked.

"Stroll onto the Marsh with me. I am a wagoner; perhaps I will see some horses to admire."

"I thought the Marsh was sheep country," I said.

He laughed. "All the more reason to admire horses if we see any."

We paid our scores. Sherlock Holmes paused outside the door for a searching look at Havenchurch, and then he turned east, towards the Marsh.

At the edge of the village, in either direction, the High Street became Havenchurch Road. To the eastward, the smooth, dusty surface changed to what the locals called "beach"—gravel—until it reached the Rye Road. Thereafter it crossed the Royal Military Canal on a timber bridge, crossed the railway at Havenchurch Halt, and went its zigzagging, rutted way through the Marsh as far as the village of Brookland.

We followed it only a short distance past the bridge. Sturdy planks, held in place by stakes driven into the ground on either side, were laid to give passage over the drainage ditch that lay along the south side of the road. On the far side, the pasture side, there was a wood barrier to prevent animals from crossing the planks. I quickly discovered that it was not horses that interested Sherlock Holmes, but their tracks. He uttered an exclamation and scrambled over the rough span. A flock of sheep had crossed there, in both directions, but his unerring eyesight had picked out of that jumble of sheep tracks the partially obliterated print of a horse's shoe. It was a startling demonstration of the marvellous acuity of his senses.

He examined the mark with his magnifying glass and searched the muddled ground in vain for more horse prints. Then he turned his attention to the barrier. One post was hinged in an ingenious arrangement. No animal could push it aside, but the farmer could swing it out of the way in an instant when he wanted his animals to cross.

Leaving the road behind us, we moved south along the canal and turned eastward when a drainage ditch blocked the way. We walked further and further onto the Marsh, which was of course no marsh at all but a magnificent pasturage. Many lands famous for sheep rated their pastures according to the number of acres required to support one animal; but there were places in these Marshes of south-east England where the grass was so rich that it would support ten or more sheep per acre and fatten them without extra food. The white-faced sheep viewed our intrusion uneasily, but they quickly sensed that we were ignoring them, and they returned to their business of eating.

There was no path for us to follow. When a lesser drainage ditch barred our way, we turned aside and followed it until we found a plank bridge similar to the first one we had crossed. The locals sometimes called the ditches "dykes," sometimes "sewers," but they all looked like ditches to me. We could have crossed the fenced railway line by crawling through the wires, but Sherlock Holmes turned north, and we soon found a crossing with neatly painted wood gates on either side. There were tracks where horses had crossed the line there, and twice more Sherlock Holmes was able to pick horse tracks out of a jumble of sheep tracks where grass was worn away at the ends of one of the crude plank bridges. We continued to move eastward.

The flat land seemed to swallow us up. Its undulations were so gradual as to be imperceptible. I had no awareness of going from valley to ridge, but we must have done so, because a tiny brick building loomed up ahead of us. It was a sheep house, or lookers' hut—as the shepherds of the Marsh were called—and it was surrounded by board fences enclosing the sheep pounds.

A roughly clothed figure had been seated beside the open door. It rose and walked towards us followed by a handsome black-and-white dog. Not until it came close did I suddenly perceive that it was a woman.

She halted a few feet away and laughed shrilly. "You lost?"

"We are enjoying a walk on the Marsh," Sherlock Holmes said genially. "Are you a shepherd?"

She spat as disgustedly as any man would have. "Looker," she said. "Been one for ten year. Took my old man's place when he died."

"You have a lonely house," I said.

She cackled. "Don't live here. Only stay here for lambing. I lives in Brookland."

"Do many people come this way?" Sherlock Holmes asked.

"Depends on who wants to go from where to where."

"Someone did, riding a horse," Sherlock Holmes said.

She spat again. "That'll be Ben Paine. Mole catcher. Rides around on a horse looking for moles."

"Has he been this way recently?" Sherlock Holmes asked.

"May have."

"We shall look for him," Sherlock Holmes said.

"Don't you wish!" she said scornfully.

"Smoke?"

Sherlock Holmes offered her his tobacco pouch. He had noticed the pipe stem protruding from a pocket. She immediately produced a charred old pipe and filled it. He lit a vesper for her, and then, as she began to smoke, he asked her a few more questions about passers-by. She answered vaguely. When we parted, she ambled back towards the odd little hut emitting clouds of smoke.

"What do you think, Porter?" Sherlock Holmes asked. "Was that a demonstration of the natural taciturnity of her kind?"

"She saw *us* quickly enough and came to investigate," I said. "I don't think anyone could walk or ride past here without her noticing. In her lonely life, every passer-by is an event."

"But at night she goes home to Brookland," Sherlock Holmes said thoughtfully. "The Marsh must be desolate indeed under darkness when even its shepherds abandon it."

When I looked back, the looker's hut had disappeared. Only the drainage ditch we were following kept my sense of direction intact. I had the feeling that if I were to angle away from it, I would soon become helplessly lost in a green-grass sea—but I already was lost. When I tried to determine my position, I discovered that the ditch had curved and the sun was not where I expected it to be.

The cardinal points of the compass were irrelevant in that land. Things were where they were, and their locations were information that the land shared with you if you were privileged. If you were not, if you were an arrogant stranger who needed to be taught humility, this land could humble you in a handful of minutes and leave you not only uncertain as to your whereabouts but in total doubt concerning the relationships between land and water or earth and sky. We continued to use the same large ditch as a guide, and I felt certain that we would have lost ourselves utterly had we wandered away from it.

We turned back, finally, and began retracing our steps. Sherlock Holmes was still intent on his search for horses' tracks, and he had us walk parallel to our guide ditch but almost out of sight of each other in order to look for tracks or horse droppings across a wide sweep of pasture. I saw neither; and when I passed close by the looker's hut, the woman was not in sight.

We were still a long way from the Havenchurch Road when we heard a horse overtaking us. Ben Paine, the mole catcher, whom I had already talked with in Havenchurch, brought his horse to a halt, swung down easily, and walked along with us.

"Pleasant afternoon," he remarked.

He was a well-built man in his thirties, good-looking in a coarse way, with quick, shrewd eyes and a mop of straw-coloured hair. His manner seemed as taciturn as that of the looker, and he kept glancing sideways as though trying to decide what to make of us, but he answered our questions readily. Sherlock Holmes, with his usual alert interest in anything that was new to him, wanted to know all about the occupation of mole catcher. He examined the tools of Paine's trade: the digging implement, and the traps, and the large bag with strap and buckle that Paine carried on his shoulder when he was working on foot.

Paine obligingly displayed and demonstrated them. "We call this a spud," he said, holding up a small spade. He showed us how he dug just ahead of a burrowing mole—never behind, or the mole, which could move fast if it wanted to, would escape—to scoop it out of the ground. He also showed us how he baited a trap with a worm and set it.

This strange occupation fascinated Sherlock Holmes. When he had fully explored the manner in which moles were caught, he asked to see the contents of Paine's bag. Paine at first was reluctant—obviously such a request came his way but rarely. When Sherlock Holmes persisted, he shook out the bag of dead moles for us. He had perhaps a dozen of them, and at least one had been in the trap longer than overnight. I lost interest when Paine opened the bag, but Sherlock Holmes's curiosity was impervious to unpleasant odours.

"You seem to make the profession pay," he observed to Paine.

"The ladies must have their fur collars," Paine said with a laugh.

"But I suppose there is more skill and knowledge involved than an outsider would suspect."

"Skill and knowledge in catching the moles and skill and knowledge in curing or dressing the skins," Paine said. "If you are thinking of trying it, don't. You have to be trained to it. My father taught my brother and me—we were catching moles and rubbing skins not long after we learned to walk."

"I suppose one would have to be familiar with the markets, also, to know when and where to sell the skins profitably," Sherlock Holmes said.

"All of that," Paine agreed.

He continued to answer our questions pleasantly enough but otherwise he had little to say. Once we had disposed of the occupation of mole catcher, Sherlock Holmes wanted to know about the Marsh's lookers, and Paine described the expertise with which they cared for their sheep. Then the conversation turned to the drainage ditches, which Paine called dykes.

"They must make work," Sherlock Holmes said, keeping to his role as an unemployed wagoner. "Don't they have to be cleared regularly?"

"That they do," Ben Paine said. "And hard, mucky work it is, and cold in the winter. But there aren't enough jobs to go around, and what there are go to the local unemployed."

When we reached the Rye Road, he parted with us as unceremoniously as he had joined us, bidding us good day, remounting his horse, and riding south. Sherlock Holmes asked me to meet him at Sergeant Donley's home that evening, and he went off on an errand of his own.

He drove himself in a punishing manner whenever a case took us out of London. He was restless enough at home, especially when he had no problem to occupy himself with; but he seemed unable to relax at all away from his comfortable Baker Street rooms, and his chemical experiments and scrapbooks and fresh editions of papers and Mrs. Hudson's patient catering. I knew that he worked both day and night, but too often there was little that I could do to assist him, once my own initial inquiries were completed, because of his secretive nature. Unless he asked, I often did not know what help he required.

He had given me no instructions for the remainder of the afternoon, but I never interpreted the absence of orders as a license to do nothing. It was a challenge to me to use my imagination and find a way to occupy myself that might assist in our investigation.

The next day's program included a visit to Sea Cliffs—unofficial and probably illegal—at a time when everyone would certainly be attending Edmund Quallsford's funeral. I did not care for the idea of meeting the family on the road on its way to church, and the public footpath we had followed to the tower also was a highly conspicuous route. I wondered whether it would be possible to walk *below* the cliffs, climb them west of Sea Cliffs, and find a less noticeable approach.

I began my walk near the school, where paths from Havenchurch and the Rye Road converged into one that led westward. The day had become warmish; I removed my coat and strolled along slowly while I emulated Sherlock Holmes's search for horse tracks. I did not know what his object was or whether tracks on this path would have the same significance for him as tracks on the Marsh, but I examined the ground carefully as I walked. In addition to sheep tracks, I found ample evidence that a number of horses had passed this way in either direction.

I had a pleasant walk for about two miles with the cliffs looming up on my right and, some distance to my left, the quiet-flowing water of the River Rother. Midway in my walk, I saw the old Quallsford tower high above me. The cliffs descended from terrace to terrace, but they looked far too precipitous to negotiate safely. I saw no paths and no place at all where an easy ascent could be made. Finally I came to a north–south road, and I quickly satisfied myself that it crossed the Isle of Graesney and would intersect Havenchurch Road somewhere west of Sea Cliffs.

Sherlock Holmes would already have that information. He normally began an investigation by acquiring a large-scale ordnance map of the district that interested him. My walk was not entirely wasted, however; I could tell him that there was no obvious short cut, and I discovered, where the path I was following intersected the road, a structure that was as interesting to me as a route up the cliffs would have been.

It was an old stone oast-house, a building for drying hops. Obviously it had not been used for that purpose for many years. The conical roof of the kiln and its revolving wood cowl were sadly decayed. The remainder of the building, however, was in fair condition. The windows of the upper floor were curtained, an indication that someone lived there, and the ground floor seemed to be in use as a stable. There were two wagons in the yard, and in a fenced area behind the building were six of the handsomest dray horses I had ever seen.

I turned back towards Havenchurch wondering what deductions I might make concerning an oast-house so remote from any hop gardens. Probably it was evidence of nothing more than change: At some time in the past, when hop prices were high, someone had tried to plant new gardens nearby. But the hop business is an erratic one, as was once explained to me in great detail by a grower in Hampshire who hired Sherlock Holmes to unravel a domestic puzzle. The periodic decline in hop prices forced many growers into bankruptcy; a few years later, the only evidences of their formerly flourishing businesses were the disused and decaying oast-houses—some of which might be restored to use with the next turn in hop fortunes.

The old oast-house was a meagre profit to show for a four-mile walk unless Sherlock Holmes decided to extend his interest in horses' tracks to horses. If he did that, I had discovered some splendid specimens for him.

When I returned to the Royal Swan, I found two things waiting for me: A note from Miss Quallsford, giving me the address of the friend she was staying with in Rye; and a dish of eels that Mrs. Werner had prepared. The eels were delicious, and I ate them with a severe guilty conscience, wondering what makeshift meal Sherlock Holmes would be consuming at that moment—if, indeed, he remembered to eat.

I often puzzled over the fact that all of his senses were superlatively developed except for his sense of taste—at least where food was concerned. Food was simply fuel for his body, and the less time wasted in taking on another load, the better satisfied he was. Dr. Watson fancied himself a gourmet, and he delighted in inveigling Sherlock Holmes to London's fancier restaurants, such as the Café Royal, or Simpson's, or Pagani's. The good doctor would have been distressed indeed had he heard some of the descriptions of those lavish meals that Sherlock Holmes regaled me with afterwards. I relished the Royal Swan's appetizing dinner while reflecting ruefully that he was probably gulping a chunk of bread and a slab of cheese and that his body would certainly function far more efficiently on such makeshift victuals than mine would on Mrs. Werner's skilled cooking.

Mr. Werner was already busy dispensing the bitter that he took such a justifiable pride in. I murmured something about an evening walk and went out to look for Sergeant Donley's house.

Sherlock Holmes had given me detailed instructions for reaching it without being seen. I walked north for a short distance on the Rye Road, found a footpath, and came to the rear garden of the small cottage just as darkness was descending.

Mrs. Donley opened the door for me. She was a tall, slender woman, and she wore a scowl and a slightly peevish air, perhaps because her husband had evicted her from her kitchen. The sergeant and Sherlock Holmes sat on opposite sides of a sturdy table with an oil lamp between them, Sherlock Holmes's lank form a droll contrast to the sergeant's bulky figure. Spread out on the table were sheets of paper covered with ornate writing, and Sherlock Holmes, with a look of intense concentration on his face, was examining one of them with his magnifying glass.

The sergeant greeted me amicably, though he was noticeably nervous. Sherlock Holmes's penchant for dramatic revelations was becoming known even to England's rural police, and the sergeant knew about it from firsthand experience. He was worried that the death he had officially proclaimed a suicide might turn out to be murder.

I seated myself and waited.

"You will never convince me that Edmund Quallsford did not write that," Sergeant Donley announced.

"It was certainly written by the same person who wrote these letters," Sherlock Holmes said.

Sergeant Donley heaved a sigh of relief. "I didn't see how it could be otherwise. Really, Mr. Holmes—I cannot understand what it is that you are investigating."

Sherlock Holmes had laid the magnifying glass aside while he held the letter up to the light. "Edmund Quallsford did not indulge himself in the stationery he used for this alleged farewell letter. The paper is three pence the packet at the local emporium of our friend George Adams."

He passed the sheet of paper to me. Under his scrutiny, I examined the few lines of writing with more than my usual care.

They read:

I cannot continue. I have attempted to honour my obligations scrupulously no matter what the difficulties, but that is no longer possible. The only solution is to end everything. I say this with regret, but I have higher obligations that I can compromise no longer.

It was signed "Edmund Quallsford."

Using my own lens, I compared the writing with that on the other pages. "Do we know for certain that Edmund Quallsford wrote these?" I asked.

"We do," Sergeant Donley said gruffly. "I collected them for the record, but I already knew his handwriting."

"If he wrote the other things, he certainly wrote this message," I said.

"What else can you deduce from it?" Sherlock Holmes asked.

"It is an exceedingly strange suicide letter," I said. "I take it that the remark about ending everything is supposed to refer to his killing himself, but nothing else in the note supports that, and the conclusion flatly contradicts it. It is the statement of a man who has decided to put something behind him and devote himself to his higher obligations."

"It is indeed," Sherlock Holmes said. "If he had been forced by honour to terminate a business arrangement, this is the letter he would have written. Surely a genuine suicide message from Edmund Quallsford would be very different. He has been described to us as a kind man who loved his wife and children. Would he kill himself in his own home without giving a thought to them? At such a moment they would be foremost in his mind. He would not deliberately end his life without leaving them a message or making some reference to them. I don't believe it. Can you suggest anything else, Porter?"

"Where was the letter found?" I asked.

"On a desk in the bedroom where his body was found," Sergeant Donley said.

"Was it folded like this?"

"Just like that," the sergeant said.

I looked at Sherlock Holmes.

He nodded grimly. "A small point, but well observed. Why would he write a suicide letter *and fold it twice* in order to leave it lying on his desk? Was he concerned that some intruder might read it? The contrary—he would want to call attention to it, and he would know that a host of strangers would be prying into all of his secrets once he was dead. Each additional piece of evidence places new difficulties in the way of your suicide theory, Sergeant."

"He might fold it from force of habit," the sergeant said.

Sherlock Holmes smiled. "Perhaps."

I said slowly, "What if the letter were not connected with the suicide? He wrote it; he decided later to kill himself."

Sherlock Holmes chuckled. "No, Porter. You cannot simplify the result by surrounding it with complications. Why would he leave a message that is *not* a suicide note and then kill himself? And if this were a normal communication, written in the way of business, surely it would commence with date and salutation. Look again— you have missed the most vital clue."

I held the paper up to the lamp, as he had, and moved it to catch the light at various angles. Suddenly I detected marks that I had not seen before. "This is the second page of a letter!" I exclaimed.

"Exactly," Sherlock Holmes said. "Because this is cheap, flimsy paper, here and there a tiny spot of ink has soaked through from the page above, and the pen has left a few faint impressions. If Edmund Quallsford had used a pencil, we could reconstruct the entire letter. Unfortunately, he did not, so I am not able to make out any words. There is just enough suggestion of format to show where the date and salutation were placed."

The sergeant looked stricken. "Then—you mean—"

"We must be fair to the sergeant, Porter," Sherlock Holmes said. "For the present, I mean only this. If you want to know what happened in Edmund Quallsford's bedroom, you will have to find the first page of this letter. There are two possibilities. One is that he committed suicide, leaving a two-page letter, and someone entered the room after he died and removed the first page. If this is true, the missing page certainly would give us a better understanding of why Edmund Quallsford killed himself.

"The second possibility is that the letter was written some time before he died. The person who received it was astute enough to recognize the opportunity that fate had handed to him in arranging a second page—in Edmund Quallsford's own handwriting and with his signature—that *almost* read like a suicide letter. All he had to do was find Edmund alone, pull the trigger, and leave this second page behind. In the latter case, if we knew what the first page of the letter said, in all likelihood we would know who murdered Edmund Quallsford and why."

"I don't believe it," the sergeant muttered.

"There is one more problem," Sherlock Holmes said. He held one of the other letters up to the light. "These examples you brought for comparison are written on expensive stationery—the best Oxford Street quality, ivory tinted, watermarked, possibly something his wife or sister selected for him. Why would he use that for routine letters and write the most momentous communication of his life on cheap paper that he normally would have used only for scribbles? There must have been a compelling reason."

He got to his feet and gave the sergeant a friendly clap on the back. "You have the two possibilities to work on, Sergeant. They are complicated by the fact that the missing page of the letter has certainly been destroyed. In order to solve this case, we may have to reconstruct its contents from other evidence—which will be difficult."

"But what am I to do?" the sergeant blurted.

"Go to your superior tomorrow," Sherlock Holmes said. "Confess having sober second thoughts about Edmund Quallsford's suicide letter—for the reasons we just gave you. Then do what Porter and I are going to do: Go back to work."

We left the sergeant's cottage by the same surreptitious route and circled around to Havenchurch's High Street. The moon had not risen yet, but the High Street and its now shadowed houses had become so familiar to me that it seemed impossible that I had seen them for the first time only two nights before while riding in the trap with Emmeline Quallsford.

We overtook the Havenchurch milkman. His cart and horse, driven by a boy, followed him along the street, and he went from door to door carrying his tin in one hand and a hurricane lantern in the other, dipping out milk with a half-pint or pint measure and pouring it into the jug left there. As we passed him, he attacked a door with a fusillade of knocks and bellowed, "If you want milk, get your jug out here!" The startled housewife rushed to the door with her jug.

"Charming cottage," Sherlock Holmes said, pausing to peer through the darkness at the house, whose looming array of Tudor black and white had been briefly illuminated by the shallow glow of the milkman's lantern. "These buildings surely have a notable history. I wonder how many murders have been committed in each of them. Could we say, on the average, one for six generations, or one to each century and a half?"

"Surely not as many as that!" I exclaimed.

"Human passions churn as violently in the country as in the city, Porter. Love, hate, selfishness, greed—never forget greed, it is the universal solvent of crime—there is no sound reason why the deadly sins should be any less deadly here even though the air is purer. I find it both awesome and appalling to reflect on all of the events that an old dwelling like that has witnessed, the famous people who have passed by and perhaps tossed a glance in its direction like a miser surrendering a crumb of bread to a beggar—"

"Queen Bess," I said, remembering Mr. Werner's lecture on royalty.

"What about Queen Bess?"

I related Mr. Werner's description of her visit to Rye and the possibility of her contributing the "Royal" to the Royal Swan.

"We are much more advantageously placed than Queen Elizabeth," he said. "If she actually did see that particular cottage, she found nothing picturesque about it. It had not yet acquired its historical charm—at that early date, it may not have seen even one murder—and Tudor buildings were hardly a novelty to a Tudor monarch. I am reliably informed that even today they quickly lose their charm for those who have to live in them."

We entered the Green Dragon. Sam Jenks, the landlord, a large, obese, untidy man, looked us over expectantly. I was about to order a pint of Real Stingo, which I had found potable though vastly inferior to Mr. Werner's home-made bitter, but Sherlock Holmes stopped me.

"Do you have French brandy?" he asked.

We carried the two small glasses to a table in a quiet corner. I had never tasted French brandy, and I sipped it as though it were an unpleasant medicine, which is what it reminded me of. Sherlock Holmes applied himself to it with the same scientific objectivity with which he approached every experience.

"It is very good French cognac," he said. "It has been watered about a hundred percent, which is a bit too much but no more than I would expect in an establishment like this."

"Is it Edmund Quallsford's brandy?" I asked.

"It may be," Sherlock Holmes said. "But the landlord probably supplied the water himself."

We sipped our brandy and talked. I told him of my search for an inconspicuous route to Sea Cliffs. As I expected, he already knew about the north-south road, but the converted oast-house interested him.

"That will be Jack Browne's establishment," Sherlock Holmes said.

"I met him last night."

"He seems to be the most enterprising carrier in the area. His horses are widely admired. He rents a stable in Havenchurch and another in New Romney where he can keep wagons and horses overnight when his rounds require that, and he is well known in all of the Marsh villages. He boasts that he will haul loads anywhere between Land's End and Inverness. I intend to call on him in the morning as an unemployed wagoner. There is one more matter that we can investigate tonight. Does Mr. Herks have a key to the Quallsford Importing Company?"

"Nat Whyte has one. I never thought to ask Mr. Herks."

"Ask him now. He will be easier to locate than Nat Whyte. Tell him there are one or two points about the inventory that you need to check, and you will return the key in half an hour or less."

As we were leaving, he paused for a word with the landlord. "Very good brandy," he said. "Do you have much call for it?"

"Very little," the landlord said. "And when this is gone, maybe there won't be any more. The man who was importing it killed himself the other day."

"Interesting," Sherlock Holmes mused as we walked along the High Street. "He said he has very little call for it—but both this afternoon and this evening he was selling more brandy than anything else."

Mr. Herks's shop was closed, and my knock went unheeded. Finally I circled around to his back door. He greeted me with a scowl.

"I have had a message from London," I said. "There are one or two points that I need to check about the Quallsford Importing Company's inventory. Could you let me have the key for a few minutes?"

His immediate reaction was to refuse. "Call in tomorrow morning," he said. "I'll take you down there myself."

"This can't wait until tomorrow," I told him. "Didn't Miss Quallsford instruct you to cooperate fully?"

"That she did," he agreed reluctantly. "But I will have to come with you."

His wife called to him. "Harry! Your dinner is getting cold."

Reluctantly he surrendered the key. A few paces down the street, Sherlock Holmes joined me. We unlocked the door of the Quallsford Importing Company and fumbled about until we found a candle. Sherlock Holmes lit it and carried it over to the table that Edmund Quallsford had used as a desk.

"Here you are, Porter," he said.

The few sheets of paper there were identical with the one that bore the supposed suicide message.

"So he wrote the letter here," I said.

Sherlock Holmes was examining the top sheet. "He certainly was not in the habit of writing his correspondence here. The only impressions I can make out are numbers that were written on the sheet above with a pencil. On the other hand, there is no other paper. If he wanted to write a letter here, he would have had to use this. The ink is the same, but so was the ink on the other letters. That only means that he made purchases for home and business at the same shop."

He seated himself at the table and bent over Edmund Quallsford's ledger. He always attempted to absorb the atmosphere of his surroundings. "I had hoped to find a sheet with impressions from that second page," he said, "but it could have been written weeks ago. We may learn more when we see the desk in his bedroom."

"But he definitely was murdered," I said.

"No, Porter. Not 'definitely' until we have explored all of the alternatives; but I can give you one assurance. If he was murdered, his murderer was no buffle-headed farm hand. The cleverest London criminal never did a more artful job of work."

CHAPTER
9

We locked the building, and Sherlock Holmes strode quickly away into the night. On Sergeant Donley's recommendation, he was staying with the schoolmaster, who lived in a small cottage behind the blacksmith's shop.

I returned the key to Mr. Herks and went back to the Royal Swan.

Mrs. Werner was dispensing drinks. I decided to conduct an experiment of my own, and I asked her for French brandy. The glass that she served me was smaller than the one I had received at the Green Dragon; the price was much more severe. I found out why with my first sip. Mr. Werner did not water his brandy, and it was sufficiently overproof to take the drinker's head off.

The landlord was talking with Ben Paine, the mole catcher, and Derwin Smith, Edmund Quallsford's rival grazier. He waved to me to join them. Their talk was about local matters, rates and road repairs, and I listened in silence while I made a show of drinking the brandy.

I had asked Sherlock Holmes whether he wanted me to obtain more information about any of the local citizens I had talked with. I expected him to express at least a cursory interest in Derwin Smith. To my astonishment, it was Taff Harris whom he was curious about

—the farm hand from New Romney who walked some ten miles to and from work.

But Taff Harris did not patronize the Royal Swan.

On this night before the funeral, talk turned naturally to Edmund Quallsford. "They say Larissa is still taking it very bad," Derwin Smith said. "Also, old Doris has gone completely off her head, and Emmeline couldn't stand her sister-in-law any longer and moved out, or maybe she couldn't face the prospect of all these Monier relations coming for the funeral. It will be interesting to see how things go without her. It wasn't Edmund who ran Sea Cliffs, you know. It was Emmeline. She knew twice what he did about farming, even though she didn't know very much. I tried to show him, once, how I could rent his land and pay him more than the money he was making with his own sheep. He halfway agreed with me, but the next time I saw him he had changed his mind. Meaning that Emmeline had changed his mind."

I could understand his jealousy of Edmund Quallsford. Smith was intelligent and successful, but he would never wear his clothes the way Edmund had, no matter how much he paid for them. No one would ever say that Derwin Smith treated people gentlemanly. Could he possibly have believed in some warped way that murdering Edmund Quallsford would change that?

"Going to the funeral?" Mr. Werner asked me suddenly.

I hesitated as though I had not yet decided. "No," I said finally. "I am sure that the church will be full. I would not want to deprive some friend of Edmund's of a place."

Mr. Werner nodded. "The church certainly will be full," he agreed. "Everyone is going. We are closing right after breakfast, and we won't open again until evening. If you ask Mrs. Werner tomorrow morning, she will give you some bread and cheese to tide you over."

"Are all of the Havenchurch shops closing?" I asked.

"I think so. It is the least we can do—a mark of respect to Edmund's memory and to the family."

"There will be very little work done in this village tomorrow," Ben Paine said. "Not that there ever is much work done here. People in Havenchurch don't wait for the excuse of a funeral to take the day off. Then they complain about how bad business is and how hard it is to make money."

"What about you?" I asked with a smile. "Are you closing?"

He answered with a shrug. "The moles will be working regardless, but I'll take the time to attend Edmund's funeral, of course. I have known him since he was a boy."

"I suppose he helped you to catch moles at Sea Cliffs when he was young," I said.

"Actually, he did not," Paine said. "That was Emmeline. For a time, she caught the moles herself and gave them to me. Edmund was always friendly to me, though. Always gentle, always generous." He got up suddenly and excused himself.

"A lot of people are cut up badly by this," Mr. Werner said quietly as we watched Ben Paine walk away. "It will take Havenchurch a long time to get over it. Edmund knew everyone, and almost everyone he knew was his friend."

I had been over this ground before. I now thought it certain that Edmund Quallsford had been murdered. If he had no enemies, and if everyone was his friend, a friend must have murdered him.

"Your mole catcher seems to be prospering," I said.

"Aye," Mr. Werner acknowledged. "Getting rich. He always has been a hard-working chap. Out there digging at all hours if there is one more mole to be found. His brother Ned is just like him. Lives at Old Romney. This year we are having a plague of moles. Heard Tom Barling talking about it just the other day. He says he has never seen anything like it. No matter how many moles Ben catches, there are always more around. Both Ben and his brother have taken on apprentices."

"I've never seen so many moles as we have this year," Derwin Smith said.

"Where does Ben live?" I asked.

"Over on the Iden Road."

"He told me that he learned the trade from his father. Doesn't he have a son to teach?"

"Sad story, that," Mr. Werner said. "Married a parson's daughter from somewhere. Nice girl but a slight little thing. She died with their first baby, and the baby died, too. That was six, seven years ago. Far as I know, he has never looked at a woman since then. Lots of girls would jump at the chance, nice-looking fellow, good income, but he can't see them. Sad story. His brother's children are too young to be of much help, so they took apprentices. You might not think it to look at him, but Ben is an unhappy man. Successful but unhappy. There is a lesson there." He savoured a long draught of his bitter and pondered the lesson.

Mr. Herks came in, responded to a nod from Mr. Werner, and took the chair that Ben Paine had just vacated.

"Talking about Ben Paine," Mr. Werner said. "Must be doing real well, but he is an unhappy man, I say."

Mr. Herks nodded gloomily. "Plenty of moles around this year, but Ben always has done well. He has a sharp temper, though. Not an easy man to get along with. His wife left him, you know."

Mr. Werner raised his eyebrows. "I never heard that."

"Went to stay with neighbours. Maybe that's why Ben felt so guilty when she and the baby died."

"I suppose a mole catcher has to know the Marsh from one end to the other," I said.

"Has to know where to look for moles," Mr. Werner said. "Has to know the underside of pastures, you might say. If you want to find out about pastures right side up, ask the lookers."

"Do you sell much French brandy?" I asked him. I had not heard another call for it since I arrived.

"Very little," he said. "It is expensive, and my customers don't seem to care for it. I don't like it myself. I suppose it takes getting used to. Mrs. Werner thinks it is classy to offer it, though, and I wanted to help Edmund's company. I hear the Green Dragon gets some call for it. Of course Sam Jenks waters it so he can sell it cheap, but don't tell him I said so."

Mr. Werner moved on to talk with other customers. Herks and Derwin Smith finished their pints and took their leave of me. A stout newcomer dropped into one of the vacant chairs, and, when I responded to his nod, introduced himself as Alvin Pringle. His round face radiated good humour. Obviously the gloom of Edmund Quallsford's impending funeral did not weigh heavily upon him.

"Heard you were here to take a look at Edmund's business," he said.

"Yes," I said. "It has turned out to be much more complicated than it seemed at first."

His smile broadened. "Everything is complicated in Kent. Especially the people. I am from Cambridgeshire. Came down here to buy a farm. These people not only think funny, but they talk a funny language. Have you noticed?"

"I have been trying to work out the difference between a ditch, and a dyke, and a sewer," I said.

"There you have put your finger on it," he said, nodding vigorously. "All of those things are simply drains. Why do they have to make up words for them? These people also think that 'manure' is 'dung,' and a 'shelter' is a privy—which is a toilet where I come from—and a 'thack' is a 'thatch.' They make out that 'gravel' is 'beach' and 'tay' is 'tea,' and you can't even take a hook and trim a verge here—they call it 'brushing.' " He laughed merrily. "They have me so confused I can't hardly make out what I am doing. According to them, 'honeysuckle' is 'woodbine,' and 'whitethorn' is a 'May tree,' and 'foalsfoot' is 'coltsfoot,' and 'blackthorn' is 'sloe.' I might as well be in a foreign country."

"It certainly is a strange place," I agreed. "One of the strangest things is that they say there is no smuggling here."

"Ha!" Mr. Pringle drank deeply and came up with his smile

unimpaired. "Ha! Whoever heard of a stretch of coast without smugglers? Do you know what an island is?"

"I have a general idea," I confessed.

"No, you don't. An island is a body of land completely surrounded by smugglers."

"Did you have smugglers in Cambridgeshire?"

"We've got no coast in Cambridgeshire, but we have smuggling just the same. Smuggling happens wherever there is money in it."

"Smuggling is something that we importers have to worry about," I said. "We bring in goods legally, and pay the full duty, and we can't compete with smuggled goods that are brought in duty-free."

He nodded. "Stands to reason."

"I have been wondering whether Edmund Quallsford's business might have done better without that unfair competition, but they tell me there is no smuggling here."

"Ha!"

"Do you personally know of any, or have you heard of any?"

"That isn't the kind of thing that gets talked about," he said. "Smugglers that talk don't stay in business long."

"But you think there is smuggling going on?"

"Where there's a sea coast, it stands to reason there's smuggling."

I finished the brandy and made my unsteady way up to my room, holding my candle so awkwardly that Mrs. Werner watched me with more than motherly concern. I tumbled into bed with my mind churning the question, "Who murdered Edmund Quallsford?"

If Sherlock Holmes stressed one principle more than any other, it was that an investigator should not theorize until his data is complete. To attempt to reach a conclusion before all of the evidence was in hand would bias the judgement, he thought. This was one reason for his aloofness from the official police: He preferred not to divulge his conclusions until he was certain that they *were* his conclusions.

But in the course of an entangled investigation such as this one, he must have tested the evidence against every possible suspect over and over again with his brilliant logic. How else could he deliver a finished case in all of its masterful completeness with such dramatic suddenness as to stun his onlookers, including the police?

The problem with Edmund Quallsford's murder was that there were no suspects. According to the evidence, no one wanted him dead.

Therefore the evidence was incomplete. I set myself the task of identifying at least one suspect before I fell asleep.

First I asked myself who stood to profit from his death.

From the evidence already collected, I could not think of anyone who did. Derwin Smith, the fellow grazier who wanted to rent Edmund's land and farm it properly, surely could have had no expectation that his scheme would be more favourably received by Edmund's widow than by Edmund himself. As for the possibility that Smith had somehow expected to inherit Edmund's popularity and social position, that took us into a realm where logic could not follow, as Sherlock Holmes would have said.

Smith merited a close look, however, because he defied local opinion and openly declared that Edmund had been murdered. This could have been a crafty manoeuvre by a clever man. If everyone else was saying that Edmund killed himself, either accidentally or intentionally, and he persisted in calling it murder, an investigator would be likely to conclude that Smith could not possibly be the guilty party. If he were, he would not be calling attention to his crime.

It was also possible that his calling the death murder was no more than an emotional reaction. Emmeline Quallsford, too, had insisted that her brother was murdered. Apart from Smith's ill-concealed jealousy and scorn for Edmund's incompetence, there was no evidence of any kind that the two men had been anything but friendly to each other.

Did Edmund Quallsford constitute a danger to anyone? The

gentlest of men might be capable of intense moral indignation if confronted by treachery or illegalities. Did Harry Herks, for example, enrich himself by falsifying the books of the Quallsford Importing Company? Or were Nat Whyte and his fellow sailors operating a smuggling ring under the respectable cover that Edmund's business provided? In either case, one of the guilty parties might have murdered Edmund to prevent a threatened exposure, but there was no shred of evidence suggesting such a possibility. It would have been difficult for Herks to commit defalcations involving any significant sum of money with such a small firm. The excisemen were not ignoramuses, they surely knew all of the smuggling dodges, and it should have been impossible to work one from a business conducted as openly as Edmund Quallsford's.

I fell asleep counting the quarter hours sounded by the clock in the old church on the hill, and the reverberating chimes hung over the village like question marks.

I took an early breakfast the next morning, and Mr. Werner entertained me with his version of the history of the Holy Maid of Kent, a sixteenth-century servant girl from nearby Aldington who was afflicted by spells of some kind during which she had visions and made prophecies.

"They made a martyr of her for being right," Mr. Werner said.

"How was that?" I asked.

"She told Henry the Eighth that if he married Anne Boleyn, the vengeance of God would plague him and destroy them both. The king persecuted everyone who opposed the marriage. He had her tortured and executed. But Anne Boleyn certainly was destroyed, and so was he after spending the last years of his life in hideously bad health, which I call being plagued. In retrospect, it seems like a remarkably effective prophecy. Doris Fowler has always been interested in the Holy Maid of Kent. For years she tried to get a shrine built to her. Tradition says that the Holy Maid was either touched in the head, or a liar, or both. Doris disagrees, and Doris knows the history of the Marsh as well as anyone. If you meet her, ask her about it. It's an interesting story. Unfortunately, Doris is a bit crazy herself, now, and it has been a long time since anyone took her seriously."

"Does Doris have visions and make prophecies?" I asked.

"Well, no. Not that I've heard tell of. If she ever did have one, it would be a ripper."

Sherlock Holmes had rented a dogcart in his role of a wagoner looking for work. I met him at the Rye Road intersection, and we rode off across the Marsh. From the comfort of the box, behind a sturdy horse, the land looked ordinary enough except that the road, which should have been able to go its unwavering way in that flat country, took unexpected jogs and twists and turnings because of drainage ditches that followed the boundaries of ancient and forgotten land-holdings. We threaded one small community after another onto our route: Brookland, Brenzett, Snargate, Appledore, Stone— and in each of them we visited the churchyard.

It was a flying visit. Sherlock Holmes did not even pause to read the apocalyptic messages on tombstones. I glimpsed a few in passing, and on one I saw the same message we had read in Havenchurch: "The angels guard my sleeping dust, 'Till Christ return to raise the just."

I pointed that out to Sherlock Holmes. "Of course," he said with evident irritation. "With thousands of tombstones to ornament, we can hardly expect an original message for each. Sententious favourites are certain to be repeated over and over."

We circled through the churchyards, made brief visits to the churches, and remounted the dogcart. I would have liked to pause in the cool, peaceful quiet of the little cemeteries to admire the ancient buildings and reflect on the centuries of human history written in fading messages there, but Sherlock Holmes was on the hunt for something. We moved swiftly, yet his keen eyes examined every tombstone, every corner of the churches' dim interiors. Only the odd, detached spire of the church in Brookland, which he had not seen before, and the sweeping view from the church in Stone, which stands on Oxney, another Isle of Kent with sea cliffs rising incongruously from the Marsh, momentarily distracted him, and that left me wondering what their significance might be. Of the many possible reasons for Sherlock Holmes to pause and study something, sightseeing was not one of them.

His only observation was to caution me about drinking water in the Marsh communities. "The wells may be unhealthy," he said, "and the water is certain to taste brackish."

We turned south for a fleeting look at the East Guldeford churchyard, and by ten-thirty, after what seemed like a long morning with little accomplished, we were approaching the Isle of Graesney on the Iden Road. The oast-house loomed up on our right, and Sherlock Holmes boldly drove the dogcart up to it and dismounted.

There was no one there. The handsome horses were away performing their owner's business of carrying. Jack Browne, at least, had not taken the day off for Edmund's funeral.

We looked into the old stone oast-house, now a stable.

"He may be an enterprising carrier," Sherlock Holmes observed, "but his stablekeeping reflects serious defects of character."

One glance—and a sniff—told me that the stable was filthy. A second glance, and I exchanged puzzled looks with Sherlock Holmes.

"What manner of ostler would shovel manure into the corners of a room when he could easily throw it out of a door?" Sherlock Holmes asked.

Manure was piled high in three corners of the cavernous room. We turned together and looked at the field where I had seen the horses. "Summer is not long past," Sherlock Holmes said. "It would be only recently that he stopped leaving them in the pasture overnight. Where has the manure come from?"

"In Kent, it is called dung," I said, remembering the previous evening's conversation with Alvin Pringle. Then I said incredulously, "Are you suggesting that they have brought manure into the stable instead of shovelling it out?"

Sherlock Holmes smiled. "Like Dr. Watson's, Porter, your powers of observation are increasing daily. Unfortunately, you fail to reason from what you see. Would you like to explain why the fresh dung is on the bottom of that pile in the far corner? Here is another pretty mystery for us. This case has already given us several that are unique."

A voice called out, "Did you want something?"

In the fourth corner of the room there was a stairway, and an elderly woman stood there peering down at us.

"We are looking for Mr. Browne," I called to her.

"He is at work," she said reprovingly. "You have to come early or late to see him."

I thanked her, and we returned to the dogcart.

"That is the proper description of an enterprising man," Sherlock Holmes said. " 'You have to come early or late to see him.' We shall certainly manage one or the other if only to inquire into his theories of stable cleaning."

"But what possible connection could that have with Edmund Quallsford?" I asked.

"Perhaps none at all, but we certainly shall have a look at the stables at Sea Cliffs to see whether the Quallsfords also store dung inside."

Our horse plodded slowly up the long slope to the crest of the Isle of Graesney, where the road intersected Havenchurch Road. We turned east, and shortly after eleven o'clock we found a lane that led down to a large barn. We tied our horse there, out of sight of the road, and made our way towards the forbidding old mansion. Sherlock Holmes insisted on pausing for a look at the stables, but the Quallsford cleanliness was exemplary.

Our expedition received a setback as we approached the house: We heard women's voices and halted cautiously. "They left the servants behind," I said.

"They may have hired extra servants or borrowed some," Sherlock Holmes said. "We have Miss Quallsford's word for it that she and her brother were the last of their line, but there has been talk about the number of relatives on Mrs. Quallsford's side who were coming for the funeral. If she has invited family and friends for a funeral dinner, she needed extra servants to prepare the food. We are guilty of an oversight, Porter. No matter—we must risk it."

He always pressed ahead boldly, relying on his inexhaustible ingenuity to deal with any contingencies that arose. Taking advantage of trees and bushes, we made our way to the front of the house without challenge, entered by the massive front door—which opened with surprising ease and quietness—and turned first to the study. The fine old desk that I had seen there contained the ivory-tinted stationery that we were familiar with but no other paper. Sherlock Holmes went through its drawers quickly, then we climbed the narrow stairs to the first floor, where he flitted from door to door.

"This looks like the room," he announced. "We must move quickly, Porter. Stand where you are and listen. I will clap my hands as loudly as I can."

The door closed. I heard a muffled sound. I hurried into the room after him and closed the door behind me.

He was examining a drawer of the desk. "Could they have heard the revolver shot downstairs?" he asked.

"No," I said. "It would have been audible in the next room, but it might not have been recognized as a gun shot."

"I suspected as much. Look here—there is more of the quality stationery but no paper like that used for the suicide note."

"Perhaps there were only two sheets and he used them," I suggested.

"It is possible, Porter, but it is also highly unlikely. This is the paper he habitually wrote letters on. Why, for that one climactic message, would he use something else when there is an ample supply of this? Look around quickly, and then we will leave."

It was evident that Edmund Quallsford had not surrounded himself with luxury. The sturdy old furniture had been handed down by his father or his grandfather. The desk had a scarred, much abused look to it. So did the wardrobe. The carpet was even more badly worn than the carpet in the study downstairs.

I looked through the wardrobe, noting that Edmund Quallsford's clothing was of good quality but of a surprisingly small quantity unless he had kept some of it elsewhere. I knelt to look under the bed, memorized the objects in sight on the bed stand and a small table, and opened drawers in a splendid old chiffonier without disturbing the contents. Sherlock Holmes was busying himself with the desk and the furnishings on the other side of the room.

The sound was so quiet that I sensed rather than heard it. I turned quickly. Doris Fowler stood in the doorway watching us. She was as hideous as I remembered her, with a disfiguring nose and a bloated face, and now her eyes were wildly staring. She wore an ugly black garment that enveloped her form shapelessly.

Sherlock Holmes also had seen her. He strode towards her.

She pointed a trembling finger. "I will call Master Edmund. He will see that you are evicted at once."

"We came to tell him about the pitahayas," Sherlock Holmes said.

She took a staggering step backward. "Pitahayas? Pitahayas?" she repeated weakly.

"Didn't you find them at Spitalfields Market? One of my agents saw you there."

"Pitahayas," she mumbled. "No problem at all with pitahayas. No one has ever heard of pitahayas."

"Who sent you to London?" Sherlock Holmes asked.

Her grin was hideous. "We must ask Master Edmund about that. 'Pitahayas' is his word."

"Master Edmund was murdered, wasn't he?" Sherlock Holmes asked.

"Dear little Edmund," she murmured. Then her body stiffened. "Yes. He was murdered. So sad. He was such a charming child. So gentle and well-behaved. Too gentle. Much too gentle. Too gentle to look after himself in a harsh world. Too gentle to claim what was rightfully his."

"Who murdered him?" Sherlock Holmes asked.

"I did it. I murdered him. Why did I do it?"

Moaning pathetically, she reeled back into the hallway and collapsed. She lay kicking at the wall and uttering scream after scream.

There was no chance that those working downstairs would fail to hear her. Sherlock Holmes reacted with his usual infallible resourcefulness. He leaped into the corridor, signalling me to follow him, and the two of us knelt beside her. A moment later there were rapid footsteps on the stairs. We looked up to see a plump, middle-aged woman in an apron looking down at us in astonishment.

Sherlock Holmes got to his feet. "We were passing by," he said, "and we heard her scream. We thought she might be ill or in trouble. Didn't you hear her?"

The woman shook her head dumbly. Doris Fowler's screams continued.

"Strange. We heard her from the road, but she may have been screaming out of a window. We thought she was here all alone. Since she is not, we will leave her in your hands. Probably she should have the doctor."

Another servant had dashed breathlessly up the stairs. We left the two of them bending over Doris Fowler.

We walked quickly back to the dogcart and drove towards the Iden Road.

"Will the servants mention finding us there?" I asked.

"Probably not," Sherlock Holmes said. "They will fear being blamed for negligence."

"Does Doris Fowler's confession mean anything, or is she demented?"

"She is demented, and her confession means something. The problem is in determining what. We gained very little this morning, Porter, but that little may be enormously important. Edmund Quallsford's supposed suicide letter was certainly written at the

Quallsford Importing Company on the only paper available there, announcing that he could not continue with something—probably a business arrangement." He paused. "That in itself is suggestive—that he would write an important letter, a business letter, on cheap paper."

"Then the letter must have been written to the person who later murdered him," I said.

Sherlock Holmes shook his head. "As yet we have no evidence, but Doris Fowler certainly knows something about it."

"Why would Doris Fowler murder him?" I asked. "He was like a son to her."

"The explanations for that and for several other things could have been found on the first page of Edmund's letter. Would you like to try your hand at rewriting it, Porter?"

"I would not know how to begin."

"We already have the beginning," he said. "Yes," he went on in a musing manner, talking to himself as much as to me. "The beginning is clear enough. What I don't understand is what went wrong. What caused the difference of opinion, why did he have to write a letter ending everything, when the business was going so well? If we can resurrect that information, Porter, we will have our case."

CHAPTER
10

Richard Cole was a wizened little man who lived alone in a tiny stone cottage that could be reached only by a steeply climbing path. His house and small garden seemed suspended on the side of the hill between the church and the village. Cole had, as he explained to us with his puckered smile, a reminder of God every quarter hour from the church bells above and more frequent reminders of the devil from what he observed in the village below.

Richard Cole had worked much of his life for the Quallsford family. Under old Oswald Quallsford, he had been an unofficial steward. He hired help, ran the farm, kept the books, and paid the debts as long as there was anything to pay them with.

Now he sat huddled in his little garden on a sunny autumn afternoon with a blanket wrapped around him. He had a woman who came in daily to do for him and fix a meal or two. His rheumatics bothered him so badly, and the path was so steep, that he rarely got down to the village. For that reason I had missed him completely, and it was Sherlock Holmes who turned up his name. To make certain that we did not overlook anyone who might have useful information for us, he had reviewed all the inhabitants of the village with Sergeant Donley.

Cole was one of the few who were available on the day of

Edmund Quallsford's funeral. His rheumatism was worse than usual, and his aching bones could carry him no further than his garden.

He had gone to work for Oswald's father, Edmund's grandfather, when he was a boy, and he worked long past the normal time for retirement. He was extremely old, and he confessed with his quaint smile that his mind wasn't as sharp as it had once been.

"I can remember when I could remember a lot better than I can remember now," he said, beaming at us.

"What sort of a man was Oswald Quallsford?" Sherlock Holmes asked.

"Stupid," Cole said matter-of-factly. "Never a thought for to-morrow. His father had plenty of money. For a long time, he had plenty of money. He never looked at the accounts. There had always been enough money for whatever he wanted to do, so he went ahead and did it and left the figuring to others. Then one day there wasn't quite enough money. He went on spending it as he always had. There came other days when there was less and less money, and finally there came days when there wasn't any money at all and he had to borrow. Then, towards the end, he couldn't borrow because he never repaid."

"What about mortgages?" Sherlock Holmes asked.

"We had them," Cole said grimly. "Everything was mortgaged. Some things were mortgaged more than once. As Oswald got more and more desperate for money, he became less and less scrupulous about how he obtained it."

According to Mr. Werner, my landlord at the Royal Swan, Richard Cole had no small measure of responsibility for the financial mess Oswald had got himself into. For one thing, Cole wasn't much of a grazier—he never had the proper training for it—and he had run Sea Cliffs badly. For another, he never stood up to Oswald about anything. A man with character might have kept Oswald from ruining himself so completely.

On the other hand, Cole always did his best and did it honestly, and it wasn't his fault if Oswald was too stupid to find a capable manager for his farm. That had been one of the first items of business for Edmund. Also, it was possible that Oswald would have ruined himself just as thoroughly even if Sea Cliffs had been better managed, though he might have taken a bit longer to do it.

The old man did not know much about Edmund's restoration of the family finances because he had been discharged before Oswald died. The first inkling he had of the turn in the Quallsford fortunes came when Edmund began paying him the pension he had not known that he had earned.

"The last months I worked for Oswald, he paid me nothing at all. Then he discharged me on the grounds that he had to save money." The old man shook his head indignantly. "Wasn't paying me anything, so he let me go to save the amount of my salary— which I will tell you had never been what anyone would call generous. After that, I certainly didn't expect a pence of pension from the Quallsfords, but Edmund started one as soon as he could and paid it regularly. Not only that, but he paid me some arrears in a lump sum for the years I got no pension and for the unpaid salary. That was how I bought this cottage.

"It was a just thing for him to do. I served the Quallsfords for more than sixty years. They were my family, I had none of my own. I helped to raise Oswald, who needed a lot of raising, and then I helped to raise his children. But to do Oswald justice, it wasn't that he didn't want to pension me. He honestly didn't have the money."

"Where did Edmund get the money?" Sherlock Holmes asked.

"He had a smart head for business," the old man said. "Not like his father. Oswald was very good at spending but no good at all at earning. Mr. Edmund, once he got out from under his father's thumb—and I will say that Oswald had a heavy thumb—once Edmund got out from under it, he soon showed what he was made of. Did something up in Lunnon and made a big success. Married well, too. And one of the first things he did with the money, even before he got all the debts paid off, was to start my pension. Was

I surprised? I was, and I wasn't. Edmund was a man of honour, and he understood priorities. We always were good friends, Edmund and I. It stood to reason that he would remember me if he could, but I never thought he would be able to do it, what with him having to start out in life with the burden of his father's bankruptcy."

"Did you know that he intended to restore the old tower?" Sherlock Holmes asked.

The old man nodded. "He talked to me about that. I couldn't see the point of it. There were things that needed doing about the house and barns, and what was the use of that tower even if it was restored? But it was a monument to something or other, and the family honour was at stake, and Mr. Edmund thought it had to be done. He wanted to know if I had any suggestions. I told him to stay away from Tuggy. Tuggy always has done shoddy work. Built the barn for the Warnleys, the one that fell down in that wind storm when Edmund was a boy. Tuggy's father built the addition to the tower, and maybe you've seen what happened to that. I told Oswald the same thing—stay away from Tuggy. Oswald didn't, and now the tower has to be rebuilt."

"What will happen to your pension now?" Sherlock Holmes asked.

The old man shrugged. "Don't know. Don't like to ask at a time like this. It will work out somehow. Things always work out. Edmund's wife comes from a rich family. Some say that is where Edmund got the money that started him out. I feel real sorry that I couldn't go to the funeral, but I would have had to be carried."

"Did you ever hear Edmund use the word 'pitahaya'?"

"That was silliness that he picked up at Oxford. The university was about to spoil him, but he met his wife through a friend he made there and got serious again."

"Why would he want to kill himself?" Sherlock Holmes asked.

"He had no reason that I know of. The vicar says it must have been an accident, and I believe him."

We returned down the steep path to a Havenchurch that looked completely deserted. Sherlock Holmes wanted to talk with Joe, but neither he nor Mr. Werner were anywhere to be seen.

"I will look for him later," Sherlock Holmes said. "We are going to need a Romney Marsh branch of the Baker Street Irregulars before this case is finished."

Sherlock Holmes and I shared Mrs. Werner's enormous chunks of bread and cheese while sitting on the bank of the Royal Military Canal. The only interruption came from Charles Walker, the water bailiff. He jokingly asked us if we had tickets to fish.

"Do we need tickets to catch sharks?" Sherlock Holmes asked with a sly smile.

Walker grinned and said if we caught any sharks in that water, he would excuse the tickets. What he really wanted was to tell us what a lovely funeral Edmund Quallsford had, and what a fine address the vicar had delivered—and how Emmeline Quallsford had refused to sit in the same pew with her sister-in-law.

He moved on, and Sherlock Holmes, after he had smoked a pipe of his rough shag, asked me to meet him at the George Hotel in Rye the next morning.

"We must call on Miss Quallsford," he said, "but this is not the proper day for it. I shall expect you at the George at nine."

He walked away southward, towards Rye, and I returned to Havenchurch with the problem of contriving a profitable use for my afternoon and evening in a village where almost everyone was taking part in the unproclaimed day of mourning for Edmund Quallsford.

It was late in the afternoon when people finally reappeared in the High Street and some of the shops reopened. No one wanted to talk about anything but the funeral and especially about how Emmeline and Larissa had not spoken or even looked at each other. I listened politely to a dozen different accounts of this. When Mr. Werner finally unlocked the door of the Royal Swan, about five o'clock,

I was very badly in need of something, and so was the rest of Havenchurch. The three public houses were crowded the moment they opened their doors.

I was peacefully enjoying my pint of bitter with a hubbub of talk swirling around me when one voice vaulted above the others in an angry snarl. "What has come over this bloody village? How is a man to wet his whistle when every slacking publican has to take the same day off? I suppose serving a half-pint of mild before evening is above you toffs."

Dead silence ensued. Mr. Werner remarked quietly, "We closed for Edmund Quallsford's funeral. Since you don't approve, we will stay open for yours."

"Quallsford! Bah! I could tell you a few things about your sainted Edmund, I could, and then maybe he wouldn't seem so sainted to you. Except that you probably wouldn't know the difference." A hulking man with long, untidy whiskers, dressed in dirty working clothes, stormed out of the crowd carrying his beer and took it to a table in the far corner.

I finished my own pint, and then I squirmed my way through to Mr. Werner, who was still glowering. "Who was that?" I asked quietly.

"Dead Pig Martley," he growled.

"Dead Pig—" I exclaimed.

"There's a story. I'll tell you later."

I nodded, accepted another pint, and made my way back through the crowd. Dead Pig Martley had his table to himself. I asked politely if I could join him. He had no chance to refuse; he was taking a long draught of beer at the time, and I was already seated when he finished.

He looked at me suspiciously. "Stranger here?"

I nodded. "I agree with you. It has been a long day. Not only was there nothing to drink, but I have had nothing to eat since breakfast. Who was Edmund Quallsford?"

"He was the bloody taradiddler who went off to Lunnon and made himself a fortune. Or so anyone will tell you. I could tell you something different."

"Tell me," I said. "I'm always ready for a good story, and this has been a dull day."

He took another draught, still eyeing me suspiciously.

I waited.

He looked at me again while wiping off the ragged hair around his mouth. Finally he leaned forward and spoke in low tones. "Edmund Quallsford was a fraud."

"I'm not surprised to hear it," I said in the same conspiratorial tone. "When a man is praised as much as he is, I begin to feel suspicious about him. Whom was he defrauding?"

Dead Pig Martley leaned across the table. "Look here. One Monday morning, early, I happened to be at Rye Station, and there was Edmund, on his way to Lunnon to pick up a few more millions. He was driven to the station by that shabby old groom, Ralph. He jumped out of the trap, grabbed his bag, and called, 'See you Friday. Late train as usual.' Ralph drove off. Edmund went for a cup of tea, which happened to be my destination. Except that the Lunnon train arrived and then left, and there was Edmund still drinking his tea."

"Slow drinker," I observed.

"That he was. Later, I saw him driving himself away from a stable in a trap that I was certain he had just hired. He headed towards Winchelsea. I went to the stable and made inquiries. The owner knew nothing about Edmund Quallsford, or so he said."

"Ha!" I exclaimed, emulating Alvin Pringle. "The Quallsfords own at least one trap of their own. I not only have seen it, I have ridden in it. They also own I don't know how many horses."

"Of course they do. Didn't I just tell you Ralph drove Edmund to the station? But if he had gone gallivanting in his own trap, his wife would have known that he was traipsing about down here when he was supposed to be in Lunnon. That was not the end of it. I chanced to be in Tenterden on Thursday, and who should I see but Edmund Quallsford, same horse and trap but now very dusty, arriving from the west. I didn't let him know that I had seen him. All of that made me curious. So on Friday night I went to Rye to meet the late train from Lunnon. I got there early and looked around carefully. There was Ralph, the groom, waiting for the train. It arrived, Ralph began looking into the carriages for his master, and suddenly Edmund came sneaking around the station building carrying his bag. 'Here I am, Ralph,' he called. Ralph said, 'Did you have a pleasant trip?' And Edmund said, 'The usual, Ralph. I would much rather stay at home, but it has to be done.' And Ralph purred, 'Yes, sir.' Like to make me sick. That told me as much as I needed to know about your sainted Edmund Quallsford. No doubt he went off and chased women when everyone thought he was in Lunnon."

"No doubt," I agreed. "But in that case, where and when did he make his money? Because he certainly did have money. Could it be that some of his business was transacted in towns to the west of here?"

"In that case," Dead Pig Martley said—when he scowled, he looked more than a little like his name—"in that case, why did he pretend to go to Lunnon? Why get himself taken to the station and met there, and then sneak off and sneak back?"

"There is that," I agreed. "And it certainly does look queer. But if his purpose was to chase women, he should have found it much more convenient just to take the train to London and do it there. There are plenty of women in London who enjoy being chased, or so I have been told, and in London, one does not have to sneak."

"Then what was he doing?" Dead Pig Martley demanded.

"I don't know," I said. "And I very much would like to know."

Dead Pig Martley had nothing more to add about Edmund Quallsford except a series of grumbles about the pious fraud he had been. He finished his beer and took himself off, and Mr. Werner came over to join me.

"What was it?" he asked curiously.

"Nothing much," I said. "He saw Edmund Quallsford driving a trap in Tenterden when he was supposed to be in London."

Mr. Werner shrugged. "Something about his business, no doubt. He told me that he sometimes had to travel about."

"That is what I thought. Tell me about Dead Pig Martley."

"Well. It happened years and years ago. Martley and his neighbour, who was a man named Hughes, each owned a pig. The pigs were enormous, handsome animals from the same litter, prize specimens, and as much alike as twins, which in a manner of speaking they were. One morning Martley's pig was sickly. Martley was very upset about it. He was fond of that pig, and it was a valuable animal. The next morning, his pig was worse, and Martley, who would rather wear money out in his pocket than spend it, was worried enough to have the vet. On the third morning, the neighbour, Hughes, went out and discovered a very strange turn of events. Martley's pig had got well as suddenly and as mysteriously as it had sickened—but Hughes's pig was dead. Everyone knew, of course, that Martley had substituted his dead pig for Hughes's well pig, but no one could prove it. Martley has been known as Dead Pig Martley ever since then, but it would be best if you don't let him hear you call him that."

"I won't," I promised.

I had no intention of ever calling him that. I felt extremely grateful to Dead Pig Martley. I had been searching for such an item of information ever since my arrival in Havenchurch, and if he had not spoken up when he did—and if his nickname had been less colourful—I would have missed it.

But I could not understand what it meant. It would be up to Sherlock Holmes to fit it into the picture he had already framed.

I was wondering why I had not met Dead Pig Martley before. "What does he do for a living?" I asked Mr. Werner.

"Higgler," Mr. Werner said. "Deals in all kinds of things. Mostly cattle. Said to be a shrewd 'un."

I walked to Rye in the morning. I found the pretty old town perched high on its hill like an illustration in a story book, and that thought remained with me all of the time that I was there. It was a story book kind of town.

I entered by the Land Gate and walked up the steep cliff road to the cobblestoned High Street, where I found Sherlock Holmes waiting for me at the George Hotel. He had taken a room there the night of his arrival and kept it even though he had been staying in Havenchurch. This did not surprise me. His secretive nature, and his fondness for changes of disguise, led him to maintain a number of rooms or apartments in carefully selected localities about London, and it was to be expected that he would arrange such boltholes here if he sensed a possible need for them.

On the previous night he had gone late to call on Jack Browne, the carrier with headquarters in the old oast-house. Browne had been home, but he offered no encouragement to a wagoner seeking work. He said he had trouble enough in finding work for the men he already employed.

"But there are indications that his business is not quite as bad as he makes out," Sherlock Holmes said with a wry smile. "He does own handsome horses."

"Probably he prefers to hire local men," I said. "It is a common prejudice."

"Common and understandable," Sherlock Holmes agreed.

Both of us had eaten breakfast, but we called for tea, and while we drank it, I told him Dead Pig Martley's story.

He nodded with satisfaction when I had finished. "Excellent," he said. "I deduced it when we were first told about Edmund Quallsford's mysterious business in London, but now we know exactly how it was done."

"Do we know why it was done?" I asked.

"Of course we do. A few more details, Porter, and the picture will be complete. Did you think to inquire as to why Dead Pig Martley had business in both Rye and Tenterden?"

"No—"

He shook his head. "Careless, Porter. You should not spoil a fine piece of work by failing to finish it off. Now we shall have to take another look at Dead Pig Martley. With a history like his, we must make certain that he does not have more than a dead pig on his conscience."

"He is a higgler," I said, quoting Mr. Werner. "He deals in all kinds of things, so he has a reason for travelling about."

"That is reason enough for taking another look at him."

Sherlock Holmes was attired as himself that morning, having exhausted the potentialities of his role as an itinerant wagoner. This often was a signal that a case was rapidly approaching a climax, and I was not surprised when Sergeant Donley joined us for a conference with one of the excisemen.

Sherlock Holmes had talked with this particular officer, whose name was More, on the evening of his arrival. It was obvious that the request for a second interview puzzled the officer exceedingly.

"I regret to inform you," Sherlock Holmes told him, "that there is a massive smuggling operation taking place in your territory. It is of course a citizen's duty to report violations of the law to the proper authorities, and I am doing so. If it is your pleasure, I will also confer with you as to the best means for securing evidence and arresting the culprits."

"Really, Mr. Holmes," the officer said. "*Massive* smuggling operation? If there were such an activity in a quiet territory like this one, we would already know far more about it than any casual visitor such as yourself could discover."

Sergeant Donley shifted his feet uneasily. He was loyal to Sherlock Holmes, but this was an assertion he could not accept. "If there were that much smuggling, Mr. Holmes, there would be a lot of unexplained money around. Where is it? There would be quantities of contraband turning up—liquor, tobacco, tea, or whatever—that no one could account for. Where is that?"

"It is true that there is no unexplained money or contraband around," Sherlock Holmes said. "That is because these smugglers have been ingenious enough to provide you with explanations."

"Who are these smugglers?" the customs officer asked.

"I am not prepared to name them yet. My next step will be to witness one of their operations. I came here this morning to extend an invitation to you to join me."

The customs officer scratched his cheek thoughtfully. "A beach patrol? We already have them, and they are as effective as we can make them."

"Not a beach patrol," Sherlock Holmes said.

"I am sorry, Mr. Holmes. I have heard of your work in London, and I know that you have enjoyed considerable success there, but you obviously are not familiar with our local conditions. We place our men at the points where experience has taught us that they will be the most effective. We cannot allow them to scurry off in all directions whenever anyone thinks he sees a smuggling operation. Nor do we like to have amateurs meddling in our work. It is your safety that I am concerned about, Mr. Holmes. Smugglers can be extremely dangerous people."

"I know," Sherlock Holmes said, getting to his feet. "These particular smugglers have already committed one murder that we know about. It was my duty to inform you, sir, and now I have done so. Are you coming, Sergeant?"

Mr. More began to experience second thoughts. "If you have evidence—"

"Any evidence I secure will be presented to the proper authorities. That is the law, is it not?"

We took our leave, and Sergeant Donley followed after us doubtfully. We moved on up the hill to Mermaid Street and the Mermaid Inn, where Sherlock Holmes startled both of us by calling for coffee. While we were waiting for it, he looked about him with satisfaction.

"There is no better place in England for a discussion of smuggling," he informed the sergeant. "In the eighteenth century, one did not have to look for smugglers in Rye. One simply arranged to meet them here."

The sergeant began to apologize for Mr. More's brusque attitude. Sherlock Holmes shrugged impatiently.

"A police officer cannot choose to ignore evidence that he has not discovered for himself, and he should not regard it as criticism of his own performance when an outsider brings new facts to his attention. It is unfortunate that Mr. More has this attitude, but we cannot allow his sensitive feelings to interfere with our own work. Are you willing to make a night foray with us, Sergeant, on the chance of seeing smugglers in action?"

"If you invite me, Mr. Holmes, I am bound to come along, but I still find it hard to believe that smugglers could work on that scale without anyone knowing about it."

"My invitation to you is proof that they couldn't," Sherlock Holmes said with a laugh. "*We* know about it. I will send for you when I need you. Eventually we will have to persuade Her Majesty's customs officers to cooperate with us, and an official witness will be useful. One more thing, Sergeant. Successful smuggling *does* produce enormous profits. You and Mr. More are fully justified in asking where they are. Because you have not seen them, you assume that they do not exist. I know that they exist, and therefore I assume that the smugglers have cleverly concealed them. Who are those persons, Sergeant? They will have far more money than their positions in life could possibly account for. No one could possess such wealth without leaving visible traces of it. You told Porter that a rural police officer knows *everyone.* You also should have a very good idea of everyone's finances."

"The only person who has made a lot of money in recent years is Edmund Quallsford. Are you suggesting that he—"

"From what I have learned, I would have to consider Edmund Quallsford a most unlikely smuggler. Could you imagine that gentle man of slight build unloading a boat and wrestling kegs of brandy across the shingle?"

"I could not," Sergeant Donley said.

"There would have to be others involved—probably a large number of people. Before we attack that problem, we must lay to rest this illusion of a wealthy Edmund Quallsford. It is true that he came into money from somewhere some seven or eight years ago, shortly after his marriage. He paid off his father's Havenchurch debts. He met the obligations that the family's honour obliged him to attend to, such as paying a small pension to Richard Cole. He paid off the outstanding arrears in the mortgages on Sea Cliffs, satisfying those creditors and removing the threat to his inheritance. He also had enough money to establish the Quallsford Importing Company.

"But that is all. He did not pay off the mortgages in full. He only reduced them to manageable proportions. With the help of Walter Bates, he has put Sea Cliffs on a sound financial basis. He did not even attempt to settle his father's London debts, however—apparently the family honour did not extend to those obligations. And nowhere, at any time, has he conducted any kind of business except in that pathetic establishment here in Havenchurch.

"I have my own extensive contacts in London's business and financial worlds, Sergeant. Edmund Quallsford was known there as his father's son but not for his own business activities because there were none. Neither did he have the lavish amounts of money that everyone in Havenchurch took for granted. He has lived in a kind of genteel poverty with a show of wealth but very little substance. Sea Cliffs is actually a threadbare manor. Apart from a few fine pieces of old furniture that he inherited, everything is shabby and worn out. He talked about restoring the tower, but that was part of the role he was playing, along with the trips to London and his supposed great success there. He played that role extremely well. He fooled everyone in Havenchurch. We shall have to look further than Edmund Quallsford to discover illegally acquired riches, Sergeant. Where is that money?"

Sergeant Donley shook his head.

"You are in a better position than anyone else to answer that question," Sherlock Holmes persisted. "Think about it."

We finished our coffee and took our leave of the sergeant. We next went to a house in Watchbell Street, at the top of the town, to see Emmeline Quallsford. She and her friend, a young woman her own age, were staying with the friend's brother, a prosperous Rye merchant, in a fine old half-timbered house in a street of fine old houses. At one end, Watchbell Street led into the square of Rye's splendid medieval church. At the other, it opened onto a view that rivalled those of Oxney and the Quallsfords' tower. Unlike the churches and views we had inspected earlier, these had no possible connection with the problem we were working on, and Sherlock Holmes ignored them both.

Miss Quallsford received us in the merchant's study, a book-lined room far more luxuriously furnished than that of Sea Cliffs. The friend showed us to the room and then discreetly vanished. Miss Quallsford, again in a very simple black dress, still looked pale and drawn from what must have been a nerve-wracking experience for her—attending her brother's funeral in the face of open hostility on the part of her brother's wife.

It was still very much on her mind. She was immensely surprised to see Sherlock Holmes, but after greeting us, she said earnestly, "When you talk with Larissa, please try to convince her that I intend to make no claim at all on the Quallsford estate. I never intended to. It should go to Edmund's children, whom I love dearly. I could not care more for Lara and Edbert if they were my own children. I cannot understand how Larissa could imagine that I would attempt to deprive them of their ancestral home."

"We shall certainly give her that message," Sherlock Holmes said. "I have one question for you. Was it after your brother's death that you visited the room in the tower?"

She nodded. "The next morning. I was trying to understand why he would kill himself. I thought I might find—something—"

"A clue?" Sherlock Holmes suggested.

"Something that would help me to understand. But there was nothing—just the old table and chair and bed and dust everywhere. I looked, and then I came away. It was later, when I had thought and thought and found no explanation anywhere, that I knew he had been murdered."

"I have important information for you. I told you in London that I could promise nothing more than an investigation into the cause of your brother's death. What ensued would depend on what that investigation disclosed. That preliminary investigation has now been completed."

She leaned forward tensely. "Yes?"

"Your own conclusion was correct, Miss Quallsford. Your brother was murdered."

She leaped to her feet, her pale face suddenly white. "Are you certain?"

"As certain as it is possible to be without knowing the murderer's name and his motive."

"What evidence do you have? I must know!"

Sherlock Holmes described our conclusions concerning the suicide letter: the paper, the place where it had been written, and our reasons for concluding that it was actually the second page of a business letter. She listened avidly.

"I should have known!" she exclaimed when he had finished. "I read it without thinking. I could not believe what had happened. I could not believe that Edmund was dead, and yet there his body lay, and there was the note, and it never occurred to me—I am certain that you are right. If he had written it in that room, he would have used his usual stationery. Is there anything else?"

"Many small things," Sherlock Holmes said. "Now we must put them all together and try to identify the murderer."

"Do so!" she said fervently.

"Perhaps you can help us," Sherlock Holmes said. "Who, among your brother's associates, could have had reason to murder him?

Whom had he quarrelled with? Who were his rivals—in anything? Who envied him?"

She shook her head dumbly. Then she said, in a voice taut with emotion, "Find out who did it, Mr. Holmes. If you don't—" Her voice broke. "If you don't, I will find him myself—if it is the last thing I do."

CHAPTER
11

Sherlock Holmes returned to Havenchurch with me. I introduced him to Mr. Werner under his own name, calling him a colleague, and he took a room at the Royal Swan—though of course he maintained his arrangement with the schoolmaster and also kept his room at the George Hotel in Rye. He believed in being prepared for any contingency.

Mr. Werner was impressed. He had never heard of Sherlock Holmes, and he assumed that my reports to Loxton & Lagg had induced them to send a superior to continue the negotiations.

"I hope that you can work something out," he said. "I heard that Emmeline was planning on running the company herself. She means well, of course—she probably would try to keep it going as a memorial to her brother—but a woman, now. I ask you!"

Mrs. Werner served us an excellent lunch. Sherlock Holmes picked at it absently, and I fear that he hurt the good woman's feelings with his indifferent appetite. Afterwards, he sent me to ask Mr. Herks for a sample of the coarse tobacco he had seen at the Quallsford Importing Company. We settled ourselves in my room and sat looking out at its sweeping view of the High Street, pints of Mr. Werner's home-made bitter at our elbows, while Sherlock Holmes energetically produced a cloud of thick, pungent smoke.

"Porter," he said finally, "this simply will not do. We have a highly successful gang of smugglers who have been operating for eight years, possibly longer, and, as far as we can determine, most of the profits have been dumped into a hole and buried. Smugglers do not behave that way."

"I might," I said.

"How would you behave, Porter?"

"Profits are one of the things that give smugglers away—didn't you just tell Sergeant Donley to try to think of someone who has money that can't be accounted for? So I would not spend the money until I was done with smuggling. Then I would never be caught."

"You would be a unique smuggler, Porter."

"Then these are unique smugglers," I said.

"They are," he agreed. "In the past, smuggling of this kind involved a loose organization of men assembled hastily to unload the boat and carry the goods away from the beach. Sometimes the leader's summons was made so incautiously that the authorities caught wind of it and were there to meet the boat. Sometimes the men were so poorly disciplined that they had to sample the brandy before they got it off the beach, and the operation proceeded in an orgy of drunkenness bound to attract every customs officer within miles. Afterwards, they would meet in favourite haunts like the Mermaid Inn to brag publicly about their deeds and flaunt their gains. That kind of operation would be impossible to conduct successfully today—which is why Mr. More was sceptical when I informed him that a smuggling ring has been functioning here for years. He did not believe that smugglers could operate so discreetly. In a quiet place like this Marsh country, their unexplained wealth and the flood of contraband would quickly give them away. Even a small amount of money, or a small quantity of smuggled goods, would attract attention."

"Then these are unique smugglers," I said again.

Sherlock Holmes said slowly, "No, Porter. It is the gang's *leader-ship* that is unique. It has combined imagination and foresight with astonishing gifts of organization and management. It has been able to enforce discipline with an efficiency that I find difficult to believe. The Marsh's rich history of smuggling is a history of smugglers' mistakes. That is why we know so much about them. This gang has made no mistakes until now. That is another mark of inspired leadership—the ability to learn from past blunders made by others."

Again he directed his attention to his pipe. Finally he said, "If you were a smuggler chieftain recruiting men who could be relied upon for discretion, and self-control, and strict obedience to orders, what kind of men would you hire?"

"Respectable men," I said. "Men with enough sense not to get drunk while unloading brandy. Men who are prosperous enough so that their profits will not cause talk even if they spend them."

"No," Sherlock Holmes said. He shook his head firmly. "Men who are prosperous and respectable are men of responsibility—but they are also men who have responsibilities. They tend to be older men. Can you see them sneaking away at night to unload boats and carry the contraband to safe hiding places? They have servants who would talk if their masters were mysteriously absent from home several nights a week. Their possible gains from smuggling would mean little to them, and they would have an extraordinary amount to lose if they were apprehended. No, Porter. Not respectable men who are well off."

"Respectable men who are not well off, then."

"Could such a man be lured into a life of crime that will certainly bring severe penalties if he is caught?"

"Respectable men who are badly off," I suggested.

Sherlock Holmes nodded. "My thought exactly. Wealth is a relative thing, Porter. The good sergeant is searching his memory for a name associated with purchases of property or the reckless squandering of hundreds of pounds, or trips to Ascot and the famous watering places, and of course there is no such person. What we need to look for is the respectable but badly off man who once had nothing but debts and now has an occasional shilling to spend. Let us talk with your friend George Adams."

Sherlock Holmes's name was known to Adams, who looked curiously from one of us to the other when Sherlock Holmes introduced himself. No doubt he was wondering what connection there could be between the famous detective and myself, the humble clerk of an importing company, but he invited us into his cramped office without question or comment.

"I am asking you to think back eight or perhaps even ten years, Mr. Adams, and see whether you have, or have had, a customer who fits this description," Sherlock Holmes said. "He is probably a family man. He is a good worker, but he has been down on his luck all of his life with a problem in finding and holding steady employment. Eight or ten years ago, he was always in debt. Even in good times, he was never quite able to pay up."

Adams was smiling sourly. "I can give you a list. You are talking about two thirds of the population of Havenchurch."

"In recent years, this particular man has done better almost without your noticing it. He began to pay cash instead of buying on credit. He gradually got his account paid off, but he is still without steady employment."

Adams was shaking his head. "No," he said. "There isn't anyone." Then he paused. "I wonder. Just a moment. I did notice—I remember thinking—"

He took down a dusty ledger and began turning pages. He kept his accounts in bright green ink, and the names were written across the tops of the pages in large, florid loops and curls.

"George Newton," he said slowly, when he had found the page he sought. "Always has been a good, honest chap, but—like you say—he never seemed to have any luck. But he never quit. He took his family to pick hops every autumn, and he paid off as much as he could. But it does seem strange now that I look back. His wife has been buying for cash—oh, for some years, now. Never very much, nothing extravagant, but she does her regular shopping here. And the account finally got settled in full, a little at a time. I just assumed—he always took any work going, you know, a day or two at a time, or a week or two—he was willing, whatever it was. But he never was very strong, and he is no hand at all with animals, so no would one consider him for full-time employment."

"Does he still take his family to pick hops?" Sherlock Holmes asked.

"That he does. Probably they are picking right now. They always go to the same hop garden over by Appledore. For some years, the Havenchurch pickers walked over and back, morning and night, but now the farmer provides a wagon for them."

"Does Newton still take part-time jobs?"

"As far as I know, he takes anything he can get for as long as it lasts. Hold a moment! I saw him working for Derwin Smith only yesterday, so he is not picking hops—but his family is. His wife and children were riding with the hops pickers a few evenings ago. Like I said, he is a good, honest chap, and he has always done his best."

"But his best was never very good until the last few years," Sherlock Holmes suggested.

George Adams nodded. "Strange that I never noticed that. But I have too many unpaid accounts to spend much time worrying about why people pay cash. I hope he is not in trouble."

"We hope so, too," Sherlock Holmes said. "Is there anyone else in a similar situation?"

George Adams turned the pages of his account book. "No one that I can think of."

"Please do not mention this to anyone," Sherlock Holmes said. "We are engaged in a complicated investigation, and we would not want to embarrass a man who has done nothing wrong."

We took our leave of George Adams, and Sherlock Holmes, whose legs at such times seemed to be twice as long as mine, strode so quickly that I had difficulty in keeping up with him. He hired a trap, and it was not until we were on our way to Lydd, bouncing over the rough, dusty road into the Marsh, that he was willing to talk about what we had discovered.

"Do you see its significance?" he asked me.

"If George Newton is a smuggler, he certainly has handled his ill-gotten money so that no one would notice. But I don't understand how a person of that class could exercise such self-control."

Sherlock Holmes shook the reins gleefully, and the startled horse stepped up its pace. "It is a masterful touch, Porter. I have not encountered the likes of it since the death of the late—but unlamented—Professor Moriarty. Who would have thought it possible in this quiet corner of England? It took a brilliant criminal intellect, and an astounding organizer, to create such an operation. He was already reaching out for London, and I hesitate to contemplate the heights of iniquity that he might have attained in that vast theatre. But fate has turned against him, Porter. What a tremendous stroke of luck it was when Radbert overheard the word 'pitahayas'! It has placed us in a position to end this criminal career here and now."

Lydd, with a nearby army camp and a flourishing brewery, was much larger than Havenchurch and far more prosperous looking. We called at the Hutchings General Store. Like Mr. Adams, Mr. Hutchings sold almost everything; as his signs proclaimed, he was a draper, grocer, clothier, and hatter, and his store was also a boot and shoe warehouse.

Sherlock Holmes's name meant nothing to him, and he flatly refused to discuss his customers' confidential accounts with a pair of strangers. Sherlock Holmes pointed out that a quiet investigation was much more easily kept quiet if the police were not involved. Hutchings finally agreed to cooperate, but not until Sherlock Holmes threatened to invoke Sergeant Donley. His initial survey of his ledgers produced emphatic negatives, but after a diligent search, accompanied by an insistent prodding of his memory, he surprised himself—but not Sherlock Holmes—by producing two names: Alfred Mitchell and Wallace Dickens.

"But it means nothing at all except that they have been doing a little better," he protested. "They both are good, reliable, honest citizens. They have always paid what they owed whenever they could."

"Have they had steady work at any time during the past eight years?" Sherlock Holmes asked.

"Well, no. They pick hops every autumn with their families, of course, and they work on the dykes, or on the roads, whenever there *is* work, and they hire out when a farmer needs hands. Come to think of it—"

He decided not to say what he was thinking.

"What it amounts to," Sherlock Holmes said, "is that six to eight years ago they began paying cash for what they bought. At the same time, they gradually paid off everything they owed, and they haven't been in debt since then."

"That is correct," Mr. Hutchings agreed.

"But in spite of this commendable solvency, their situations with regard to work and income did not change."

"As far as I know, they are still working whenever they find work. They must be earning a bit more money, now—that is all. I cannot believe that either of them would do anything dishonest."

"I don't know that they have," Sherlock Holmes said. "That is why we are making a private investigation. Please say nothing to anyone. If they have done nothing dishonest, the investigation will be kept private."

We returned to the trap and headed for New Romney, which was also larger and far more prosperous looking than Havenchurch. There we called at the general store of A. H. Smith, a smaller establishment than the emporiums of Hutchings in Lydd and Adams in Havenchurch. Sherlock Holmes applied the same measures of persuasion and mnemonic prompting that had moved both Mr. Adams and Mr. Hutchings, and Mr. Smith eventually produced the names of two of his own former debtors: Evan Banks and William Allen.

"But they are honest, hard-working men," he protested.

They had also experienced a very modest prosperity in recent years—inexplicable because it was based upon a motley assortment of temporary jobs. We thanked Mr. Smith, pledged him to silence, and returned to the trap.

There Sherlock Holmes hesitated.

"Five should be sufficient," he said finally. "There may be twenty or thirty more cleverly scattered about the Marsh, but we should leave *some* work for Sergeant Donley."

It was late afternoon when we reached the sergeant's home in Havenchurch. He had just returned himself, probably from a frustrating investigation involving a hayrick fire or a missing pig. He looked irritated, and it took some time for him to grasp what Sherlock Holmes was explaining.

"I don't believe it," he exclaimed when Sherlock Holmes presented his list of names. "Evan Banks? I saw him only this afternoon, loading hay for Eben Warnley. George Newton? I went to school with him. He asks me regularly where there is work going. Last week one of Derwin Smith's men smashed a foot, and George is taking his place. He will have maybe two months' steady employment there. That is why he isn't picking hops. If he were making money smuggling, why would he be looking for work? Why would he send his family hop picking?"

"Tomorrow," Sherlock Holmes said, "you can visit other merchants and add to the list. This afternoon—right now—you have something more important to do. I want you to call on all five of these men."

"Now?" the sergeant wailed with dismay. "Two of them live in Lydd, and two of them live in New Romney. They may not even be home. And what am I to call on them about? Can I make a police case over their paying out a shilling or two instead of buying on credit?"

"That," Sherlock Holmes said, "is the diabolical cleverness of it."

"But really, Mr. Holmes—a master criminal? Here in Marshes? That just is not possible. There is no money here to support smuggling on that scale."

"The fact that we have smuggling on that scale proves that there is, and the smugglers have made arrangements to ship their surplus contraband to London. They may already have begun. Come, Sergeant. This must be done *now*."

"What am I to say to them?"

"We will come with you and talk with George Newton," Sherlock Holmes said. "I will show you what to say. Where will we find him? At Derwin Smith's farm?"

"He may be home by now. I know that his wife is at home. The hop pickers finished early today."

George Newton, as befitted an honest man who had never had steady employment, lived in a tiny cottage that only too obviously had been converted from a small stable. It was located in the rear of a dilapidated larger cottage on the extreme outskirts of Havenchurch.

Sherlock Holmes rubbed his hands with delight when he saw it. "Perfect!" he exclaimed. "The master's touch again! I want you to make a careful note, Sergeant, of the exact locations where these men live. I am confident that you will find all of them situated so that they can slip away at night without causing comment among their neighbours."

Sergeant Donley shook his head in bewilderment.

George Newton's wife, a tiny, thin woman with a care-worn face, looked us over curiously as we marched up the path to her front door, but she asked no questions. She went to call her husband.

George Newton had been lying down, and he came to the door blinking his eyes sleepily. He was a small man of slight build—small without the wiriness that some men of his stature enjoy. Certainly this was not a man who could endure heavy work or handle a rumbustious horse, but he had been working regularly. His face had the weathered look of a farm hand.

Mrs. Newton followed on her husband's heels, and stood behind him in the doorway, watching. George Newton's eyes flitted uneasily from one of us to the other and settled on the sergeant.

"These gentlemen want a word with you, George," Sergeant Donley said.

He jerked his head, and the three of us turned and walked a short distance down the path. Newton hesitated for a long moment, and then he edged after us. His face was too sun-burned to show it, but there was a dismal pallor in his manner.

"This is Mr. Sherlock Holmes, from London," the sergeant said when we were out of his wife's hearing.

Sherlock Holmes fixed Newton in a piercing stare, but his manner was not unkind. "This is not an official call, Newton," he said. "That will come later. The sergeant is an old friend of yours, and he thought you ought to have this advance warning."

Newton was having difficulty in swallowing. His lips were trembling.

"The excisemen and the police know all about it, Newton," Sherlock Holmes went on. "Very soon they will come down heavily on the entire gang. But we can understand why you were led to this—how hard things were for you. Why don't you turn informer? That would make it much easier for you and for your family. Think about it. You will have to act soon, or it will be too late."

Sergeant Donley patted Newton on the back in a friendly manner. "Think about it, George," he said. "Mr. Holmes is giving you an opportunity to get off easy. You aren't likely to have another one."

The three of us turned away.

As we walked towards the High Street, Sherlock Holmes told the sergeant, "Take our trap. If a man is not at home, say to his wife, 'Tell your husband I was looking for him. I want to talk with him. He will know why.' If the husband is home, adopt a sympathetic manner. You are an old friend, giving him some timely advice. Say nothing more than I said to Newton. If he protests that he does not know what you are talking about, say, 'Of course you do. I told you—the police know all about it.' Call on those four men whose names I gave to you and then come directly back here. And hurry! We may have a long night's work ahead of us."

The sergeant drove off at a fast clip, and Sherlock Holmes went looking for Joe. He found him in the stable behind the Royal Swan and spoke to him tersely. Joe left at a run.

It was dusk; the trees around the old windmill at the edge of the village served as a rookery, and a cloud of birds formed over it, wheeled far out over the Marsh, flying low, and returned flutteringly to their roost. Sherlock Holmes stood watching them absently.

He said, "I should have kept the trap. No matter, we will hire another. Edmund Quallsford's widow should be facing up to her sadly altered life by now. It is time that we had a talk with her."

At first she refused to see us. We waited in the shabby study, now lit by a single flickering candle, and Sherlock Holmes was patiently persistent with the young servant girl, sending her back three times with similar messages. Finally Larissa Quallsford stepped into the room and faced us indignantly as we rose to greet her.

She was as pale as I remembered her, with the same stylish grace about her black costume. She had come prepared to silence Sherlock Holmes, as she had me, with an outpouring of accusations, but he gave her no chance. His manner was kindly but nonetheless firm.

"Madam, you have gravely misunderstood my intention and that of my assistant," he said. "I have only one commission—to discover the truth about your husband's death."

"He died by his own hand," she said bitterly. "I shall always believe that his sister drove him to it, but it is all one to me whether he did it accidentally or intentionally. He is dead, and the truth cannot change that."

"I regret having to bring these tidings to you, but it is better that you should hear them now, before they become a matter for official police concern. Your husband was murdered. I shall soon know who did it, and the police will cooperate in seeing that the murderer is apprehended and properly punished. We need your assistance."

She stared at him for a moment. Then, slowly, she stepped to a chair and sank into it. "You mean that," she said wonderingly. Her voice still sounded accusing.

"Indeed I do," Sherlock Holmes said. "You may not be familiar with my reputation in such matters—"

"I am familiar with it," she said. "I asked my brother about you when he was here for Edmund's funeral. Please be seated. It seems that I must talk with you."

Sherlock Holmes took the chair opposite her. I discreetly placed myself at one side, out of her line of sight.

"Murder sometimes has deep roots, madam," Sherlock Holmes said. "It is necessary to probe deeply in order to discover them. Your husband was poor when you married him?"

"He was poor when I married him. He was poor when he died. He had satisfied some of the indebtedness left by his father, and we are no longer in danger of having the roof snatched from our heads. Sea Cliffs produces a good profit, now, but much of it still goes to pay old debts."

"How large an allowance did your husband make to his sister?"

"I do not know that he made her any allowance. She had no need for one. She had some money in her own right, left to her in trust by their mother, and she had no expenses except for her clothing. Edmund had a similar bequest, but he drew upon it when he went to Oxford."

"Do you know that your husband had the reputation of making large sums of money in London?"

"I know nothing about his reputation. I only know the truth. From time to time he did make some money—he was able to pay off the worst of the debts early in our marriage—but he worked hard for it, and the strain of risking the little wealth he did have in speculations told on him. In time, it began to affect his mind."

"When did your husband first start behaving strangely?"

She hesitated. "Immediately after our marriage I found that he occasionally went out in the evening and returned late. I thought that he was visiting friends, but he said nothing about were he went and I did not want to question him. I do not know whether he was already visiting the old tower, or if that came later. I suspected all manner of things, but between such incidents he was completely normal, and he was happy. We were happy. Years went by before I finally discovered that he was brooding in the tower at night." She choked down a sob. "Brooding, alone in the dark. His mind became more and more unbalanced."

"Did he ever talk with you about financial matters?"

"Before we were married, he told me frankly what the Quallsford financial position was. I knew that it would take him years to restore the situation. And he was doing so. I do not understand why you dwell upon money, Mr. Holmes. Money was never a problem for us. I did not expect luxury from him. I know that he went through very difficult times early in our marriage, but he never left his family in want of anything. Of course we could not indulge in lavish entertainments or city-trained servants, and some of these furnishings are shabby and becoming more so, but that has been no deprivation to me."

"Did he ever have strange visitors—people obviously not of his social class?"

"Who in Havenchurch *is* of his social class?" she asked scornfully. "But I was never aware of his having *strange* visitors of any class. In a small village, one soon knows everyone. The local people have resented me because of my foreign background, but I have had no cause to return that resentment. They are good people for all their narrowness. The vicar has been an enormous help to us. I feel that this is my home, because it was Edmund's home, and this is where my children should grow up."

"Did Edmund have any enemies?"

"If you had known him, Mr. Holmes, you would not ask that question. He was a man who could not have enemies. Where there was a need, he tried to help. Where there was enmity, he made peace. Who could be the enemy of such a man?"

"Your sister-in-law sends a message to you. She makes no claim of any kind on the Quallsford estate. She never intended to. She cannot understand how you could imagine that she would attempt to deprive Edmund's children—whom she loves dearly—of their ancestral home."

Larissa Quallsford flushed and then turned paler. "The vicar told me that I not only had judged her harshly but that I had pronounced judgement on her for actions she had not committed. He conveyed the same message to me, and I have already written her an apology."

"Your sister-in-law brought my assistant here when he first arrived in Havenchurch. You met them at the door and told her that she had driven your husband to kill himself. She had made him do it. What was the reason for that statement, Mrs. Quallsford?"

She smiled wanly. "Perhaps my own mind was disarranged by grief. I always was just a little jealous of Emmeline. She and Edmund had so many things in common that dated from their childhood—little games they played with words, memories of events from long ago. They talked together frequently, and though they were never secretive about it, it seemed to me that I was excluded. Then—when Edmund died—I wanted to blame someone, I suppose. I had thought that Emmeline intended to remain at home that day, and it seemed to me that she could have prevented his death if she had been here. But I, too, could have prevented his death if I had been here."

Larissa Quallsford stifled a sob with her handkerchief. "I felt that she had been pushing him to become more successful. I had always felt it, and at that moment it seemed that she had pushed him more than his mind could stand. It was just a combination of many small things, you see, and I regret very much that I said that to her."

Sherlock Holmes nodded. "Your husband frequently used the word 'pitahaya.' Do you know where he got it or what he meant by it?"

"That was not his word," Larissa Quallsford said.

Sherlock Holmes stiffened. "It was not? Many people heard him use it."

"It was my brother's word," she said. "It was just a—a nonsense word. My brother used it in joking. Edmund picked it up from him when they were at the university together."

Riding back to Havenchurch, Sherlock Holmes let the horse follow the dark road in its own time. He leaned back and said to me thoughtfully, "It is easy to understand Larissa Quallsford's unpopularity. Sea Cliffs should be a social centre for the wives of gentry in Havenchurch and the surrounding communities. Probably it always was in the past. Edmund's wife could not carry on that tradition because there was no money for it. She comes from a wealthy family, and the worn carpets and shabby furniture must be an embarrassment to her even when entertaining close friends. By her standards, it is an impoverished home, and she has been unwilling to invite the women of Havenchurch to it. For that reason, few of them have invited her."

"Now that her husband is dead, she may receive no invitations at all," I observed.

"We must make every effort to preserve the reputation that Edmund Quallsford built for himself," Sherlock Holmes said. "That may not be possible, but we must attempt to apprehend his murderer in such a way that he is not destroyed a second time. He has already paid what sensationalists like to call 'the extreme penalty.'"

"Was he involved in the smuggling?" I asked.

"Deeply. But I intend to reveal no more about that than circumstances require."

CHAPTER
12

When Sergeant Donley returned, looking as sweated as his overworked horse, he found us at the Royal Swan talking with Mr. Werner. Sherlock Holmes ordered a pint of bitter for the sergeant and resumed his conversation with the landlord.

He was inquiring into the antecedents of Dead Pig Martley. Sergeant Donley listened with growing impatience. He was eager to report, but of course he could not do so while Mr. Werner was present.

"What was the official police view of that case of the dead pig?" Sherlock Holmes asked the sergeant finally.

"That was long before my time," Sergeant Donley said, "but I don't believe that Hughes ever made a formal complaint."

Sherlock Holmes touched his fingertips together meditatively. "The history surely contains one gross exaggeration. The pigs are described as unusually large, but they could have been no larger than medium size and probably were much smaller. If they had been as enormous as the legend suggests, Martley could not have made the transfer without leaving highly conspicuous evidence. Even an average large pig would weigh well over five score. On the other hand, the tale would lose its impact if they were described as *baby* pigs. It is the storyteller's instinctive grasping for effect that gives them size. Far too many historical accounts are similarly exaggerated. I have often thought, Porter, that a useful and interesting pastime for one's old age would be the deductive rewriting of history."

Mr. Werner was gaping at him. He was unaccustomed to having his stories subjected to deductive analysis. "They were certainly not baby pigs," he protested tartly. "I have always heard them called large. Maybe 'large' means something different in Lunnon where people have all of that garbage to feed their pigs."

"Perhaps so," Sherlock Holmes conceded with a smile.

Mr. Werner, still ruffled about the size of the pigs, went off to talk with other customers. Sergeant Donley leaned forward. "I saw Mitchell and Banks. I told them exactly what you said. Both of them started protesting, and I turned and walked away. Dickens and Allen weren't home, and I left the message with their wives. What happens now?"

"Your wife will have dinner waiting for you. Go home and eat quickly. By the time you return, we will be ready to leave. Or—"

"Or what?"

"Or we will not. Eat quickly and come back. Tell your wife you will either be home soon or she is not to expect you until tomorrow."

The sergeant hurried away.

"Mr. More's advice was sound, Porter," Sherlock Holmes said. "We may have a dangerous night ahead of us. It is true that these particular smugglers have never behaved violently, but they have never been threatened until now."

"Wasn't it the smugglers who murdered Edmund Quallsford?" I asked.

"We have two problems, Porter, and the links between them are not fully tested. Certainly Edmund Quallsford was not murdered in the kind of mad frenzy a gang of smugglers might display if it found itself cornered. His murder was deeply premeditated. Did you bring a revolver with you?"

"No, sir."

"I should have suggested it, but perhaps it is just as well that you did not. Firearms are unreliable weapons in the dark, and we are likely to have some fog to contend with before morning. A stout stick may be more useful than a gun. Ah! Here is Joe."

The boy had poked his head in the door, and he grinned when he saw us. He had been commissioned lieutenant of the Romney Marsh Irregulars and permitted to recruit his own force. I had received no hint as to what this unlikely group was doing. Sherlock Holmes went to talk with him, and he returned rubbing his hands with satisfaction. "We have no time to wait for the sergeant. Let us collect him and be on our way."

We told Mr. Werner that we were off to meet friends in Rye, and we might stay the night there. If we had not returned by midnight, he was not to expect us. The overcast sky had forecast a dark, moonless night, and now it was upon us. We felt our way through the murk to the sergeant's house.

He had already finished his hasty meal, and he met us at his front gate. His wife stood in the open doorway looking after him; probably she had entertained him while he ate with reminders that a policeman's lot is not a happy one.

"If you don't mind, Mr. Holmes," he said, "I would appreciate it if you would give me some idea of what I am supposed to be doing."

"Nothing," Sherlock Holmes said. "I want you to do nothing. Remember that. If things go as I expect, you will see smugglers at work. It is important to restrain your official indignation. The only thing the three of us can do about a large smuggling operation is to observe it surreptitiously. It would be dangerous to attempt more. At the most, we would be able to apprehend one or two of the smugglers, at considerable risk to ourselves, and our objective is to capture the entire gang, including the leaders. In the morning, you will return to Mr. More and give him an eyewitness account that will stir him to action. I will send my own report to officials in London by telegram. Between the two of us, we will marshal enough force to settle this gang with one well-planned raid."

We walked out along the Havenchurch Road into the enveloping darkness of the Marsh. The plank bridge that we had crossed earlier was located only by a cautious, fumbling exploration along the bank of the ditch, even though we knew its approximate location. Sherlock Holmes paused there.

"Have you observed this bridge?" he asked the sergeant.

"Of course I have observed it," Sergeant Donley said irritably. "I come past here almost daily."

"What do you make of it?"

"Well, it is a—plank bridge. What else could one make of it? There has been one here as long as I can remember."

"Has *this* bridge been here as long as you can remember?"

"Of course not. Planks rot and have to be replaced, if that is what you mean."

"You observe, Sergeant, but you do not reason from what you see. Porter is excused because he is not familiar with rural ways. Tell me, how often does a farmer build a plank bridge—or anything else —that is far wider, and far sturdier, and far more expensive, than is necessary? This bridge is even double-planked in the center, but you cannot discover that without a careful examination of the underside—which I took the trouble to make. I was curious enough about this particular bridge to inquire. The farmer, one William Lander, disavows it. He noticed one day that his narrow, somewhat rickety plank bridge had been replaced. He assumed that the Parish Council, or the Lords of Romney Marsh, or the Drainage Board, or some nebulous governmental authority, was responsible. Or so he says. If the government chooses to construct at this point a much sturdier and wider bridge than anyone's common sense would allow, what concern is it of his? A substantial bridge is a useful thing to have. It was built a number of years ago, and it has been kept in good repair. He never noticed when that was done. One day the bridge was here, and he has gratefully used it ever since."

"Why not?" the sergeant asked.

"Why not, indeed? It so happens that the Parish Council has no knowledge of this bridge—nor of any of the other similar bridges that have mysteriously appeared across the Marsh. One day they were there, one at a time, in unlikely locations, and the lookers and farmers have used them gratefully. They assumed, as Lander did, that some nebulous government agency, probably the one responsible for the Marsh drainage, had built the bridges. At least that is what they say. Lander and the other farmers almost certainly know that smugglers are responsible. Probably they are paid to see nothing and say nothing. Every place we look, we encounter the touch of a master. Is not this case a classic?"

The bridge felt solid enough as I crossed it, but I could see nothing at all.

The darkness was stifling, and I knew that invisible wisps of fog were already rising from the drainage ditches. Sherlock Holmes had counted his paces—on our afternoon walk or on subsequent excursions—and he knew exactly where he wanted to go. We stumbled after him, moving with quick assurance or slowing when he did.

Sergeant Donley muttered, "How is anyone going to *see* smugglers on a night like this?"

"They will have to show some kind of light even if only intermittently," Sherlock Holmes said. "I am wondering how they will manage it."

He had unusually acute night vision and an uncanny sense of direction, but I doubted that even his eyes could penetrate the blackness that now enfolded us. He slowed his pace and edged forward as we approached a ditch, and though he rarely missed a bridge by more than a few steps to one side or the other, we had to feel about cautiously for the animal barrier that marked its exact location, and it was like creeping along the edge of an abyss blindfolded.

We struggled forward in the darkness, and for a time I was not aware of the strangeness that had enveloped us. Then, as we pressed deeper and deeper into that disturbing landscape, I began to feel nervous. The senses develop an unnatural acuity under such circumstances. They hear and see and even feel things that in normal surroundings they would miss. The imagination becomes a sixth sense that overwhelms the other five with false impressions. Soon there were smugglers looming up all about me, and I seemed to hear the cackle of the old woman looker trickling through the darkness.

We stumbled on as quietly as we could.

The light loomed up so suddenly that it brought the sergeant and me to a gasping halt. Sherlock Holmes, who knew where he was, chuckled.

"It seems that our looker spends more nights in the Marsh than she let on," he said. He added, "I wonder. Wait here."

He moved off with his long, silent strides. We waited, watching the light. It shone with ghostly radiance, our first clue that the fog was drifting around us. After what seemed to be an interminable silence, we heard Sherlock Holmes's soft chuckle. His call was little more than a whisper reaching out of the darkness. "Sergeant! Porter!"

We moved to join him.

"Look!" he said softly, indicating the window from which the rectangle of light extended. "A lighted hut—but no one is here. Our looker has penned her sheep and gone home to Brookland. But she left her hut lighted, and that candle is of a size to burn all night. This is a classic, Porter! Professor Moriarty could not have bettered it!"

"Do you mean that the lookers are in the pay of the smugglers?" I asked.

"They would have to be, Porter. They are the only persons in a position to notice these night-time incursions of their pastures. Sooner or later they would be bound to develop a certain curiosity about them. The smugglers not only have bought them off, but they have recruited them. A candle left burning in a window converts every looker's hut into a lighthouse. The allusion is a very real one. Navigating this land at night can be a worse problem than sailing uncharted seas—as you surely have noticed."

"Let me snuff the candle," the sergeant muttered. "That will fix them."

"It will also fix us," Sherlock Holmes said sternly. "We don't want to arouse their suspicions. Come!"

We turned our backs on the reassuring light and moved on.

Some distance beyond the looker's hut—stumbling along in the darkness, it seemed like an enormous distance—Sherlock Holmes reached the place he had been aiming for. The ground was irregular, with shallow hollows that could shelter us at least superficially. The sergeant wanted to know why we needed cover in that heavy darkness, and Sherlock Holmes made no reply. His long-established penchant was to leave nothing to chance.

He placed us with care. When my turn came, he said quietly, "The problem is that we don't know how precisely they will keep on course, and we must take positions as close to their route as possible or we won't be able to witness much."

"If there are many of them, we should be able to hear them," I said.

"Her Majesty's customs officers may require a more exact description than our ears could provide. Are you agile enough to get out of the way of a gang of smugglers, Porter?"

"I should hope so," I said indignantly.

"I should hope that our agilities will not be tested. Make yourself comfortable. I expect that we shall have a long wait."

He moved to his own position, and I was left alone in the darkness.

I first set about making myself comfortable. I sat with crossed legs, like an Indian fakir, wrapped my arms around my knees, and began to rock slowly as a silent means of keeping myself awake. At the same time, I fixed my gaze along a line of sight and tried to determine whether I could make out anything at all. After ten or fifteen minutes, I decided that I could not.

From that point, I could only guess at the passage of time.

An uncanny quiet engulfed me. I had not even a general idea of where Sherlock Holmes and the sergeant were. The darkness had swallowed them up. Once I thought I heard the sergeant muttering a complaint, but the sound, if there was one, was fleeting.

Sherlock Holmes thrived on such tests of endurance. Despite his restless, volatile nature, he could manifest infinite patience when he was on the hunt, whether the problem was one of meticulously searching for clues or of stalking his prey. If his calculations had somehow gone wrong on this night, and the smugglers failed to appear, he would philosophically resort his data, make new calculations, and try again. On my first assignment as an Irregular, when I was eight years old, Sherlock Holmes gave me the task of watching a pawnbroker's establishment from dawn until long after dark for eleven consecutive days in the expectation that a thief might appear there—he did not—and in the process I learned that the fundamental technique every detective must practise is patience. Under Sherlock Holmes's tutelage, that technique had been honed to perfection.

But I felt sorry for Sergeant Donley, whose career—revolving as it did around hayrick fires and lost pigs—had not prepared him for sitting in a black, fog-enshrouded Marsh on a chill fall night watching for an event that might or might not happen. After a couple of hours had passed, his muttering became audible, Sherlock Holmes spoke sharply to him, and he subsided.

No matter how tensely one has been waiting, when a long-expected event finally occurs, it often comes as a complete surprise. This one did not. I saw a distant flicker of light. When next I saw it, it had come much closer, and it took the form of a small spot of brightness floating on the ground. Not until it had come near to me did I realize that the smugglers were not moving in single file but side by side. The muffled footfalls of men and animals were briefly audible on the soft turf of the pasture, the horse at the end of the line came within a few feet of me, and then the sounds moved on to fade into the distance while the spot of brightness floated ahead of them and seemed to bounce over slight irregularities in the ground.

It vanished, and the unremitting blackness reasserted itself. Somewhere off to my left, Sergeant Donley shifted his position noisily. Sherlock Holmes did not stir, and neither did I.

To my astonishment, there suddenly came a sharp flash from the direction in which the smugglers had disappeared. A few seconds later, the light flashed again.

The night closed in on us, darker and more silent than before. My breathing sounded thunderous to me. We had seen what we had come for, and there seemed no reason to wait longer, but still Sherlock Holmes did not stir.

In the direction from which the smugglers had come, I saw a flicker of light as though a downward-directed spot of brightness had moved over a small hummock. When next I saw it, it was dancing over the ground as the first light had. This second group of smugglers had veered slightly to the south and did not pass close to me. I heard, faintly, the muffled tread of men and horses, then they were gone.

We continued to watch. Again there were two sharp flashes and, some time later, the flicker of brightness that heralded the approach of more smugglers.

Either the third group followed a more northerly course or it was spread out more. I was trapped before I realized it. A horse passed behind me, and, an instant later, a heavily laden walking man stumbled over me. I rolled to one side, took several running steps in a crouch, dropped to the ground again, and began to crawl away on my knees. The flash and report of a gun ripped the darkness, and the ball passed perilously close to my ear. I changed my direction, ran again at a crouch, then rolled to one side.

Before I had stopped moving, there was a scream of rage behind me. "Put that away, you idiot!"

A voice that sounded vaguely familiar began a whining explanation. The words were indistinguishable, and the first voice quickly cut it off. "Nonsense! There's no one out here! You know the rule —no guns. You stumbled over your own feet."

The second voice whined again.

"All right, maybe it was a dog. We've had enough rumpus. Come along."

The gunshot had startled the horses. They reared back, hauling at their leads, and the smugglers were milling about uncertainly. Finally they re-formed their line and moved away. No more lights flashed, and, although we waited for another two hours, no more smugglers appeared.

It was a long time before my pulse returned to normal. I understood why Sherlock Holmes had led us so far into the Marsh to observe the smugglers' passage. Their leader was certain that they would meet no one amidst this vast emptiness.

Finally Sherlock Holmes spoke. "We can move on, now," he said softly.

He led the way—not towards Havenchurch, but in the direction from which the smugglers had come. We stumbled deeper and deeper into the Marsh in a journey that was tortuous even though led by a man with superb night vision and a clear recollection of our route. Each ditch crossing was a perilous hazard. Finally light showed ahead of us, and we came to another hut in which a looker had left a candle burning.

"We can rest here for a time," Sherlock Holmes said.

The sergeant did not seem grateful for the revelation that Sherlock Holmes had arranged for him. "Why didn't we wait at the

Havenchurch end?" he complained. "Maybe we could have followed them and seen where they were taking the stuff."

"That can be dealt with later," Sherlock Holmes said. "It was important to see how they cross the Marsh, and it was also important to wait for them at a place where they would not expect to be observed—as you noticed. My apologies, Porter. That slight miscalculation on my part could have had serious consequences. Since there were none, I am pleased that it happened. It gave us an important insight into this gang's operations. What did you think of their light, Sergeant?"

"Some trick with a lantern," the sergeant grumbled. "We could have observed it just as well from the road."

"You would have seen very little from the road, Sergeant. They doused their light long before they came within sight of it. What about the voices? Did you recognize either of them?"

The sergeant hesitated. "One was George Newton's," he said. "The other—I could not place the other."

"The enraged outburst that you heard may not resemble his normal voice," Sherlock Holmes said.

Without disturbing the candle, we composed ourselves to rest as best we could. The sergeant took the rude cot, Sherlock Holmes the hut's one chair, and I settled myself into a corner. We were on our way again before first light, and as dawn touched the Marsh, the going became much easier. People were stirring when finally we made our way into the town of Lydd, and Sergeant Donley quickly arranged for a trap to take us to Rye. There we made use of Sherlock Holmes's room at the George to tidy ourselves. This was especially important for me—when one has been rolling in a sheep pasture, one is likely to need a great deal of tidying.

Sherlock Holmes busied himself with a telegram to be sent to London and a note for Mr. More, the customs officer, and then the three of us caught a few hours' rest under more comfortable circumstances than those spent in the looker's hut. By the time we reached

Mr. More's office, the sergeant's testimony was no longer needed—a fact that he must have noted ruefully, though he said nothing. Mr. More had received a telegram of his own, prompted by Sherlock Holmes's wire to London, that ordered him to extend full cooperation to us.

Sherlock Holmes insisted that the sergeant tell his story regardless. When he had finished, Mr. More asked, "What is it that you want?"

"This is a large gang," Sherlock Holmes said. "It is superbly organized. Its operations have an efficiency that could only come from meticulous planning and long practice. I am certain that it leaves nothing to chance. When it has to use a road or cross one, it probably sends out sentries for a considerable distance to make certain that the way is clear. By travelling in widely separated groups, it makes it impossible for the authorities to ambush the entire gang at once. In any event, I don't fancy a night battle with smugglers, which would certainly result if we attempted to interrupt an operation such as the one we witnessed. The Battle of Brookland occurred some eighty years ago, between smugglers and the excisemen of that day, but it still offers worthwhile lessons. It would be far better to identify the smugglers and arrest them individually."

Mr. More responded with a puzzled protest. "I have no quarrel with that, but I still cannot understand what this gang does with its contraband."

"My suggestion is that we first identify as many members of the gang as possible. The sergeant and his constables can spend the day adding names to the five we already have. If he works carefully, he may be able to frighten one or two of the underlings into turning informer without alarming the remainder of the gang. Following that, we shall need a large enough force to raid their storehouse and pick all of them up at once."

"I am certainly in favour of avoiding night battles," Mr. More said. "Have you any idea at all as to who the leaders are?"

"Of course," Sherlock Holmes said. "But ideas are not evidence.

It will be immensely helpful if one or two members of the gang can be induced to talk."

"Very well," Mr. More said. "I accept your guidance. I shall give you whatever help you need."

Sherlock Holmes shook his head. "I shall be pleased to give you any assistance that I can, but the smugglers are your responsibility. I have finished with them. I came here to solve a murder, and that murder proved to be so intertwined with the smuggling that I have made very little progress on it. Let Sergeant Donley proceed with his ferreting out of members of the gang, and then I will help you to plan the next step. In the meantime, Porter and I will get on with this business of identifying the murderer of Edmund Quallsford."

We arrived at the Royal Swan to the accompaniment of a cascade of church bells. I turned to Sherlock Holmes in surprise. The only bells I had heard previously had been the clock chimes.

"It is Sunday," he reminded me.

Mr. Werner greeted us with amazement. "Did you go to a party or to a fight?" he asked.

"A bit of both," I told him grumpily.

We had eaten lightly at the George Hotel, and I had planned to ask Mrs. Werner for a late breakfast. "She has gone to church," Mr. Werner told me. "I can give you some cold food if you want it."

He promised that Mrs. Werner would feed me well when she returned. He also mentioned that there would be rack of lamb for Sunday dinner, so I decided to wait. Sherlock Holmes went to have a conference with Joe. When he returned, I followed him up to his room.

He generously suggested that I sleep the remainder of the morning—he never seemed to need rest, whereas an all-night adventure left me tired for days afterwards—but I declined emphatically.

He considered the smuggling case closed. All that remained was ordinary police work: Identifying the members of the gang, persuading one or two of them to turn informer, singling out the leaders, organizing the final raids that would arrest the lot of them.

His long-established principle of keeping his conclusions to him-self until a case was finished no longer applied. That meant that I finally could ask for, and get, a full explanation of what had happened.

I helped myself to a chair, crossed my legs, and announced, in the tone of voice that he so frequently used on me, "The smugglers. I want to know all about them."

CHAPTER
13

S herlock Holmes arranged his lank form on the chair beside mine. *"All* would require a lengthy discussion," he said. "What is it that you want to know?"

I wanted to know about the mastermind whose touch rivalled that of Professor Moriarty and how Sherlock Holmes had in a few days laid bare a smuggling operation that had gone undetected for years.

"Even if several of the members turn informer, the complete details about this gang's activity may never be known," he said. "The lesser members, those whose principal function has been carrying the contraband across the Marsh at night, may know very little about the advance planning and how the goods were disposed of. I had scant information to go on myself. As you are well aware, deduction is not possible without facts. The only recourse left to me was surmise. You know my methods. I balance probabilities with the scientific use of the imagination and choose whatever result seems most likely."

He packed his pipe with deliberation, lit it, and folded his long legs into a more comfortable position. Because he had arrived several days after me, he had been assigned the inn's second-best room. It was smaller than mine, and it overlooked the low building that housed the establishment of William Price, who dealt in corn and fertilizers.

"Smuggling," Sherlock Holmes mused. "If I sided with criminals instead of the law, I should write a monograph upon the subject. Smugglers—those who work in gangs and attempt to bring in contraband in wholesale quantities—have long been among the most consummately stupid of the entire criminal class. They inevitably prefer the bludgeon to the rapier. They have succeeded temporarily, in certain times and places, because of special local conditions, but they have never survived a concentrated and intelligent effort to put an end to their activity. Tell me, Porter. Have you ever been at Charing Cross when the Continental Express arrives?"

"No, sir," I said.

"You should have that experience. I will make a point of sending you there after we return to London. If you arrive just before the train does, you will find an alert group of Her Majesty's customs officers already on the scene, waiting to inspect passengers and baggage with professional skill. Why? Because those passengers and their baggage are arriving from outside the country, of course.

"Now consider another example. Have you ever been at Euston when a train—any train—arrives from Birmingham?"

"Yes, sir."

"Did you see any customs officers?"

"No, sir."

"If you were to study these two situations from the point of view of a smuggler, what would you conclude?"

"If I wanted to bring contraband into London, I should be well advised to do so by way of Birmingham rather than by way of Dover, and I should be especially well advised to avoid the Continental Express."

"Precisely. Logic is life's greatest illuminator. We are fortunate that few criminals are capable of applying it. Unfortunately, few police officers are capable of applying it, either. You would find, however, that you had almost as much difficulty in transporting your smuggled goods to Birmingham—so that you could bring them into London unmolested—as you would have were you to bring them here directly. But the principle is one that the intelligent smuggler would be well advised to contemplate.

"Now consider the gang of smugglers whose acquaintance we made last night. If I were to write my monograph, Porter, the ideal smuggling scheme that I would describe would very closely parallel the one that was followed here—except that this gang created original touches that I might not have thought of."

He continued to talk, pausing at intervals to send up thick, swirling rings of smoke. He considered it likely that this smuggling operation commenced as a small, very tentative venture, and that it was born out of a desperate need for money on the part of normally respectable people who otherwise would have been unable to imagine themselves committing criminal acts. Many law-abiding citizens saw nothing particularly wrong with smuggling. Charles Lamb had said that the smuggler was the only honest thief, since he robbed nothing but the revenue.

These novice smugglers—and Sherlock Holmes thought the nucleus of the present gang had existed from the beginning—saw nothing criminal in an innocuous breaking of the law to save themselves from destitution. They tried it, they had the good luck not to be caught—since they were novices, it probably took them time to develop the techniques that they now used so effectively—and they must have been astonished at how profitable a smuggling operation could be.

"Was Edmund Quallsford one of them?" I asked.

"His certainly was a desperate financial situation, and he must have been in on the scheme from the beginning. His eminently respectable position would be of great value to any group of smugglers. But I do not believe that Edmund Quallsford was the genius who applied the logic, developed the remarkable system, and built a smoothly running organization that could employ thirty or more men in an operation such as we witnessed last night."

The smugglers' first problem was to land the contraband safely on English soil. However that was accomplished in the beginning, the genius of the gang's leader quickly refined it into an art. Mr. More, the customs officer, had mentioned his beach patrols. Sherlock Holmes felt confident that these smugglers knew more about those patrols than Mr. More did. They knew when patrols were made, and where, and by whom. They knew what public houses would be visited to relieve the tedium of patrolling, and when, and for how long. They watched and studied the patrolling activity on their favourite sections of beach every night—not just on the nights a small boat was scheduled to arrive from the Continent. Only a Professor Moriarty of smuggling would devise such a touch.

"Perhaps we will never know for certain, but it would surprise me very much, Porter, if this leader does not have a position to fall back on for every contingency. The gang was singularly fortunate in the landing of contraband—due in large part to excellent planning and the study of patrols—but what would have happened if a landing had been surprised by customs officers? Nothing."

"Nothing?" I echoed in astonishment.

"Nothing. My surmise is that every boat out of France has been fully equipped with proper papers, and that there would have been a convincing story about an accident, the boat having drifted ashore with a broken mast or some similar disability, and papers would have been produced showing the proper consignment of goods to the Quallsford Importing Company. In that case, Edmund would have presented those papers at Rye in the morning, paid the duty, and apologized for the stupidity of the sailors, saying resignedly that such things will happen from time to time when one employs small boats and makeshift crews."

When the contraband was landed, at a time and place carefully chosen to avoid the patrols, the smugglers would meet it with a well-practised manoeuvre. They would quickly move it to safe storage away from the beach and far enough inland to escape the close surveillance of the excisemen but not too far to be reached quickly without causing comment. Then they would remove all traces of the landing and disperse. Their leader knew the history of smuggling well, and he knew that the downfall of smuggling gangs often had been rooted in their inability to land goods and move them to safety without parading them on public roads and through villages. A concealed cellar under an isolated barn or looker's hut, located no more than a half-mile from the beach and probably closer, would be an ideal place.

"I found one of those hiding places," Sherlock Holmes said. "There may be several. The one that I inspected was empty. After last night's expedition, probably all of them are empty."

The next step, in terms of Sherlock Holmes's illustration, was to move the goods to Birmingham—or to any safe place further inland from which they could be sold to those who wanted them. Again it was necessary to avoid public roads and villages, but these smugglers were fortunate in having the Marshes at hand, populated at night only by sheep and an occasional looker. They were an infernally difficult place to find one's way about in, even in the daytime, as I had learned myself. Here the leader's genius asserted itself again, for the Marshes also were an infernally difficult place for the excisemen to find their way about in.

The routes—and Sherlock Holmes was certain that a leader of that calibre would have prepared more than one—were laid out meticulously. Bridges were placed where needed. The whole system was mapped. Navigators were trained, because crossing the Marsh at night would be as much a problem in navigation as crossing the sea. Lookers were brought into the scheme with small payments for which they had to do nothing but leave a candle burning when told to do so and, the next day, remove any traces left in their pastures by the smugglers. One of the oldest dodges in the colourful history of smuggling in England was to obliterate the tracks of smugglers and their horses by driving a flock of sheep over them.

The smugglers certainly made practice runs at night—carrying nothing—merely to gain experience in going from one place to another and to train their horses to cross the narrow bridges. This explained Sherlock Holmes's interest in Taff Harris, the man who walked to and from work all the way across the Marsh. The smugglers' routes through pasture land were longer and more difficult than Harris's route by road, but neither was a hardship to a man accustomed to walking. If one of those practice runs had come to the attention of the authorities, no harm would have been done. There was no law against taking a short cut through the Marsh at night.

"It sounds like an enormous amount of trouble," I said.

"Exactly. That is why only a genius would think of it and have the patience to make such meticulous plans and carry them out. And that is why the authorities have not even suspected it. Once it was accomplished, the rewards were enormous and well worth the trouble. You saw how they travelled in three small groups instead of one large one. This is another touch of genius—if one group got into trouble, the other two could slip away. It would cut the gang's losses, and, by having each group signal occasionally to the one behind it, probably to show the location of bridges, only the first group needed a skilled navigator. You saw how they walked side by side when crossing the pastures. That is another touch of genius. Men and animals walking in single file make a path. Walking side by side, with each group taking a slightly different route, kept the marks of their passage to a minimum."

The recruiting of respectable workers for the gang demonstrated a similar touch of genius. They were moved into dwellings that they could slip away from at night without causing comment. They must have been paid a regular but modest wage—a powerful incentive to those hard-working men who had never experienced any luck in life—and it made their newly found prosperity so inconspicuous that no one noticed it. They were trained and taught severe discipline. The snarl of rage we heard when one of them rashly fired a revolver at me was a sobering illustration. The leader had wisely forbidden firearms.

If any members of the gang were caught, they were instructed to submit peacefully. The authorities would take little note of the arrest of a nondescript smuggler or two, and their punishment would be mild. The gang would continue to pay them wages, their families would be taken care of, and, after a suitable pause, the operation could continue as before. Smugglers who fought back with revolvers would raise an alarm that would shock London and bring the full force of Her Majesty's government down on the quiet Marsh country, which would be very bad business indeed. Months or years might pass before the smugglers could resume.

"They will have their own special form of punishment for Newton," Sherlock Holmes said. "His rash act put the entire operation in jeopardy."

Once the goods were safely inland and away from the more stringent activities of the excisemen, the problem became one of distribution, and there we saw the most fantastic touch of the leader's genius: Edmund Quallsford's Importing Company. *Edmund Quallsford was importing—legally—exactly the same goods that the smugglers were bringing into the country illegally.* He imported other odds and ends as well, and he perfectly created the illusion that the leader wanted him to create—that of a wealthy, well-intentioned, somewhat bungling idealist pursuing a noble but hopelessly impractical idea. He was so respectable, and so honourable, and so finicking in his attempt to follow the law in its every particular, that the customs officers—once they had assured themselves that his tiny business was genuine—paid small attention to him except to regard him with affectionate amusement.

Edmund Quallsford developed wide support for his noble project and sold small quantities of his legally imported goods at the lowest possible prices throughout the Marsh area and into eastern Sussex. At the same time, he—or someone—sold huge quantities of identical but smuggled goods to a carefully selected list of less reputable merchants who already had bought from Edmund as a cover. The Royal Swan supported Edmund's business by offering French brandy to its customers. No one would suspect Mr. Werner of handling smuggled goods. He would send for the authorities if anyone were to suggest it, and he would be horrified to know that he was rendering valuable assistance to smugglers by handling Edmund's brandy, but it was true. He did not sell much of it, and it was not necessary that he should. The Royal Swan, respectable and fully legal, lent credibility to the nearby Green Dragon, where Sam Jenks sold an enormous amount of brandy, and almost all that he sold was smuggled.

"Note this well," Sherlock Holmes said, underscoring another touch of genius with his long fingers. "If the customs officers came to investigate, Jenks would show them one or two kegs with bills of lading from Edmund Quallsford's importing company, and if they investigated further, Mr. Herks, who keeps Edmund Quallsford's records with such fine precision, would show them the exact date or dates when those two kegs were purchased. All Sam Jenks had to do was keep his reserve supply hidden and refill those two legal kegs when necessary."

Smuggled goods were brought inland from the coast by men and horses who surreptitiously crossed the Marsh at night with great skill. They were transported back to coastal villages—and everywhere else—openly, by carriers who had bills of lading to cover them.

"Do you understand how that was done?" Sherlock Holmes asked.

"No," I said. "Surely it would be obvious that the carriers were transporting far more goods than the Quallsford Importing Company had imported legally."

Sherlock Holmes thought not. If a ship were surprised in a landing, the crew would have papers consigning the goods *to* the Quallsford Importing Company. A carrier would haul smuggled brandy openly with bills of lading *from* the Quallsford Importing Company. If the excisemen investigated, the carrier was transporting legally imported kegs and had the documentation to prove it.

If no one investigated, he would quietly unload the smuggled brandy, with a very different billing, at a public house that already had documentation to sell the brandy legally. The next day he could transport more smuggled kegs to a different public house, again with bills of lading to cover them.

Eventually, for appearances' sake, the Quallsford Importing Company would import more brandy legally, and the customs officers would smile again at the preposterous little business. And that was how the scheme was worked. Much of the time that Edmund Quallsford was supposed to be getting rich in London, he was travelling about looking for new customers to add to the respectability of the Quallsford Importing Company. Sherlock Holmes was uncertain as to whether he also made the contacts and took orders for the smuggled goods. It seemed like an unlikely role for him.

"The scheme has been operating for eight years or more," I said. "You detected it almost immediately. What gave it away?"

"I suspected smuggling before I arrived here. I knew something that the customs officers had not bothered to discover—that Edmund Quallsford's supposed financial success in London was a fiction. His sudden wealth was unaccounted for, and, as you know yourself, one immediately thinks of smuggling when there is unexplained wealth in a coastal area. The source of that wealth became obvious when we visited the tower. Its position so conspicuously overlooking the Marsh made me think of an ancient lighthouse—but lighthouses are built to attract ships safely to port as well as to warn them away from hazards, and the tower was ideally situated for signalling. One glance at Edmund's retreat confirmed that—he had been using a spout lantern."

"What is a spout lantern?" I asked.

"A smuggler's tool. If you had ever seen one, you would never forget it. It looks like a watering can with a long spout. The spout makes it possible to aim the beam of light at a pre-arranged spot. Smugglers have long used it for signalling to ships. From the marks on the tower window, I suspected that Edmund employed a specially designed rack with his lantern that enabled him to aim it accurately along pre-arranged lines of sight. It served as an excellent navigational signal to those crossing the Marsh. If an outsider did chance to notice, it was only one more star in the sky. Edmund may have brooded in the tower, but while he brooded, he also signalled."

"Signals from the tower did not help them last night," I said. "The smugglers could not have seen them through the fog."

"By this time, after years of experience, the tower signals would be more of a convenience than a necessity. They surely have developed other methods of navigation, and probably they have several men who can lead a group across the Marsh with their eyes closed. They know the paced breadth of every pasture and where every bridge is located.

"But they did use spout lanterns last night, Porter. The small light on the ground that served to keep the group together must have been thrown by some kind of down-turning spout that utilized a mirror—a fantastically ingenious touch that provides an inconspicuous light for a group of smugglers to follow and one that must look supernatural if glimpsed from a distance. Country people are naturally superstitious, and no Marshman seeing that floating light would feel inclined to investigate it more closely.

"Once the picture was clear to me, I was able to trace one of the smugglers' routes all the way across the Marsh and, by following it backward, discover one of their initial hiding places for contraband. I could also prepare a list, Porter, of places in southern Kent and Sussex that are selling brandy and tobacco and silk illegally. I have had an active three days."

He had been talking freely for some time, and I attempted to slip in what I knew was a forbidden question. "Why was Edmund Quallsford murdered?"

He smiled. "There we pass into the realm of pure conjecture. Your hypothesis is as likely to be correct as mine."

"I have no hypothesis," I said. "Was his murder connected with the smuggling?"

He shrugged and took the time to spin more smoke rings. "The facts about his death are still obscure. The one thing that is perfectly clear is that Edmund's honour no longer permitted him to take part in a smuggling operation, as the surviving page of his letter demonstrates. Why that sudden decision after eight years or more? Was it because the gang was about to extend its operations to London?"

He lapsed into silence.

"Perhaps he was murdered because he wanted to withdraw," I said. "His resignation threatened the gang."

Sherlock Holmes shook his head. "No, Porter. Edmund Quallsford really was a man of honour. He would never have given his confederates away—not even to save himself. They would know that positively. No, we must look for another reason for his murder. Edmund's resignation certainly came at an inconvenient time, but they would not murder him for that. Perhaps he refused to take the message to Spitalfields Market, and a substitute messenger had to be found. Or perhaps he sent the old governess because for some reason he could not go himself. Such speculation is useless because we have no idea of the import of the message or to whom it was addressed."

Again he lapsed into silence and worked furiously at his pipe.

"I have difficulty in connecting Doris Fowler with a gang of smugglers," I said.

"Do you?" Sherlock Holmes asked with a smile. "I have encountered far more unlikely connections. But in this case, she may have been innocently doing a favour for Edmund. The old woman at Spitalfields was not as totally incapable as the one we met at Sea Cliffs. Her derangement could have been due to Edmund's death."

"So we are left where we started," I said. "We have a murder to investigate."

"When we started, we did not know that it was murder. At least we have made that much progress, and we have turned up a number of points of interest, but the matter has proved to be far deeper than I suspected. The smuggling operation was a distraction. Now that it is disposed of—"

There was a firm knock on the door. Neither Mr. Werner nor his wife rapped with such authority.

I opened it. Sergeant Donley entered the room with one long stride. He wore an expression of indescribable gloom. "Bad news," he said. "George Newton's body has been found in a dyke. Drowned, but he was hit on the head first. He was murdered."

Sherlock Holmes slumped back into his chair. He said nothing at all, leaving it to me to make the sergeant comfortable and fetch another chair from my room. Then he listened without comment while the sergeant recounted the details.

A comparative stranger like Sergeant Donley found his apparent indifference bewildering. Only one who knew Sherlock Holmes well could have properly interpreted that sullen taciturnity. He was as angry as I had ever seen him.

"Would you like to see the body?" the sergeant asked finally.

Sherlock Holmes shook his head. "Has his wife been informed?"

"Yes," the sergeant said unhappily. "I had to tell her myself. She feels that I—that the three of us—are somehow at fault, because we called on him yesterday, and he was mightily upset afterwards. I couldn't get any explanation from her as to what she thought that had to do with his death."

"She was right," Sherlock Holmes said. "The three of us are somehow at fault. The poor little trapped rat. But was he murdered because we talked with him or because he unwisely fired that shot at Porter? This opens a new chapter, Sergeant. Before I can comment, I must have a talk with Mrs. Newton."

We made our way back to the tiny cottage we had visited the day before, where we found a widow who was not dressed in black. Perhaps she had no black garments, or perhaps she had not yet given thought to the proprieties. Her care-worn face now was ravaged with weeping. Two small, frightened children clung to her skirts;

an older child, also with a ravaged face, peered out at us with mingled fright and curiosity.

Mrs. Newton chased the children to another part of the house and resentfully invited us in. Sherlock Holmes, with a friendly, relaxed manner that common people always responded to, quickly put her at her ease.

He apologized for disturbing her at such a tragic time. "We are determined that those responsible for your husband's death shall not go unpunished," he said. "Anything you can tell us about his activities will be helpful."

"The sergeant knows all about it," she said bitterly. "George died for his country, and the sergeant knows it and pretends he don't."

"The sergeant knows," Sherlock Holmes repeated, "but we don't. Please tell us how your husband died for his country."

"He worked for the customs," she said. "He guarded the beaches at night to keep smugglers off. Precious little they paid him, too—only ten shillings a week for all that danger, with him risking his life every time he went out, and he had to take work during the day so we could get by."

"I see," Sherlock Holmes said thoughtfully. "How long had he been working for the government?"

She was uncertain, but she calculated from the birth of her second eldest child and made it seven or eight years.

"How many people knew about this?" Sherlock Holmes asked.

"No one knew it but me. He had to keep it secret because the smugglers would do him in if they found out. He went and came after dark, and we never told anyone, and now they found it out anyway and he is dead."

"Did he ever talk about his experiences guarding the beaches?" Sherlock Holmes asked.

"Never," she said. "Kept it to himself so's I wouldn't worry, but I worried all the time. I knew this would happen. Smugglers think nothing of killing people."

The previous night, her husband had slipped away as usual after dark. Before he left, he talked about an appointment he had with Mr. Herks the next day, today, to discuss some garden work. He always returned long before dawn, but this time he never came back at all. She had been so worried that she had not taken the children to pick hops. When her husband was found, the police would not even let her have his body, which she thought cruel. Sherlock Holmes spoke a few words of consolation, and we took our leave of her.

"Poor woman," he said grimly, as we walked back towards the Royal Swan. "The natives of this region learned horror stories about smugglers in their cradles. In the eighteenth century, gangs of two hundred or more terrorized the countryside and so effectively intimidated the authorities that smuggling was carried on openly, during the day, with no attempt at interference. Tales of the bloodthirsty Hawkhurst Gang probably have become folklore, and there may be people still alive who remember the infamous Blues and the Ransleys of Aldington. No wonder that Mrs. Newton worried about her husband's heroic occupation."

"I suppose the wives of all of those men were told the same thing," I said.

Sherlock Holmes nodded. "The ingenious planning of every small detail is awesome. At a single stroke, the husbands accounted for their illegal wages and nights away from home and frightened their wives into total secrecy. We add to our knowledge, Porter. Here is one more touch of genius. A long list of poor devils who were down on their luck were paid a regular wage for working at smuggling whenever they were needed. They were moved to living quarters where their night activity would cause no comment, but of course they had to have a tale for their own families—and what better one than to say that they were guarding their country from smugglers and their lives depended on secrecy?"

"The pay seems surprisingly low," I said.

"I don't agree, Porter. Ten shillings is a good wage for a few hours of night work a few times a week. Some of the work was not hard at all. Part of the time they actually were 'guarding the beaches'—meaning that they were watching Mr. More's patrols. The men were encouraged to find day work when they could and to take their families hop picking in season, which was such an effective blind that not even the merchants they did regular business with suspected them of having an illegal income. I will wager that they even continued to draw their winter poor relief. It is the master's touch again, Porter—but something has gone wrong."

He said nothing more until we had returned to his room at the Royal Swan. Then he sent me down to Mr. Herks to buy a full pound of the Quallsford Importing Company tobacco.

Mr. Herks was surprised at the request. "It is not very good tobacco," he said. "No one buys it twice."

I told him that a colleague of mine liked it.

"Is that so? I will make you a present of as much as you want. Larissa will have nothing to do with the importing company, and I have not seen Emmeline since Edmund died except at his funeral. Of course I could not talk business with her there. If your firm wants to make an offer, I hope that it does so soon."

We walked together along the High Street to the Quallsford Importing Company, and Mr. Herks packed a generous bag of the tobacco for me.

"Is it true what they are saying about George Newton?" he asked suddenly.

"I don't know what 'they' are saying," I said. "It is true that Newton is dead."

"He fell into a dyke and drowned?"

"I heard that he had drowned," I said evasively. Sergeant Donley probably had not made public the fact that he had been murdered.

"Incredible," Mr. Herks said. "George could swim like a fish."

I took the tobacco to Sherlock Holmes and told him what Mr. Herks had said about it.

"It is miserably poor shag," he agreed, "but I will use it for penance, and I will save the remainder in order to give myself an occasional lesson in humility. I have gone badly astray somewhere, Porter, and a man has died because of it. If Edmund Quallsford had lived, this gang of smugglers might have operated for many more years and extended its activity to London undetected. It could have shipped its contraband disguised as Appledore runner beans, or Ashford wool, or whatever went to London from other inland communities, and that would have been the equivalent of smuggling by way of Birmingham. Making connections with Spitalfields Market instead of Covent Garden, the logical outlet for goods arriving at Charing Cross, was another touch of genius. The gang was immensely successful, and it was poised to magnify that success. Then Edmund was murdered, and that seems to have left the ship adrift with no hand at the helm. The gang's discipline has failed utterly. Is it possible that he *was* the genius behind it? There is no other way to account for George Newton's senseless murder. Someone remains in command—the operation last night proves that— but instead of the master touch, we have a brutal attempt to rule by terror. And yet—and yet—I cannot believe that Edmund Quallsford exerted that much influence. My instinct is against it. I must have erred somewhere."

He filled his pipe, lit it, and exhaled with a grimace of distaste. "I have a long work session ahead of me, Porter. Please tell Mr. Werner that I do not want to be bothered by anyone."

"Is there anything that I should be directing my attention to?" I asked.

"Yes," he said. "The missing first page of Edmund Quallsford's letter. That letter was completely out of character for him. All of our uncertainty about the murder and its connection with the smuggling gang may be resolved when we can explain why he wrote such an important communication on cheap paper."

CHAPTER
14

I took the message to Mr. Werner.

He was agog with the rumour of George Newton's murder, though he did not call it that. "Drowned, they said. Probably got drunk and fell in a dyke. Out carousing, I shouldn't wonder. Mrs. Newton didn't even know where he had gone. Her neighbour told me that for a fact. Your friend doesn't want to be bothered? Who would bother him? Never mind—I will see that no one goes near him."

When Sherlock Holmes said that he did not want to be bothered by anyone, that included me. It gave me another free afternoon, and I racked my brains to think of something to do that might advance our investigation. First I went to see Joe on the chance that I might learn what the Romney Marsh Irregulars were up to. It was wasted effort; Sherlock Holmes had sternly imposed secrecy on him.

We talked for a time. He told me that Mr. Werner had hired him only a week before I arrived.

"What did you do before that?" I asked.

"I worked for Mr. Pringle," he said. "Bird scarer."

"*Bird* scarer?" I echoed.

"I scared birds away from his corn. He paid me sixpence a day, and I had to take an examination with the Board of Guardians so I could leave school."

"How did you scare them?" I asked.

"Rattles and clappers. But that only lasted through the summer, and sixpence wasn't much. My father said he couldn't feed me for that. A friend of mine got a job as wagoner's mate. He gets ten bob a week, but he's fourteen. Mr. Werner only pays me four bob with meals thrown in."

I smiled at the thought of Mrs. Werner's meals being thrown in. "The meals are very good," I said.

"They are," he agreed, licking his lips enthusiastically. "But I would rather be a detective."

I told him to keep working at it, and I went off to try to be a detective myself. I considered questioning Richard Cole again to find out whether the old servant of the Quallsfords had seen anything suspicious from his eyrie above the village; but I reminded myself that the comings and goings of George Newton and his confederates would have been covered by darkness.

I also considered having a talk with the vicar. Sherlock Holmes had demonstrated an unaccountable interest in churches and churchyards when he first arrived, and that had set me thinking. It finally occurred to me that he had been looking for possible hiding places for smuggled goods.

The case against the smugglers would not be complete until their cache of contraband was discovered, so I decided to pursue this. Remembering what Sherlock Holmes said repeatedly about the value of a knowledge of the history of crime, I asked Mr. Werner whether vicars or curates had been involved in any of the area's legendary smuggling activities.

"Probably," he said. "There were times when almost everyone had a part in smuggling, one way or another. If the vicars were not directly involved, they certainly knew about it. No doubt they thought it best to turn a blind eye. I do believe I have heard tell of smuggled goods hidden inside of a church—Brookland or Snargate or some place up that way. Of course that would not necessarily mean that the vicar was involved. It could have been a church warden or a sexton."

If I had been a smuggler looking for a church in which I could fashion a hiding place for smuggled goods, I would have chosen one with box pews, which offered a variety of advantages in concealment. St. John Havenchurch had box pews. After lunch, I took the long, climbing road up to the vicarage and the church; but the vicar's housekeeper told me that he was not at home.

"He is with the poor family of the man that died," she said.

I thanked her and decided that I would have had small success with the vicar in any case. The problem of surprising or intimidating a man with his self-assurance into a confession was better left to Sherlock Holmes.

I walked back to Havenchurch, and then, for the want of anything else to do, I followed Havenchurch Road across the Marsh towards Brookland. I paused for a close look at the plank bridge that Sherlock Holmes attached such importance to. It was indeed double-planked underneath. I wondered what had moved him to examine the underside. Probably he would have said that he found the reinforcing planks only because he was looking for them.

The afternoon had become warm, so I removed my coat and walked slowly along the road, enjoying the sunshine. Havenchurch Halt, which consisted of platforms and a shed, looked so totally deserted amid the encompassing strangeness of the Marsh that I was inclined to doubt that trains ever passed that way.

I walked on. The road gave me assurance. However much it meandered, as long as I did not stray from it, I could not get lost. I saw sheep in the distance but no humans, and the rich green pasturage filled every horizon.

The land looked flat, but new configurations loomed up repeatedly. Suddenly one of them contained two horses, and before I could quite grasp this phenomenon, a voice hailed me.

It was Ben Paine, the mole catcher, at work with his two appren-

tices, likely-looking young men of fourteen or fifteen. A drainage
ditch separated us; I seated myself beside it and watched the boys
work. One of them wielded a spud like the one that Paine had
showed to us, and he scooped out a mole with commendable expertise. He dispatched it with a rap on the head and held it up proudly.
Ben Paine spoke quiet words of praise that I could not catch and
added the mole to the bag that he carried.

The bag looked to be almost full.

"A good catch," I said.

"Quite good," he agreed. "This is the easy part of the job. The
hard part comes later—skinning the moles and curing the skins."

He seated himself on the opposite side of the ditch. "Where is
your friend today?"

"Resting," I said.

"He seemed powerfully interested in mole catching."

"He is interested in everything."

"If he would like to try his hand at it, I will take him along
tomorrow."

"I will tell him," I said. Then I added, "Did you know George
Newton?"

He looked up quickly. "What do you mean—*did* I know George
Newton? Of course I know George."

"You didn't know that he is dead?"

"No. I didn't know that. I saw him yesterday morning, and he
seemed in good health. How did it happen?"

"He drowned."

Paine looked at me levelly for a moment. "There is something
improperly queer about that," he announced. "George was a good
swimmer."

"Mr. Werner said he was drunk and fell in a dyke."

"That sounds even queerer. One pint of ale was George's limit.
I have never seen him drunk. Where did it happen?"

I told him I did not know.

"He was a good family man," Paine said. "He had a nice wife and four fine children. How is Meg taking it?"

I assumed that Meg was the wife. "About the way you would expect," I said. "Hard."

He nodded. "Life takes cruel turns. George and Meg were fond of each other. People said he was a poor husband because he never found steady work, but it was not true. He always did his best, and they got along, even if they never had much."

Suddenly he leaped to his feet and darted away. "That's the way to ruin a good tool!" he shouted. He bent over a cringing apprentice, who raised his arms as though to ward off a blow.

I wondered afterwards whether it was my presence that saved the youngster a beating. Paine relaxed suddenly and said, in a sarcastic voice, "Not like that. Like this." And then he went through the operation very patiently, a step at a time. He came back mopping his brow.

"Apprentices," he said wearily. "They are valuable once they understand what is expected of them, but they can try a man's patience when they have to be told over and over. About George Newton. Something ought to be done for his family. I'll talk to the vicar."

I asked him a few questions about mole catching, and he answered absently while keeping an alert eye on his apprentices. Finally they finished with the pasture they were working. Paine got to his feet; the two apprentices were waiting by one of the horses. He took his leave of me and joined them, and they rode off, the apprentices on one horse and Paine on the other. I remembered the sad tale of the death of Paine's wife and child, and I wondered whether Newton's death had a special poignance for him for that reason.

When I got back to the Royal Swan—tired out and feeling dissatisfied with myself for the wasted time—I found Mr. Werner in a dither. "Sergeant Donley was here," he said. "He wanted to see your friend. I know you said he wasn't to be bothered, but I didn't think you meant the police. I tapped on the door and asked if he wanted to see the sergeant, and the way he bellowed at me raised hair I didn't know I had. Then twenty minutes later he was shouting downstairs for Joe, and he bellowed again because Joe wasn't here."

"Is Joe back yet?" I asked.

"Came back long ago. I sent him up, and your friend talked with him for all of half an hour and then he told me he was hiring him for the rest of the day. Fine state of affairs when I don't have access to my own help."

"But that is what Joe is here for, isn't it?" I asked him. "To be available when your guests need a boy for something?"

"In a manner of speaking, I suppose so. But what if someone else wants him?"

"But I am the only other guest," I said. "If I need Joe, and he is not available, I will complain to my friend."

"Be careful how you complain," Mr. Werner said. "I have heard enough bellowing and shouting for one day."

I regretted that I had missed it. Sherlock Holmes rarely raised his voice in conversation. Either his afternoon's work had been frustratingly futile, or Sergeant Donley had arrived at a crisis in his reasoning; but the fact that he had sent for Joe shortly afterwards sounded promising. I considered announcing my return, thought better of it, and pushed a note under his door. "I will be in my room when you want me."

Then I went there, stretched out on the bed, and attempted to perform a feat of reasoning of my own. It came to nothing.

Sergeant Donley returned to see whether Sherlock Holmes was available yet, and the landlord sent him to me. He treated me to a lengthy restatement of a complaint I had already listened to, and when Sherlock Holmes joined us a short time later, he repeated it.

"We should have apprehended some of the smugglers last night," he said. "We would have had them in the act, with evidence. Now what can we do? We can't arrest a man because he suddenly stopped buying on credit six years ago. We have more than twenty names on that list, and we are still working on it—and making a lot of merchants unhappy by dragging them away from their families on Sunday—but there really is nothing we can do except try to frighten some of those men into turning informer, and we aren't likely to have any success with that. Someone made an example of George Newton, and his murder has all of them terrified. We should have grabbed a couple of them last night."

Sherlock Holmes patiently pointed out again that the three of us could have accomplished very little against thirty or more men with horses. "If we had confronted one group, the other two would have vanished, and there is no way of knowing how many of the men were armed. In addition to George Newton, your constables would have had the unpleasant task of fishing the bodies of their sergeant and two nosy London visitors from a dyke, and there would be no more evidence for those murders than you have for the other."

The sergeant was not convinced. "If we could have grabbed just one of the smugglers and held onto him, we would have had a case," he lamented. "If you catch a man out, you can bargain with him. There is no case at all when you can't connect your suspect with anything that has been smuggled. All of those men and horses walked right past us loaded with contraband, and what did they do with it?"

"I know what they did with it," Sherlock Holmes said.

"You do?" the sergeant exclaimed.

"Of course. I knew where they were taking it. I had the crossroads watched to make certain that they went where I expected them to go, and I also had their hiding place watched to make certain that they arrived there."

"You did?" the sergeant exclaimed again. "I'll be somethinged! But why didn't you say so? Why didn't you tell us so we could raid the place?"

"Because the case was not ripe," Sherlock Holmes said. "Breaking up a large gang like this one takes scientific planning. If we move too soon, some of the members will escape."

"I don't care if it is planned scientifically, or magically, or with the direct intervention of the Almighty, just so the work gets done. Who did the watching last night?"

"Some of the boys from the village."

Sergeant Donley looked at him severely. "You shouldn't set boys to following smugglers. They could have come to harm."

"They weren't following them," Sherlock Holmes said. "They watched from hiding places that I selected myself. They were perfectly safe."

"When is the case going to be ripe?"

"Perhaps tomorrow," Sherlock Holmes said. "Continue your interviews with the merchants. You should be able to pick up another ten names, at least."

He told me to make a copy of the new names that the sergeant had compiled. Then Sergeant Donley left, and I described my conversation with Ben Paine and repeated his invitation to take Sherlock Holmes mole catching.

"My bag tomorrow will contain rats rather than moles, and my expectation is that they will be live rats," he said.

We went downstairs to feast on the rack of lamb that Mrs. Werner had prepared for us. It was a delicious meal, and Sherlock Holmes ate heartily, but I doubted that he tasted any of it. He obviously had much on his mind; he ate in silence and several times failed to hear remarks that Mr. Werner addressed to him.

He remained unusually silent afterwards when we joined several local men who were enjoying Mr. Werner's home-made bitter. The talk was about George Newton, with them saying kind things about how hard he worked to support his family and tactfully not mentioning how he usually failed.

"I heard he was supposed to work for you today," I said to Mr. Herks.

Herks shook his head gloomily. "He was going to stop by and talk about some work. Mrs. Herks had some things she wanted done in the garden to get ready for winter. George was very capable at that sort of job, and he seemed to enjoy doing it. He would come and work evenings whenever we needed him. It always surprised me that he didn't find himself regular work as a gardener. Of course there aren't any opportunities for a full-time gardener in Haven-church, but he could have found something if he had looked around."

"Did he tell you he wasn't coming?" I asked.

"How was he to know he was going to drown?" Herks demanded. "He told me he *was* coming. I talked to him about it yesterday just before closing when he stopped in to buy an ounce of my headache preparation. He wasn't looking well, but he thought he would be all right today."

The vicar stumped into the room, greeted everyone expansively, and took the chair that Derwin Smith pulled out for him. He called for French brandy, which occasioned loud laughter.

"This would be an excellent time for your sermon on temperance," Smith remarked.

The vicar shook his head. *"Not* an excellent time. I have had a difficult day, and sherry would be less than adequate."

"Have you been with Mrs. Newton?" Smith asked.

"That I have. What a tragedy! But even in tragedy, life is one surprise after another, and so is death. I told her not to worry about the expenses of the coffin and having the grave dug. The parish would see to that. She told me, with more pride than I suspected her of having, that the Man from the Pru would pay for it. Imagine —she has the whole family in an insurance. I wonder where she got the pence week after week."

"Simple," Smith said. "Money went there instead of for other things. That is why George was always in debt."

Sergeant Donley came in and whispered something to Sherlock Holmes. He then went to the far corner of the room where two games were in progress, dominoes and darts. He pretended to watch the darts game for a few minutes before he seated himself at a distant table. Eventually we were able to detach ourselves from the discussion and join him.

He spoke hoarsely. "There has been another murder. Wallace Dickens, of Lydd, was found dead in a dyke just like George Newton. He was last seen with another of your suspects, Alfred Mitchell. Mitchell denies knowing anything about it. He says they separated and he came home alone. How many more murders will we have before we are able to do anything about this?"

"I don't know," Sherlock Holmes said wearily. "We are very near the end. The problem is evidence—not evidence of smuggling, but evidence of murder. We can act against the smugglers tomorrow morning. I have sent a message to Mr. More about combining the strengths of the customs officers and the police. We shall want enough men to raid the cache and also to arrest everyone on your list. Once you have them in custody, one or two of them should be willing to talk."

"Then we will have a case," the sergeant said with a sigh of relief. "But what is the problem with the murder evidence?"

"I was hopeful that I could solve the murder of Edmund Quallsford before tomorrow is done. Once that is accomplished, the other murders will fall into place. But I still cannot see my way to the evidence."

"Did the same person do all three?"

"That is my conclusion, Sergeant. If I had been able to move more quickly, I could have saved two lives. This case will not rank with my more conspicuous successes. It was a mistake for me to allow myself to be identified. No doubt one of the leaders knew me by reputation, and the gang viewed my presence here as a threat."

"Never mind," the sergeant said gruffly. "You would only have been saving them for gaol. Some families would rather see them dead."

After the sergeant left, Sherlock Holmes said to me, "We have been neglecting Miss Quallsford, Porter. After all, she *is* our client.

If she were close by, we could have kept in contact with her, and she might have had useful information for us. It is awkward having her stay in Rye. We owe her a report. Will you write it?"

"What do you want me to say?" I asked.

"Report what has happened. It will be sad news for her that we have connected her brother with a large gang of smugglers, but she must be told. Let her know that there is no doubt whatsoever. We have already identified many members of the gang. We expect to arrest them all in the next few days. Her brother's murder must have been connected with the smuggling, but as yet we have no evidence as to which member of the gang is responsible. Does that put the situation fairly?"

I thought that it did.

"Ask her again about her brother's associations. List the names that Sergeant Donley has identified. We need to know whether there was hostility between any of those men and her brother. If she can recall a single incident, it might solve the case for us. Ask her to reflect carefully upon each of those names. Until now, she has been certain that no one wished her brother ill, and she has not attempted to remember. Make it emphatic that there was someone and that it could have been one of the names on the list. Her memory may respond to that."

"Very well," I said.

"When you have finished, bring the letter to my room. I will be composing a telegram. Joe can take both of them to Rye."

My letter writing was interrupted. Sergeant Donley returned. We went together to see Sherlock Holmes, and the sergeant said breathlessly, "Ralph, the Quallsfords' groom, brought me a message from Larissa. Doris Fowler has disappeared. Do you suppose that she has been murdered?"

"No, I don't suppose that," Sherlock Holmes said. "Perhaps she simply wandered off. She has been deranged since Edmund died. On the one occasion when we were able to speak with her, she claimed that she murdered him herself."

"No!" the sergeant exclaimed. "I don't believe it!"

Sherlock Holmes shrugged. "It illustrates her mental state. Perhaps now she has decided that he is still alive and gone to look for him."

"In that case, we are very likely to find her drowned in a dyke," the sergeant said gloomily.

"Possibly. But it is much more likely—" He paused. "In any event, you will have to search for her."

"We have already started. I suppose I ought to have some men out there on the Marsh, too, just in case the smugglers come again tonight."

Sherlock Holmes shook his head. "No, Sergeant. They will not come tonight. I promise you that. My own belief is that they wanted to clear their contraband out of hiding places near the shore and move it inland to a place they consider safer. Having done that, they will certainly suspend all operations until things have quieted down and Porter and I return to London. The good people of Havenchurch have accepted us as representatives of an importing company, but the smugglers know who we are. I can guarantee that. It has already provoked reactions, and it may provoke more."

Sergeant Donley heaved a sigh. "I can't help thinking, Mr. Holmes, that I wish you had stayed in London. This was a peaceful place until you arrived."

Sherlock Holmes wagged a finger reprovingly. "Come, Sergeant. You know better than that. It was Edmund Quallsford's murder that brought me here. If you are suggesting that things might have been managed better, I must agree with you. But a place with a large, active gang of smugglers who had already committed one murder can hardly be described as 'peaceful.' "

CHAPTER
15

Early the next morning, a boy on a bicycle brought Sherlock Holmes a letter from Emmeline Quallsford. The perspiring youth looked badly shook up—the Rye Road, though surfaced with beach, was too rough to serve as a race track for bicycles. Sherlock Holmes glanced through the letter and gave a nod of satisfaction.

"Please tell Miss Quallsford that I will see to everything," he said.

He gave the boy a shilling and started him on his bumpy ride back to Rye.

"Does she have suggestions?" I asked.

"She offers one excellent suggestion. I felt certain that your style of writing would be more likely to stimulate her memory than mine, Porter. The objectivity that I cultivate rarely strikes a responsive note with the feminine mentality, whereas you have no compunction about distorting facts when your very commendable compassion requires it. You will remember that the appeal I made to her brought no response at all. Probably she had difficulty in comprehending it. Logic has unpredictable effects upon women. Your letter persuaded her that she actually might know something concerning her brother's murder. Once persuaded, she was able to remember. She has now given me what I need to close this case."

He would say nothing more. As we left the Royal Swan, he paused to inform Mr. Werner that we would be returning to London early the next morning.

He had arranged a conference in Rye with Mr. More. At the risk of being late, he insisted on meeting the train from Ashford that brought London passengers.

Rye Station was not in the town proper, which perches so impressively upon its crowded hill. One of the strangenesses about the Marsh country was the way that the railway seemed to ignore the towns and villages that were its proper destination. Ham Street, Appledore, Havenchurch Halt, Rye, Winchelsea all were stations with varying remotenesses from the communities that gave them their names. The railway veered around the Rye hill as though determined to miss the city altogether.

One passenger on the train that morning was familiar to us. He was a trim, muscular man in his thirties, and not even his drab tweed suit could disguise a bearing for which a uniform would have been more suitable. He swung down and strode towards us, gripping first Sherlock Holmes's hand and then mine. It was Stanley Hopkins, a police inspector with whom we had worked on a number of cases.

His manner was grave. "Your wire stirred up a hornet's nest, Mr. Holmes," he said. "A triple murderer! When I left, my superiors were still trying to make one and one add up to three. Who is the third victim?"

"Everything will be made clear to you in good time," Sherlock Holmes said. "Did you bring the warrant?"

"That I did. Understand, no one at the Yard is disposed to argue with you, but your arithmetic is puzzling. The two deaths that we know about are grisly enough."

"By tomorrow, you will be able to work in the third. Come along—we have a busy day ahead of us."

We found Mr. More talking with Sergeant Donley. The customs officer was in a petulant mood. He said, without even waiting to be introduced to Stanley Hopkins, "Mr. Holmes, I still have no idea of what you are planning to do, but *someone* knows. Charles Jordan, a solicitor from Tenterden whom I know only by reputation—he is a wily old bird—called on me first thing this morning. He understood that I had arrested some clients of his for smuggling. I told him that I had arrested no one. He said in that case he would wait until I did. He informed me that his address would be the same as that of Mr. Sherlock Holmes—the George Hotel."

Mr. More thumped his desk bewilderedly.

Sherlock Holmes burst into laughter and rubbed his hands together with delight. "The smugglers have been keeping a closer eye on me than I suspected! I have already told Porter that this case deserves to be a classic, and every new development bears that out. For several days, the gang has been floundering, but now the master's hand is at the helm again. Have you ever heard of George Ransley, Mr. More?"

"Of course," More said. "Everyone knows about the Aldington smugglers. He and his gang were tried for murder and transported. They should have been hanged. But that was a long time ago—back in—"

"Eighteen twenty-six," Sherlock Holmes said. "History repeats itself. Especially criminal history repeats itself. When criminals take to studying criminal history, it repeats itself exactly. George Ransley was affluent enough to keep his own solicitor on retainer. The solicitor's name was Platt, of the firm of Langham & Platt, Ashford, and he not only protected George Ransley from such minor inconveniences as fines, but the vigorous defence he was prepared to enter against the murder charge was instrumental in the Crown's decision to accept guilty pleas for lesser offences. Now we have another gang of smugglers with the foresight to retain a solicitor in advance. The sergeant has been attempting to frighten the members we have identified by informing them that their arrest is imminent, and he has perfectly succeeded. It must be your awful visage that impressed them, Sergeant, since you had no evidence to confront them with. Obviously they have been instructed to inform their solicitor if they are arrested or threatened with arrest, and they have done so. I am telling you, gentlemen—this is the ultimate classic!"

"That is all very well, Mr. Holmes," Mr. More said sourly. "But we still have not arrested *anyone.*"

One of Sherlock Holmes's remarks had impressed Stanley Hopkins. "You said, Mr. Holmes, that for several days these smugglers were floundering, but now the master's hand is at the helm again. Does that mean that the gang's leader has been away?"

"That is one of the questions that must be resolved today. If you are ready, gentlemen, we will begin by collecting evidence that there has in fact been a gang of smugglers operating. Mr. More prefers to actually see the contraband before he begins preferring charges."

"I do indeed," Mr. More said.

"Do you have the necessary warrants?"

"I do."

Sherlock Holmes belatedly introduced Stanley Hopkins, and two raiding parties were organized. The smaller was sent north on the road to Havenchurch; we joined the other on the Iden Road.

Raiding a smugglers' lair sounds adventurous and possibly even dangerous, but this raid proved to be a tepid anticlimax. Long before we reached the old oast-house, I had guessed our destination. The building had a mouldy, deserted look about it in the bright sunshine, but police and customs officers swooped down and surrounded it as though they expected to find an army hidden there.

Jack Browne's splendid dray horses were missing. When I pointed that out to Sherlock Holmes, he answered that he had received a report from Joe's minions before we left Havenchurch. Jack Browne and two of his men had departed at dawn on their carrier errands. Browne had travelled south. One of his men had led a team to the Havenchurch stable, hitched it to a wagon there, and headed east. The other had gone north towards Wittersham.

"Those horses are of interest," Sherlock Holmes said to Sergeant Donley. "With one exception, they are the only evidence I can discover of a member of the gang spending money conspicuously. It is puzzling that the leader permitted it. Perhaps it was because good horses were needed to transport the smuggled goods. Nevertheless, it was a mistake, and the horses should have aroused your curiosity. They aroused Porter's and also mine. Never mind," he went on, when the sergeant began to protest. "An old woman lives upstairs. Do you know anything about her?"

"That is Jack Browne's mother," the sergeant said.

"She is certain to arrange some kind of signal when she finds out who we are. Watch for it."

As we entered the stable, he said to Mr. More, "It is Browne's peculiar ideas about stablekeeping that interest us. When an otherwise tidy establishment has manure piled inside, the owner certainly is concealing something. The manure is piled in three corners, so we have three choices. I choose that one." He pointed.

"Why that one?" Mr. More wanted to know.

"When we called on Mr. Browne a few days ago, there was dried manure on the top of that pile and fresh manure underneath, which is not the normal arrangement. It suggested that the manure had been removed and then carelessly replaced. Look for a shovel—ah, the constable has found two."

Before we could set to work, the old woman's voice called down to us. "What are you wanting?"

"We are police," Sherlock Holmes called. "We are wanting Mr. Browne."

"He has gone to Winchelsea."

"We will look for him there," Sherlock Holmes said. "We also intend to look here. We have a warrant."

The old woman watched until we began shovelling the manure. Then she went back upstairs.

Sergeant Donley went outside and circled the building. "She has drawn all the curtains," he announced when he returned. "What do you want me to do?"

"Nothing," Sherlock Holmes said. "You will take Jack Browne

and his men long before they come close enough to receive that message."

The manure pile concealed a stone-topped trap that opened on a flight of descending steps. The enormous old cellar was crammed with smuggled goods. Mr. More surveyed them with mixed emotions. He was pleased that the evidence he required was finally in hand and staggered to see the enormous quantity of contraband produced by a smuggling operation he had not even suspected.

Sergeant Donley was still doubtful as to how the suspects on his list were to be linked with the evidence, but he was willing to accept Sherlock Holmes's assurance that it would be done. As he mounted his horse, Sherlock Holmes called a reminder to him.

"Five o'clock at the Royal Swan, Sergeant. The most important part of our work is still ahead of us."

He also invited Mr. More and Stanley Hopkins to join us that evening. Then the two of us walked back to Havenchurch by the River Rother footpath. The second group of police had posted itself where the footpath intersected the Rye Road to prevent an escape in that direction, and we relayed Sergeant Donley's message to them that the oast-house had been deserted and they could proceed with the business of arresting the smugglers.

After lunch at the Royal Swan—with a Mr. Werner who sincerely lamented our news that nothing, alas, could be done for the Quallsford Importing Company—Sherlock Holmes said jubilantly, "We have the afternoon free, Porter. I suggest that we take advantage of the vicar's invitation to enjoy the beauties of St. John Havenchurch."

Strolling along the High Street for almost the last time, I glanced about at the now familiar buildings. Life in the village went on as usual. The blacksmith was shoeing a horse while a farmer looked on. The baker had completed his baking for the day and the butchers their slaughtering. I could see Mr. Cole, wrapped in a blanket in his garden on the hillside, looking down and reflecting on human folly and the devil while the church bells reminded him of God.

"Did you really think it possible that smuggled goods might be hidden in the church?" I asked, as we started up the hill.

"It certainly was possible that they might be hidden in *a* church," he said. "There is a long tradition of that in the Marsh, and these particular smugglers have a detailed knowledge of the region's smuggling traditions. I doubted that contraband would be hidden in this particular church. Why go to all the work of carrying it up the hill and then carrying it down again when there are so many churches on the Marsh levels? I looked at several of them—and their churchyards—to see what possibilities they offered to the smugglers, but you had already located the most likely place."

He gave me credit even though I had not suspected that the old oast-house hid smuggled goods. It was enough that I had brought it to his attention.

The vicar, Mr. Russell, saw us coming. He stumped down the path to meet us, and he was delighted to serve as our guide when he learned what our errand was. For the next two hours we drifted after him through the cool vastness of the church while he discoursed on alterations to the fabric in the fourteenth century, of fifteenth-century windows that replaced their Norman predecessors when the church was damaged by fire, of the classic style of the perpendicular tower, of the probable dates of wall paintings, of the possibility that the stone font might be much older than the almost illegible carving on it suggested.

The flowing enthusiasm of his voice at first stimulated and then had a soporific effect, but I refused to allow him to lull me. When it became necessary to mark time in a case, Sherlock Holmes often took an afternoon off to attend a concert, or to visit an art gallery, or merely to read a book, and this excursion to the church could have indicated nothing more than his inclination to make profitable use of a few hours that otherwise would be wasted.

It was also possible that the vicar, Mr. Russell, was marked down for some role in this drama that Sherlock Holmes had set in motion and that was now unfolding all across the Marshes, and I kept a wary eye on him.

Nothing happened except that we received a very detailed guided tour of St. John Havenchurch. The vicar responded enthusiastically to Sherlock Holmes's intelligent and informed interest.

Before we left, I went to have a last look at the grave of the unfortunate young man my own age who had drowned in 1842. That date was only a few years after the conviction and transportation of the notorious Ransleys. He had been too young to be aware of it when it happened, but he certainly heard all about it as he grew older. "Let this vain world prevail no more" applied both to him and to the Ransleys and also to those smugglers whom Sergeant Donley's constables were rounding up at that moment. They would be taking their leave of this vain world for a number of years, and the murderer would be leaving it permanently.

We returned to Havenchurch. Walking along the High Street towards the Royal Swan, I asked Sherlock Holmes whether he wished to acquire any more of the Quallsford Importing Company's tobacco before we returned to London. He answered that the supply he already had should be ample for any penances his conscience might require of him for years to come, or so he sincerely hoped.

We stopped at Mr. Herks's Chemist's Shop, which surprised me, and Sherlock Holmes inquired about the proprietor's own remedies, which he understood were sought after not only in Havenchurch but also in surrounding communities. Mr. Herks dropped his dry manner and expanded on the virtues of his concoctions. The headache remedy that George Newton had bought the day before his body was found was one of the most popular. Mr. Herks also offered a powder that had proved efficacious for foot problems, a tonic for expecting mothers, a mouthwash for toothache, a laxative that worked so effectively that he could not recommend it for any but the most stubborn digestive malfunctions, and what he called a medical effusion. The last was a strongly scented liquid much favoured by ladies as an antidote for faintness.

Sherlock Holmes purchased samples of the remedies for headache and toothache, and he promised to order more by mail if he found them satisfactory. If Mr. Herks had heard that we were leaving Havenchurch without completing our negotiations for the purchase of Edmund Quallsford's business, he made no mention of it. Neither did he mention the raid on the smugglers' cache earlier that day, but it probably would not become common knowledge before evening.

Sherlock Holmes warned me to prepare for an active night's work. There was a murderer to be captured. The trap had been set, but he had no presentiment at all of how long we might have to wait for the bait to be taken or how much resistance we would have to overcome. I slept for more than an hour when we returned to the Royal Swan.

When I awoke, I found him with Sergeant Donley discussing strategy for the night's adventure. Sherlock Holmes wanted constables carefully positioned on the Sea Cliffs estate. They were to be hidden some distance from the old tower, and they were not to interfere in any way with anyone approaching it. He was adamant about that. If the murderer suspected that the place was under observation, the case would be ruined, and all of the smugglers the sergeant had diligently arrested during the day would have to be released.

The constables were to remain under cover and make no noise of any kind. Their role was to make certain that no one escaped after the trap was sprung.

The sergeant nodded glumly. His conscience was severely disturbed by the fact that he still had no evidence to connect the smugglers with the smuggled goods, and he could not imagine what kind of manoeuvre Sherlock Holmes might have devised to remedy that. There was ample evidence against Jack Browne and his wagoners, but they were not talking.

None of the smugglers were talking except to Mr. Jordan, the solicitor from Tenterden, and the sergeant was gloomy about the obstacles to the smooth course of justice that Jordan would probably erect in behalf of his clients.

"Make certain that there are no mistakes this evening," Sherlock Holmes told him, "and you can forget about Mr. Jordan."

Mr. More and Stanley Hopkins joined us for dinner, and we took a table in the most remote corner of the Royal Swan's dining room. Mr. Werner, surmising that we had private matters to discuss, left us undisturbed after he brought our food; but no mention was made of the business at hand except that Mr. More added his own complaint about Mr. Jordan and the reticent smugglers. He, too, was uneasy about the lack of evidence.

"We can't leave until it is quite dark," Sherlock Holmes said. "When we go, we must move silently. We can take lanterns, but under no circumstances can we light them until the climax comes."

We ate the remainder of our meal in silence, almost as though we were practising for the ordeal ahead.

It was another overcast night. We took the shortest possible route to the tower, going by horse to Sea Cliffs, where we dismounted out of sight of the mansion and turned the horses over to one of the sergeant's constables. Four mounted constables had taken up positions along the road in the event that the murderer should escape our trap and a chase should ensue. They were given stern instructions to keep their mounts—and themselves—quiet.

We made a wide circuit of the Quallsford mansion and barns, and, moving cautiously in the thickening darkness, we approached the old tower without incident.

Sherlock Holmes whispered his instructions, and all of us mounted the stairs. We did not climb far. At the point where they curved out of sight of the ground level, he seated himself with Sergeant Donley beside him. Next came Mr. More and Stanley Hopkins; then a constable and myself with a pair of lanterns beside us ready to be lit. The sergeant had brought a dark lantern, but Sherlock Holmes would not permit him to light it. He was concerned that the murderer might sniff the burning oil and hot metal and be warned off. The six of us, he whispered grimly, ought to be able to restrain even the most desperate murderer. He would signal when the moment for action came by going into action himself. Until then, we were to breathe silently and listen.

An hour passed. The stone stairs made a painfully hard seat, but no one stirred, and I could hear no one breathing. Another hour passed, I thought. I kept straining my ears to hear the church chimes, but they were too far away, or the wind was wrong, or both.

Suddenly I heard heavy footsteps. Someone had entered the tower. He carried his own dark lantern, and he risked a flash of light to make certain that the vast room was deserted. Evidently he saw no need for silence; he paced back and forth with a normal stride, and I passed the time by counting his footsteps.

That went on for fully half an hour, I thought, but afterwards Sherlock Holmes estimated twenty minutes. Then a lighter step was heard.

A man's voice said, "There you are."

A woman's voice said, "You fool! You have done everything wrong! Why did you murder them?"

"They were weaklings, both of them," Ben Paine, the mole catcher, said. "They would have talked. I had to shut their mouths."

"Why did you murder Edmund?" Emmeline Quallsford demanded. "Did you think that you had to shut his mouth?"

There was a moment of silence. "What got you onto that?" Paine demanded.

"Never mind. I know you did it. Why?"

"He was quitting us. He threatened to sell us out."

"Nonsense," she said scornfully. "Edmund never would have talked. Never. His honour was involved. Surely you knew that. Where did you get the revolver?"

"Bought it from a chap in Rye."

"That was a mistake. We agreed in the beginning—no guns."

"I know. That was one of the reasons I had to kill that little rat Newton—he got jittery and carried a revolver with him. Fired it at a dog or something when we were crossing the Marsh. It was different with Edmund. He was going to give us an ultimatum. He said the smuggling had served its purpose. If we didn't stop, he would peach on all of us. He had to die, and I fixed it so the police wouldn't suspect a thing." Suddenly his voice became pleading, as though he knew that he faced a great wrath there in the darkness. "It had to be done, and I had that letter—he was of no more use to us, he had made that clear enough, and you know yourself that when a man is of no more use, he is a danger. I have heard you say it."

"Yes. I have said that. How did you manage it?"

"I met him to argue with him about his quitting us. It was no go—he had made up his mind. Finally he said he had a headache and wasn't feeling well and he was going home to try to sleep. He had mentioned that Larissa had gone somewhere with the children, and I knew that you had gone to see old Emma, so there was no one else there but the servants. I followed him and got into the room without him hearing me, and—"

"And pulled the trigger."

"Well, yes. It had to be done. I was certain that you would see it my way when you had thought about it."

"I have thought about it. You are a murdering fool, and you have ruined everything. When you pulled that trigger, you destroyed yourself and all that we were working for."

"Nonsense. The police have no suspicion of me. We can wait this out and find a way to start again."

"*I* can wait it out. You are doomed. If the police don't suspect you, I will tell them myself."

"You little traitor!"

There was the sound of a blow being struck, of a struggle, but it was mingled with the sounds of Sherlock Holmes and the police going into action. I snatched a lantern and lit it, but they had already seized Ben Paine and wrestled him away from his intended victim by the time I descended the stairs and flashed light on the scene.

Emmeline Quallsford stood at one side, looking on with a grim smile. She wore a man's clothing, and her hair was tucked away under a man's hat.

She said, still smiling grimly, "I told you, Mr. Holmes. If you did not catch him, I would."

"I believed you," Sherlock Holmes said quietly.

It required a moment for Ben Paine to comprehend what she had said. Then, with a roar of rage, he wrenched himself free from Stanley Hopkins's grasp and flung himself at her. He was quickly wrestled to the ground, where he threshed and shouted curses.

"She did it!" he gasped. "She planned everything!"

"I did it," Emmeline Quallsford said. Her smile had faded. Now she merely looked grim. "I planned everything—except the murders. That stupidity was his doing. My stupidity was to invite Mr. Sherlock Holmes to Havenchurch. I won't make that mistake a second time. Good-bye!"

She slipped out of the door before any of us could move.

Those who were not occupied with Ben Paine scrambled after her, but she had already reached the sheer drop of the old sea cliff and disappeared. My lantern's beam was too feeble to penetrate far down the rocky face. I had to clutch the sergeant's arm to prevent him from trying to follow.

"Did she jump?" Sergeant Donley asked.

"I don't know," I said soberly.

I returned to tell Sherlock Holmes what had happened.

Ben Paine bellowed again. "Jump? She doesn't need to jump. She has been running up and down that cliff since she was a baby. She can do it in the dark with her eyes closed. You will never catch her now."

Sherlock Holmes and I returned to the edge of the cliff, where the sergeant was still staring downward and flashing the lantern. "I sent word to the men with horses," he said. "They'll cover both the Rye Road and the Iden Road, and one way or the other they should be able to overtake her. She will have quite a start, but with her on foot—"

From the plain below, we heard the sound of a horse's hooves. They pounded quickly out of hearing.

"There is your answer," Sherlock Holmes said. "The master's touch. She will have thought far beyond her escape from the tower. Ned Whyte, or another old sailor like him, will be waiting for her somewhere with a boat. Doris Fowler will be with him. Miss Quallsford's share of the smuggling profits—and it must be a considerable sum of money—is already abroad."

Back in the tower, we found that Ben Paine, still raging, had turned his fury on his confederates. He was delivering as full and detailed a confession as any criminal had ever divulged, naming names and places and describing events in a flow of words that would float him to the gallows and the others, including his brother, the mole catcher at Old Romney, to prison cells. Mr. More had called for a lantern and was writing busily.

Paine had murdered Edmund Quallsford, he said, because Edmund opposed his marriage to Emmeline. "Wasn't having his sister marry a mole catcher," he said bitterly. "Was so disgusted at the idea that he wrote me that letter announcing that he was quitting smuggling. Even threatened to turn us all in. If he had kept his mouth shut, everything would have been all right. Emmeline would have married me eventually, I know that she would, and we would have had money to buy us a big estate and set up like gentry."

He was a good-looking man, intelligent, hard-working until he had turned to smuggling, and, like Derwin Smith, he would never be able to understand why financial success had not made him a gentleman and why Edmund Quallsford would never accept a mole catcher as a brother-in-law.

But his greatest delusion, I thought, was his notion that eventually Emmeline Quallsford would have consented to marry him. He saw no reason for her refusal. He was her lieutenant, and they had worked together successfully for years.

Unlike her brother, his status probably meant nothing to her. She could work with a mole catcher as an equal—but she would not marry any man.

Sherlock Holmes touched my arm. "Come, Porter. None of this concerns us. We have to make an early start tomorrow."

CHAPTER
—◄— 16 —►—

Joe was impatiently waiting for news at the Royal Swan. He listened wide-eyed while Sherlock Holmes tersely described the capture of the murderer.

"Cor!" he exclaimed. "All those goings-on and no one knew anything about it! I won't let it happen again, Mr. Holmes."

"I am certain that you won't," Sherlock Holmes said solemnly.

We congratulated Joe on his work and assured him that the mystery could not have been solved without his help. Sherlock Holmes rewarded him with an entire pound for himself and his assistants.

We went up to our rooms, and I lingered at my door, waiting to see whether he felt an inclination for talk, but he did not. "London tomorrow," he said. "Remind me to send Radbert a telegram when we get to Rye." He wished me good night. Probably he was exhausted. He had been working intensely for almost a week without sleep. He never showed fatigue except in an unexpected willingness to go to bed.

We arose early and breakfasted together, and as we assaulted the plentiful meal that Mrs. Werner provided, it seemed to me that for once he was enjoying his food.

The landlord of the Royal Swan had been cool towards us since

Sherlock Holmes performed the deductive analysis of his Dead Pig Martley story, but he and Mrs. Werner were genuinely sorry to see us go—and not merely because of the loss of business. The village's dream of prosperity to be brought by the Quallsford Importing Company died with our departure—the last of Ben Paine's murders.

Sergeant Donley, Mr. More, and Stanley Hopkins came to Rye Station to see us off. Despite their enormous success in bagging a large gang of smugglers and a murderer, the three of them seemed more mystified than elated. As Sherlock Holmes frequently had occasion to point out, the police were likely to be restrained in their enthusiasm when a private detective solved crimes for them that they did not know had been committed.

Stanley Hopkins had not finished his work in Rye. He promised to call on Sherlock Holmes the moment he returned to London for a complete explanation of what had happened. Sergeant Donley and Mr. More had the resigned attitudes of men who expected to remain mystified.

I managed a few private words with Stanley Hopkins. "What was the name on your warrant?" I asked.

"Ben Paine," he said. "Just as Mr. Holmes requested in his telegram. How did he do it?"

"I don't know," I answered truthfully.

The train arrived. We found our seats, and a few minutes later it was whirling us through the Marsh country. Seen from a train window in the clear light of early morning, the land looked quite ordinary except that the green pastures were divided by ditches instead of fences or hedges. My thoughts were of my journey the week before in the company of Emmeline Quallsford, and I wondered where she was.

Sherlock Holmes bought all of the available newspapers at Rye and again at Ashford. He read diligently for an hour, attempting at one swoop to make up for the time away from London. Finally he bundled the papers into a ball and tossed them into the luggage rack.

He knew that I had been waiting patiently for this moment. "Did you suspect Miss Quallsford, Porter?" he asked.

"No, sir," I said. "Why did she call on you? That was what caused her downfall. We never would have made the connection between Spitalfields Market and the Marshes if she had not made it for us. Why did she do it?"

"It caused her downfall," Sherlock Holmes said thoughtfully. "It also exposed her brother's murderer. I feel certain that she considers that a fair exchange. Why did she call on me? For all of the success that she achieved in running that gang of smugglers, she was a novice in crime—and she underestimated me. You heard her. She will not make that mistake again.

"My newspaper advertisement must have intrigued and also alarmed her. She felt certain that it was somehow linked with her project to bring contraband to London because 'pitahayas' was an important code word used to communicate with the London gang she had made contact with. Doris Fowler said, 'No problem with pitahayas. No one has ever heard of pitahayas.' It would have been one of several unusual key words chosen for that reason. No outsider was likely to confuse a communication by employing one of them inadvertently—as would have been a very real danger had the word been 'plums,' for example.

"Suddenly, only a fortnight after an emergency 'pitahayas' message was sent to Spitalfields Market, there the word was in a London newspaper. She suspected a connection, and she had to know what it was. She was confident that she could handle me. That young woman will never lack confidence about anything."

"But why did she invite you to Havenchurch? Surely that was the worst thing that she could have done."

"She wanted to find out how much I knew, and she chose that ploy on the spur of the moment. At the time, it probably seemed like a clever manoeuvre. She was certain that I would return to London after a cursory investigation, convinced that Edmund had committed suicide—because she believed that it was true! *She did not know that he had been murdered.*

"The farewell message was unmistakably in her brother's writing, and he had recently demonstrated a disgusting weakness of character by attempting to resign from the smuggling operation. Only a fortnight previously, he had disrupted their London plans and made it necessary to have the old governess carry the emergency message. No doubt there had been harsh words between herself and her brother. Larissa Quallsford overheard the tone of those conversations, if not their substance, and thought Emmeline was pressing her brother to work harder. After that prolonged emotional tension, Edmund's suicide did not seem implausible to her. It never occurred to her that a trusted subordinate was being ruled by more powerful emotions.

"Her contempt for her brother had been growing over the years, Porter. Originally, all of the profits from smuggling had gone to restore the Quallsfords' fortunes—*his* fortunes. Once the most pressing debts had been satisfied, he would have been content to disband the gang; but Emmeline's ambition was fed by success, and the friction between them grew. I surmise that eventually she put him on a salary like the other members of the gang—larger than George Newton's but still modest—and reserved most of the profits for herself. That was why Edmund's position, and the family's reputation, were restored only up to a point. The village was able to gossip about Edmund's great success, but behind the facade were the shoddy furniture and worn-out carpets.

"Emmeline's grief was genuine, but even in that grief she was resourceful. She attempted to make use of her brother's death to find out why I used the word 'pitahayas.'"

"I still find it difficult to imagine her taking an active part in the smuggling," I said. "She was so lady-like."

"She fancied herself as capable as any man, Porter, and she was right. Her problem was that Ben Paine could not stop regarding her as a highly attractive woman. The fact that she and the old governess occupied one wing of Sea Cliffs by themselves made it easy for her to slip out of a window at night, either to make plans with Paine or to join the gang. You heard Paine's confession: She wore men's clothing and worked with the smugglers only at night, and none of the other members of the gang knew who she was or even suspected that she was a woman."

"When did you start to suspect her?" I asked.

Sherlock Holmes smiled. "As you know, Porter, I make it a firm principle never to trust any woman completely. I actively suspected her the moment she mentioned the word 'pitahayas.' When her subsequent activities that day—the calls on the draper and the barrister—proved to be innocent, I became curious as to what she had been doing in London the night before. I started my inquiries before the two of you departed for Havenchurch. She left her hotel shortly after her arrival. She remarked to the porter and also to the driver of the cab she took that she was joining a party at the Café Royal. The cab actually took her to the restaurant, and, two hours later, another cab picked her up there and took her back to the hotel. But she did not enter the restaurant. As a young woman alone in the city, she had to act with circumspection, and that was the manoeuvre she decided upon. A confederate would have been waiting for her near the restaurant with a carriage. After a conference —perhaps to repair the damage done by her brother's vacillation— the confederate returned her to the Café Royal.

"I suspected her involvement from the first. I was negligent in failing to identify her as the gang's leader until Sunday afternoon, when I suddenly recalled your report that she and the old governess lived apart from the other members of the household. Then I perceived that the gang's apparent lack of direction was due to the fact that she had moved to Rye. At Sea Cliffs, there were very few restrictions on her movements. Since the wing she and Doris Fowler occupied has only ground-floor rooms, she could come and go as she chose at night, and no one would have thought anything amiss if she were seen during the day chatting with the mole catcher. The move to Rye effectively took her out of contact. It isolated her at a critical time, and the result was disastrous, but probably she felt that she had no choice. It was essential for her to maintain her social position, and she could not risk being seen slipping out of the house in Rye during the night or consorting there with a man of low status."

"Then it was her quarrel with Larissa that brought about the gang's downfall," I said. "Emmeline must have realized that in Rye she would be cut off from the others. Perhaps that was why she was so upset about it. She was afraid that something would happen, and it did. It let Paine get out of control."

Sherlock Holmes smiled. "We may charitably say that it was upsetting to her in a number of ways. We may also say that she was an accomplished actress."

"Ben Paine," I said. "When did you begin to suspect him?"

"When I first heard of him. A mole catcher has such freedom of movement that he would be certain to be an invaluable asset to a smuggling operation. He could work at four in the morning or take a lantern to check his traps in the middle of the night, and no one would think anything of it. People would become curious if they saw anyone else prowling about the Marsh at those hours, but with Paine, it merely meant that he was an exceptionally hard-working mole catcher. Someone had to contact the merchants who were handling the contraband, and there really are few men in a rural community who can travel wherever they like, whenever they like, and seem to be earning a living while doing it. Paine's position was so ideal that I suspected him at once.

"Two things made his involvement certain. One was the plague of moles. Such distortions of nature do occur, but in this instance, it strongly suggested that formerly reliable mole catchers had not been doing their work for several years. Both Paine and his brother were too busy smuggling and disposing of the contraband to bother with a tedious and far less remunerative occupation. Only belatedly did they come to understand that their mole catching was critically important to them as a cover, and they acquired apprentices, but the mole population already had got out of hand.

"The second thing was the bag of moles that he displayed to us. No respectable mole catcher would be carrying moles that had been dead for some time. A mole has to be skinned as quickly as possible after it is caught, and processing of the fur begun at once, or it will be spoiled. Many mole catchers like to skin the animals in the field and carry only the skins home. At least one of Paine's neighbours noticed that in recent years Paine has had fewer and fewer skins on his line. He wondered what Paine was doing with them. If Sergeant Donley had made occasional use of his eyes and nose, all of these things should have made him curious if not actively suspicious.

"I used mine, and I knew at once that Paine's smuggling had taken precedence over his mole catching. When Newton's body was found, I knew that he had extended his activities to murder. In his favoured position, he had to be one of the leaders, and his short temper was well known—his wife had left him several times during a brief marriage, and he had a reputation for not getting along with people. You were right in concluding that your presence saved his apprentice from a beating when you were watching them catch moles. He was mild enough when he was calm, and he may even have been fond of the men he killed, but his history was that of a man who could lose control of himself with fatal consequences.

"Miss Quallsford knew that, too. Once she was convinced that her brother had been murdered, she knew instantly who the murderer was. That was why she told me that she would catch him herself if I did not. Your letter convinced her that the smuggling gang was finished. She immediately notified Mr. Jordan, of Tenterden, so that everything legally possible would be done for her men, and she devised a plan to expose the murderer of her brother before she made her own escape."

"How did you know that the smugglers would be transporting goods on Saturday night?"

"I put Joe and his friends to watching Jack Browne's horses. Browne had an isolated stable near New Romney—conveniently near to prime smuggling beaches and also to the places where I suspected the contraband was hidden—where he kept a team or two overnight when work took them to that side of the Marsh. When Joe reported that all of his horses were at the New Romney stable —along with other horses the gang had access to—I could confidently predict that the smugglers would be out that night."

"Why did the old governess say that she murdered Edmund?" I asked.

"Perhaps she did," Sherlock Holmes murmured. "Perhaps she did. She knew the history of that country only too well, and it was her tales about smugglers that turned Edmund's and Emmeline's thoughts to smuggling. Whether or not she played an active role in the smuggling, she certainly gave them the idea that smuggling was a romantic pastime followed by respectable people, which pointed Edmund towards his death as surely as though she had pulled the trigger herself.

"But Edmund's own character was a contributing factor. He was gentlemanly to everyone, always—except to a mole catcher who wanted to marry his sister. He showed his contempt for Ben Paine by writing that momentous letter on the cheap scraps of paper that he used for figuring. In the end, that helped me to identify his murderer. He might conceivably have written such a letter to Derwin Smith, but he would have used his Oxford Street stationery.

"We have witnessed the final act of a great tragedy, Porter. The villain was Oswald Quallsford, who squandered a fortune and left his children penniless. The Quallsford inheritance was abject ruin and grinding poverty. Emmeline, growing up with a genteel heritage and the humiliation of no money to sustain it, also grew up with a deep and fierce determination to escape from that poverty. And she has done so, Porter. She certainly has done so. I wonder whether that will satisfy her or whether we will meet again."

He glanced at his watch. "Charing Cross in ten minutes. It has been more than a week since we have seen Radbert. He should have accumulated several oddities for us."

I had more questions. "Did you arrange for Miss Quallsford to escape?" I asked.

"No, Porter," he said. "She arranged it herself and very capably, too."

"Mr. More suspected that you arranged it," I said. "He didn't say anything, but I could see that he suspected it."

Sherlock Holmes chuckled. "If he had wanted to capture her, he had every opportunity to do so. I told him that the smugglers were his responsibility. I was there to catch a triple murderer."

"Are you going to give this case to Dr. Watson?" I asked.

"No, Porter. The doctor has never been able to accept the fact that no sex or class or age is immune to evil. Iniquity's thorny blooms flourish in unexpected places—for profound reasons, or for tragic reasons, or for sordid reasons, or for no reason—and they must be contended with wherever they are found. Dr. Watson idealizes the fair sex. This case would disturb him, and he would be tempted to change things. I shall leave this one for your memoirs. Perhaps by the time you attain an age of discretion, you will be worldly wise enough to handle it."

ACKNOWLEDGMENTS

An American author is well advised to undertake a novel containing English characters and a Victorian setting with considerable trepidation. This book could not have been brought to a successful conclusion without the interest and active assistance of a number of good friends, acquaintances, and generous strangers in England, several of whom read the manuscript and rendered invaluable assistance by helping to cull my vulgar Americanisms.

Charlie Marchant, of Appledore, Kent, a retired wagoner with an astonishing memory, reminisced at length with me on life in the Romney Marsh at the turn of the century.

Fred Judge, of Appledore, a retired farmer, shared ale and his lifetime of rural experiences with me at Appledore's Red Lion, selected a rural flower for Rabby to wear, helped me to speculate on the 1900 price of Damson plums, and entertained me with a long discussion of the art and craft of mole catching.

Author William F. Temple and his wife, Joan, of Folkestone, friends of many years' standing; and Robert Morrison, of Reading, whom I first met at the Royal Albert Hall in 1945, his wife, Sylvia, and his daughter, Norma, all assisted with research problems and provided editorial support.

The hospitality of Appledore's Red Lion sustained me during a memorable week in the Romney Marsh.

I am grateful to a host of people, including librarians Margot Petts and Richard Knight, of the Holborn Library in London, for their toleration of and assistance to an excessively curious stranger.

Miss Anne Schofield, of Lamberhurst Quarter, enabled me to survive to write the book through her assistance to a traveler stranded in a driving rainstorm.

Special thanks are due to Sir John Winnifrith, of Appledore, for memorable hospitality at Hall House Farm and incomparable support as both a historical and an editorial consultant.

Not all of the assistance came from the English side of the Atlantic. As an example of the contributions from many sources that go into the making of a book, I gratefully acknowledge the kindness of a University of Michigan astronomer who prefers to remain anonymous. He generously took the time to calculate phases of the moon and times of moonrise in the Romney Marsh in September 1900.

Finally, no latter-day book of Sherlock Holmes is complete without acknowledgment and thanks to Sir Arthur Conan Doyle, the creator of one of literature's most memorable and remarkable characters. Monuments of stone may crumble, but the great detective, Sir Arthur's monument, emerges with renewed fascination for each succeeding generation.